ANITA M. LOVETT

The Devil's Double

Phoenix
PUBLISHING HOUSE
Out of the fire will come your greatest creation

Contents

One

JEREMIAH CROSS

I stood in my office adjusting my collar, trying to silence the hum
of nerves in my chest. Preaching had never made me nervous—
not once in twenty-seven years—but this morning carried a
heaviness I couldn't shake. Kingdom Rising felt... fragile. Watching
the congregation fracture under the weight of rumors and pressures
had worn me thin.

Malik hovered near the bookshelf, pretending to look over his
notes but mostly avoiding my eyes. He'd always been that way—quiet
strength, steady spirit, and a softness he tried to bury whenever I
pushed too hard.

"We need to talk before service," I said, breaking the silence.

He looked up. "Dad... can this wait? The choir's lining up."

"No, it cannot." I moved closer, lowering my voice but not my
conviction. "You need to step up, Malik. We're past the point of
waiting. This church needs an assistant pastor, and it ought to be you."

His shoulders tensed. "I'm not sure I'm ready."

I felt the frustration rise. "Not ready? Son, you've been sitting under my teaching since you were old enough to walk. You breathe ministry. You were made for this."

"Deacon Russell Hargrove doesn't think so," Malik muttered.

I froze, the irritation immediate.

"Rusty," I said with a scoff, "can go straight to hell."

Malik's eyes widened. "Dad—"

"I said what I said," I snapped. "Rusty means well, but that man is loyal to tradition, not transformation. Loyal, yes. I'll give him that. But controlling as a chokehold."

I paced toward my desk, the weight of years pressing on my back. "Kingdom Rising is growing. Times are changing. We cannot run this ministry like it's still 1998. Rusty wants everything his way—every hymn, every meeting, every decision." I shook my head. "He keeps things running smoothly, sure, but that doesn't mean he runs this ministry. He does not. **I** do."

Malik shifted uneasily. "He helped raise me in this church, Dad."

I turned sharply. "I raised you."

My voice cracked harsher than intended, but the truth sat bitter on my tongue.

"I raised you," I repeated, quieter. "I tried to raise Marcus too. God rest his soul, I tried." My gaze drifted to the framed photo of the boys on my bookshelf—one smiling bright, one forced into it.

"But he…" I swallowed hard. "He had something in him I couldn't reach. That boy came into this world with a shadow on him. The devil was sitting behind his eyes before he ever learned to speak."

Malik lowered his head, like even the memory of Marcus still carried heat.

I cleared my throat, pushing away the ghost of my failures. "You are not him, Malik. You're steady. You are the Cross legacy. And Kingdom Rising needs you to step into your place."

A knock sounded at the door—Harmony announcing five minutes

till service—but my gaze stayed locked on my son.

"You're ready," I said. "Even if you don't believe it yet."

Harmony's soft knock faded down the hallway, and Malik had gone quiet again, staring at the floor like it held answers I hadn't given him. I was about to press him one more time—gentler, maybe—when another knock sounded at the door. This one sharp. Familiar.

I sighed and pinched the bridge of my nose.

"Come in, Mother Lavvy."

The door cracked open and Mother Laverne Bolton stepped in, hat tilted like a crown, purse clutched like she was smuggling the Ten Commandments inside it. Her eyes scanned the room fast—me, Malik, the tension in the air. She took it all in before I could even greet her.

"Pastor Cross," she said, breath slightly winded, "I know you 'bout to preach, and normally I wouldn't trouble you before service..."

I nodded. "Yes, ma'am."

"...but the Holy Ghost been tuggin' at my spirit something *serious* this mornin.'"

Lord help me.

Malik looked up, trying not to smile.

Lavvy stepped farther inside, lowering her voice like the walls were listening.

"I don't know if it's because some of these choir members were out on Saturday doin' things they ain't had no business doin'..."

I closed my eyes for a beat. "Mother Lavvy—"

"Or," she continued, lifting a finger, "it *might* be because Sister Pearl Jenkins's manipulative spirit is runnin' rampant again. You know that woman don't get enough deliverance during altar call. Always in somebody else's business, never in her Bible."

Malik coughed to hide a laugh.

Lavvy ignored him and leaned against my desk like she owned it.

"But Pastor, I said, 'Let me go on in here and give my shepherd a

3

heads-up before all hell breaks loose in the sanctuary.' Mm-hmm."

I rubbed my temple. "Mother Lavvy, is there a specific issue, or—?"

"The issue," she said dramatically, "is discernment. And mine is hollerin' this mornin.'"

I wanted to tell her my discernment had been hollering for the past six months, but her voice ran right over mine.

"And don't you worry," she said, adjusting her hat and squaring her shoulders. "Because the Lord didn't raise no coward. I am part of the Holy Ghost FBI, Pastor Cross. Fully trained. Spirit-led. Tongue-certified."

Malik's shoulders shook with silent laughter.

Lavvy pointed toward the sanctuary.

"I will be on the front row—front and center—praying, intercedin', rebukin', repristin'—whatever the Spirit leads. Yes indeed."

I exhaled slowly, forcing a polite smile.

"Well… thank you, Mother Lavvy. I appreciate your vigilance."

"You welcome." She stepped back toward the door but paused, lowering her voice once more. "Pastor… just keep your eyes open today. Something ain't right in the atmosphere."

A chill spread across my shoulders before I could push it down.

Lavvy opened the door, waved two fingers in the air like she was spreading anointing oil through the doorway, and glided out with purpose.

The moment she left, Malik looked at me sideways.

"You okay?"

"No," I said honestly. "And yes. And… I don't know anymore."

Because the truth was, Mother Lavvy wasn't wrong.

Something had shifted in the atmosphere.

And somewhere deep inside me, a part of my spirit whispered something I refused to name:

This is just the beginning.

I straightened my robe, smoothing the fabric like it could iron out the worries knotting in my chest. The sanctuary lights glowed through the office door windows, flooding the hallway with a warmth that usually settled my spirit. Usually.

Today... I felt something prickling underneath my confidence.

A shift.

A warning.

A weight I didn't recognize.

But I refused to feed it.

I was Jeremiah Cross—pastor of Kingdom Rising, shepherd of thousands, a man God had raised from nothing and set on a hill for all to see.

Untouchable.

At least, that's what I told myself.

I opened the door and stepped into the narrow back hallway, Malik trailing close behind me. The closer I got to the sanctuary entrance, the heavier the air felt. Like someone had opened a window in my spirit and a cold wind had blown through.

I paused, hand on the doorframe.

Something was off.

Not wrong.

Not dangerous.

Just... unfamiliar.

The kind of off that made the hairs on my arms rise and my heart tap a strange rhythm against my ribs.

I tried to pinpoint it—

the sound,

the feeling,

the source—

but it slipped away like smoke every time I reached for it.

Maybe it was nerves, though preaching had never shaken me.

Maybe it was Lavvy's warning stirring up foolishness in my mind. Maybe it was the board whispering behind my back.

Or Marcus's ghost tugging at a place in me I didn't dare touch.

But no—

I shook my head as if the movement could break the thought in half.

This wasn't fear.

This wasn't judgment.

This was the Holy Ghost getting ready to show up and show out.

Yes.

That had to be it.

Kingdom Rising had been drifting, and God was positioning me to pull us back on course. Something big was coming—revival, outpouring, cleansing. The kind of move that breaks churches open and remakes them in fire.

I rolled my shoulders back, lifted my chin, and stepped toward the light spilling from the sanctuary.

The choir was already humming, warming up with the kind of anticipation that made the walls vibrate. Harmony caught my eye from the front row—gave me a slow, knowing nod. Winter waved at Malik, smiling too hard. Simone stood stiff near the side aisle, arms folded, assessing everything like a hawk.

None of it settled me.

None of it eased that strange weight.

But pride can masquerade as faith when you're determined enough.

I pressed my palm to my chest once, whispered a quick prayer I barely meant, and pushed through the doors.

God's about to do something,

I told myself.

And I'm still His chosen man to do it.

But as the sanctuary erupted into applause, the unease didn't leave. It crawled deeper.

Sat heavier.

Rooted itself.

Like it had been waiting for this exact moment.

The sanctuary lights poured over me as I stepped behind the pulpit, and for a moment, my confidence returned. The congregation rose to their feet, some clapping, some crying, some reaching their hands toward me like I was the miracle they'd been waiting on instead of a man running on fumes and denial.

I opened my Bible, though I didn't need it. I'd preached this text a hundred times.

But today it felt heavier.

Sharper.

Almost prophetic.

"Family," I began, my voice echoing through the room, "today we are declaring the Year of Restoration!"

A wave of applause broke out. Harmony was already rocking, eyes closed, whispering, *Yes, Lord... restore us.*

I continued, pacing slowly.

"The enemy..." I pointed toward the rafters like the devil himself was perched there, "...has tried to steal some things from Kingdom Rising."

"Amen!" someone shouted.

"He tried to steal your joy!" I said louder.

"YES, SIR!" a deacon called back.

"He tried to steal your families—your faith—your future!" I thundered.

People were standing now, some crying, some stomping, some waving their hands like they were fanning the fire I'd just sparked.

"And if I be honest this morning," I added, lowering my tone for dramatic effect, "he tried to steal *me* too."

A hush.

A shift.

Almost a tremble in the room.

I swallowed hard, feeling the words cut deeper than I intended.

"But God—" I said, tapping the pulpit once,

"—is in the business of giving BACK what the enemy thought he stole!"

The church erupted.

Shouts.

Cries.

A tambourine somewhere in the back losing its mind.

I raised my hand for quiet.

"Joel 2:25 tells us, '*And I will restore to you the years that the locusts have eaten.*' That means every year of pain… every year of lack… every season where you thought God forgot you…"

I felt the fire rising in me now.

"…He is restoring it RIGHT NOW!"

Harmony hollered.

Winter jumped clean up out her heels.

Simone even gave a stiff nod.

I leaned forward.

"The enemy may have tried to break my family…

He may have tried to break THIS church…"

My voice softened, trembling with something I didn't want to name.

"…but what the enemy tried to steal—God is giving BACK."

The congregation roared again, drowning my doubts.

I closed my eyes.

Raised both hands.

"And I prophesy this day—"

My voice deepened.

"—restoration is coming to the Cross family!"

A lie I needed to believe.

"And restoration is coming to—"

The sanctuary doors slammed open.

Not lightly.

Not like someone late for service trying to sneak in.

A full, heavy swing.

Gasps rippled across the pews as several men in dark jackets marched down the aisle — badges glinting under the lights.

I blinked, unsure if my eyes were betraying me.

Surely this wasn't happening.

Not here.

Not today.

"Pastor Jeremiah Cross?" the lead agent called out over the murmuring crowd.

The room shifted.

The fire in my chest evaporated.

Something cold and hollow settled there instead.

I gripped the pulpit.

"This... this must be a mistake," I said, trying to keep my voice steady.

The agent raised a document.

"We have a federal warrant for your arrest."

Chaos broke out.

Mother Lavvy jumped to her feet shouting, "THE DEVIL IS A LIE! NOT MY PASTOR!"

Harmony began praying in tongues so fast the ushers froze.

Simone covered her mouth, already calculating how this would affect the church board.

Winter pulled Nova back as she instinctively tried to move forward.

Malik stood motionless near the front row—

his face drained of blood—

eyes widened with a fear I hadn't seen in him since he was a child.

I lifted a hand toward him, trying to reassure him, trying to reassure

9

myself.

"Everything's alright," I lied.

But as the agents approached the pulpit, the unease I'd felt earlier crystallized into something undeniable:

This wasn't the Holy Ghost showing up.

This was the beginning of everything falling apart.

I tried to keep control.

"Uh- church... saints... let us continue to praise—"

"Reverend Jeremiah Cross, you're under arrest for federal financial crimes including money laundering, wire fraud—"

Gasps ripple like a wave.

Nova dropped her bible.

Kyrie cut the mic in panic.

Mother Lavvy screamed.

"I KNEW IT! I FELT IT IN THE SPIRIT THIS MORNIN'!"

I was hancuffed mid-sentence as the livestream rolled on tens of thousands of screens.

The church erupted into chaos.

And Malik— stunned, breathless—realized in that moment his life would never be the same. It was written all over his face. He was terrified. Not of just was unfolding, but because he had not choice but to take over.

Two

MALIK CROSS

The moment I stepped into the sanctuary, something in my spirit tightened—like the air had thickened, like the room was breathing slower than it should've. Kingdom Rising wasn't usually quiet before a sermon. Folks loved to whisper, laugh, catch up, gossip about nothing and everything.

But today...

It felt like the church was holding its breath.

Mother Lavvy sat in the front row fanning herself with one of those laminated funeral-home fans. She wasn't even doing it fast—just slow and steady like she was stirring something unseen.

"Mm-mm-mm," she mumbled, barely loud enough for anyone else to hear. "Something ain't right. Something ain't right in here today."

I swallowed, trying to shake it off.

Nerves.

Stress.

The weight of being Jeremiah Cross's son on a Sunday morning after a week full of rumors.

That's all it was.

But the feeling lingered, crawling up the back of my neck like a warning I couldn't interpret.

I took my usual seat near the front, scanning the room out of habit. And that's when I saw him—a man standing alone in the balcony. Hood up. Leaning on the rail. Still as a statue.

Watching.

Not the choir.

Not the congregation.

Not the pulpit.

Watching *me*.

My breath stuttered for half a second.

Did I know him?

Was he new?

Security issue?

Something darker?

Before I could place it, Harmony brushed past me and leaned forward to whisper to Lavvy. Winter rolled her eyes toward the choir loft. Simone was already judging the entire back row with her arms crossed.

Kingdom Rising was, for a brief moment, its usual chaotic self—just enough to convince me I was overreacting.

I tore my eyes away from the balcony.

Probably nothing.

Probably nerves.

Probably exhaustion from trying to keep the church together with tape and prayer.

I turned back toward the pulpit where Dad—Pastor Cross—was stepping up, Bible in hand. Strong. Confident. Untouchable. Always untouchable.

And still, that uneasy weight pressed against my chest.

Dad started preaching.

"The Year of Restoration: What the Enemy Tried to Steal!"

The congregation roared like the words were oxygen. He held the room in the palm of his hand. He always did.

But while the church shouted, something cracked open inside me— spiritual, emotional, maybe even psychological.

His voice echoed, but I felt... disconnected.

Like I was in the room but not rooted in my body.

Like something old was shifting.

Like something buried was clawing upward.

I pressed my palm to my thigh, grounding myself, forcing steady breaths.

Dad thundered, "God is giving BACK what the enemy tried to steal!"

The church shouted.

My heart pounded.

And something invisible in the atmosphere trembled—like the truth was brushing past me, but I wasn't ready to recognize it.

I tried to look back at the balcony.

The man was gone.

And that's when the sanctuary doors slammed open.

They slammed open so hard the sound tore straight through my father's sermon. It wasn't the kind of noise you could ignore—not a latecomer, not a crying baby, not even Lavvy rebuking a demon only she could see.

This was different.

Sharp.

Final.

Like the sound before a storm breaks.

Dad froze mid-sentence.

The choir stilled.

Even the air seemed to pause.

Then I saw them—dark jackets, steady strides, badges glinting under the stage lights. A cluster of federal agents moving down the aisle like they'd rehearsed it.

Every muscle in my body locked.

"Pastor Jeremiah Cross?" the lead agent called out.

Dad gripped the pulpit. "This must be a mistake," he said, voice low, steady…but I heard the crack beneath it.

The woman beside the lead officer lifted a folder. "We have a federal warrant for your arrest."

Lavvy screamed, "THE BLOOD OF JESUS!"

Harmony clutched her Bible like a shield.

Simone sat down so hard the pew squeaked.

My heart stopped in my chest.

My legs felt like water.

"What… what are the charges?" Dad asked.

The agent didn't flinch.

"Federal financial crimes, including money laundering, wire fraud—"

My knees buckled.

Just gave out.

If Winter hadn't been behind me, I would've hit the floor. The room spun—sanctuary lights blurring into halos, faces melting into panic and disbelief.

Wire fraud?

Money laundering?

My father?

Dad looked at me—just briefly—and there was something raw in his eyes I'd never seen before. Not fear.

Not guilt.

Something worse.

Recognition.

Like he had known this moment was coming.

"No—no, this isn't—" I tried to speak, but my throat collapsed around the words.

An usher grabbed my arm, steadying me, whispering, "Breathe, Pastor Malik—just breathe."

Pastor.

As if the title meant anything while everything around me fell apart.

The agents stepped onto the pulpit stairs.

Dad held up a hand. "I'll come willingly," he said, voice breaking on the last word.

The moment his wrists were pulled behind his back, something inside me shattered.

It wasn't just seeing him in cuffs.

It was seeing him small.

Human.

Unraveled.

"This is Kingdom Rising!" someone shouted.

"You can't do this here!"

"What's going on?"

"Pastor didn't do nothing!"

Chaos swallowed the room whole.

Through the noise, Dad kept staring at me.

His eyes said everything:

I'm sorry.

I failed you.

You're on your own now.

My breath came in ragged bursts, chest tight like a fist had closed around it. My hands trembled, my vision blurred, and for a flicker of a second I felt... hollow. Split open.

Like something spiritual and emotional inside me had been holding too much for too long—and the dam finally cracked.

15

I dropped to the pew behind me, clutching the wood till my knuckles burned.

This couldn't be real.

This couldn't be happening.

Not to him.

Not to us.

Not here.

Not in front of the whole church.

As the agents led him down the aisle, Dad mouthed something to me.

Take care of the church.

My stomach twisted.

Because I didn't know how.

I wasn't ready.

I wasn't enough.

And somewhere in the back of the sanctuary—high up in the balcony where I couldn't see anymore—I felt watched again.

Like someone had been waiting for this moment.

Like someone had been waiting for *me* to fall.

The doors closed behind the agents, and for a moment, the silence inside Kingdom Rising felt like the aftermath of an earthquake—dust still settling over a place that would never look the same again.

Then, all at once, the noise hit.

People shouting.

Crying.

Questions flying.

Accusations.

Rebukes.

Prayers.

Panic.

Winter shouted, "Everybody calm DOWN—" which of course made

folks yell louder. "LORD— CUT THE LIVE!"

Harmony was on her feet calling on every angel she could name.

Simone kept saying, "This is unacceptable — this is unacceptable," like she planned to take it up with Heaven's HR department.

I forced myself upright, though my legs still felt weak, a tremor running through them like electricity still hadn't finished settling.

You're the pastor's son, a voice inside me whispered. *They're looking at you.*

And they were.

A sea of frightened eyes, searching mine for answers I didn't have.

I stepped forward anyway.

My voice barely came out at first, cracking like a teenager. "Church... church, please—listen to me—"

No one did.

So I raised my voice again, louder this time, pushing past the tightness in my throat.

"Family! Please sit down. Everyone—just sit down!"

Something in my tone must've touched a nerve, because one by one, people returned to their seats. The noise softened from chaotic to frantic whispers.

I swallowed hard, stepping closer to the pulpit but unable to actually touch it. It felt... wrong. Like it still belonged to Dad. Like placing my hand on it would make everything too real.

I kept my distance.

"I know... I know you're scared," I said, scanning faces. "I'm scared too."

A ripple went through the room—surprise that I'd admitted it so plainly.

Harmony nodded slowly, as if giving permission for the truth to breathe.

"We don't have all the answers," I continued, "and we don't know what's going to happen next. But what I *do* know is that we're Kingdom Rising. We don't fall apart. And we don't turn on each other."

Lavvy shouted, "That's right, baby!"

Someone else started crying again.

Simone dabbed her eyes, pretending it was prayer and not panic.

I took a shaky breath.

"My father…"

My chest tightened again at the word, but I pushed through.

"My father will address these charges when he can. But until then, we're going to stay together. We're going to pray together. We're going to trust God together."

Whispers quieted.

Heads bowed.

Slowly, the room settled.

But I could feel another kind of tension rising, something heavier, something spiritual shifting in the atmosphere like a storm cloud gathering behind my ribs.

"And until Pastor Cross returns," Simone's voice cut across the sanctuary, sharp and pointed, "*who* exactly will be leading us?"

I froze.

The question hit like a slap.

All eyes turned to me.

A spotlight I didn't ask for.

Didn't want.

Didn't feel worthy of.

My mouth went dry.

Before I could even think of an answer, Harmony rose from the front row—slow, deliberate—and placed a gentle but firm hand on my back.

"This boy," she said, voice strong, "been groomed for leadership his whole life. God knew this day before any of us did. Malik Cross gon' stand."

I felt my lungs seize.

Stand?

I could barely breathe.

Lavvy nodded, waving her fan like a sword. "He's anointed, even if he don't know it yet!"

People murmured approval.

Simone didn't look pleased.

I opened my mouth, unsure what would come out.

"This… this isn't about me," I said, voice breaking. "It's about all of us. And I'm asking—please—let's dismiss calmly. Get home safe. And… and pray for Pastor Cross."

It wasn't eloquent.

It wasn't powerful.

But it was enough.

People began filing out slowly, still whispering, still shaken, still looking at me like I had answers I'd never find.

As the sanctuary emptied, I stayed rooted to the spot, staring at the pulpit. Dad's Bible was still open. His sermon notes stacked neatly beside it.

The Year of Restoration.

I didn't feel restored.

I felt like I was cracking open from the inside.

Yet everyone kept calling me "Pastor Malik" on the way out.

And somewhere in the balcony—

I felt watched again.

By the time I looked up, the man was gone.

As the last few members trickled out of the sanctuary, I finally sank into the front pew, elbows on my knees, head in my hands. My heart was still racing, my ears ringing with fragments of panic, prayer, and Simone's thinly veiled power grab.

I just needed a minute — one minute — to breathe, to think, to—

My phone started vibrating in my pocket.

Then again.

Then again.

Buzz after buzz, so fast it felt like the thing might catch fire.

I assumed it was church members texting — checking on me, asking questions, wanting answers I didn't have. But when I pulled the phone out, my stomach dropped.

130 notifications. All from Facebook.

The livestream.

The arrest.

The comment section.

It was blowing up.

I opened the app, and the first thing that hit me was the sheer speed at which rumors spread — wildfire in a digital forest.

The top comment screamed at me:

"Jeremiah got enemies OUTSIDE the church... REAL ones!"

My throat tightened.

Another comment appeared beneath it:

"The church finances ain't been right for YEARS. Y'all surprised?"

Someone else replied:

"They been saying the IRS was investigating Kingdom Rising. I guess it wasn't the IRS. It was the FEDS!"

I gripped my phone tighter.

This wasn't just gossip.

This was a full-on digital crucifixion.

Another thread popped up:

"Everybody KNOW Jeremiah been laundering cartel money through Kingdom. They literally started building AND remodeling almost overnight. No building fund service or nothin'! It's

been suspect!"

No.

No, no, no...

My chest hollowed out.

A different user commented under that:

"At least we know why it was going around that he was at Taz Moreno's club a while back."

I stared at the screen, frozen.

Taz.

Of all the names that could've resurfaced today...

A cold weight settled over my shoulders.

Someone else chimed in:

"I saw him with Taz myself. Thought it was weird back then. NOW it makes sense."

"He wasn't ministering in that club... he was laundering SOME-THING."

"Y'all blind — Kingdom Rising been moving funny."

"Malik better pray they don't come for HIM next."

My vision blurred.

I scrolled faster, heart sinking deeper with each swipe.

Memes.

Screenshots.

People tagging each other like this was entertainment.

"God don't like ugly!"

"I knew Jeremiah Cross wasn't right!"

"This why I stopped going to church."

I felt sick.

My father had always warned me:

People don't wait for truth. They feast on scandal.

But hearing the words...

seeing my family's name ripped apart in real time...

21

hearing Taz's name thrown into the storm...

seeing strangers rewrite our history with venom and certainty...

It broke something in me.

I shut the screen off, but the notifications kept coming — buzzing against my thigh like an alarm I couldn't silence.

Lavvy passed me on her way out, patting my shoulder. "Don't read that mess, baby. The devil live in comment sections."

I tried to nod, but the words echoed anyway —

the lies,

the half-truths,

the assumptions,

the things I'd never known to question.

Dad with Taz?

Cartel rumors?

Wire fraud?

Laundering?

My pulse hammered in my ears.

I stood too fast, nearly stumbling as the weight in my chest tightened.

Something had snapped — spiritually, emotionally, maybe even mentally — when those handcuffs clicked on my father...

...and now the world was tearing apart the scraps that remained.

I needed air.

I needed answers.

I needed—

My phone buzzed one more time.

A private message request.

No name.

No profile picture.

Just one line:

"You're next."

Before I could make it out of the sanctuary, three board members rushed me so fast I thought *I* was about to be arrested next.

"Malik—we need a meeting right now."

"We can't let these rumors spread unchecked."

"Come on, son, the executive board room. Hurry."

Their voices overlapped in panic, and somehow I found myself being herded down the corridor like livestock headed to auction. I barely had time to breathe, let alone recover.

The executive board room sat on the second floor—glass walls, long polished oak table, gleaming chrome light fixtures, and leather chairs so expensive they squeaked when you moved wrong. Today, the room felt like a fishbowl with sharks circling.

When the door swung open, the chaos slapped me in the face.

People were already shouting.

Mother Lavvy fanning herself like she was trying to cool the gates of hell.

Simone pacing with her iPad like she was preparing for a coup.

Deacon Rusty sitting stiff and red-faced, jaw locked, arms crossed like a bouncer at a gospel nightclub.

Pearl Jenkins whispering into her phone and pretending she wasn't.

Kyrie from media typing furiously, eyes wild.

Security hovering near the door like they expected the Feds to storm in again.

The accountant sweating through his shirt.

The church lawyer rubbing his temples like he regretted passing the bar exam.

Scandal wasn't just in the room—

It was choking the air out of it.

Mother Lavvy waved her fan at me the moment I stepped in.

"Baby, come sit by Mother. Your spirit's tremblin'."

My spirit wasn't the only thing trembling.

People started firing questions before I could sit.

"He can't be guilty, can he?"

"They took him out ON CAMERA, Lord have mercy!"

"We ain't never gon' recover from this, never!"

"What happens to the money?"

"The building fund—oh Jesus—the building fund!"

"Who got access to the accounts?"

"Where's the treasurer? Somebody call the treasurer!"

The noise rose until it felt like the walls were vibrating.

Pearl Jenkins pointed a sharp acrylic nail across the table.

"I BEEN saying something was funny 'bout the finances. But noooobody wanted to listen to me. Now look where we at—Jailhouse Kingdom instead of Kingdom Rising!"

Simone snapped her fingers at her.

"Pearl, hush. You don't know anything."

"I know enough to keep my receipts!" Pearl fired back.

Rusty slammed his hand on the table so hard the pens jumped.

"I DON'T LIKE NONE OF THIS!" he hollered.

Silence rippled for half a second.

Then Lavvy muttered, "Ain't nobody asked you, Rusty."

Rusty glared.

Lavvy glared right back.

I prayed silently for peace, but God must've been busy.

Before Rusty could bark another complaint, Mother Lavvy stood up suddenly, hands shaking like she'd been hit with revelation lightning.

"MOVE!" she shouted. "MOVE OUT THE WAY—I got a revelation brewin', and I need a SEAT!"

Mind you, she was already in one before hopping up. But I guess she had to seat at the head of the table so all eyes could be on her.

Chairs scraped everywhere as people scrambled back like she was about to lay hands or pass out—no one knew which way the Spirit was about to take her.

She dropped dramatically into a chair, fanned herself once with authority, then pointed around the table like an investigator in a crime procedural.

"The call didn't come from outside." She narrowed her eyes. "It came from **INSIDE THE HOUSE.**"

Half the room gasped.

The other half rolled their eyes.

Rusty muttered, "Oh, Lord..."

Pearl leaned forward like she was listening to a divine conspiracy.

Simone whispered, "This is unproductive," which encouraged everyone else to talk louder.

Kyrie from media raised a shaking hand, "Um—should I prepare a statement?"

Pearl cut her eyes his way.

"A statement? Boy, we need a miracle."

Simone snapped, "No—what we need is *facts*. Malik—what did your father tell you before service? Did he warn you?"

A dozen pairs of eyes turned on me at once.

My throat tightened.

My chest caved in.

I felt exposed—as if I was already being framed as the next Cross they'd drag out in handcuffs.

"I—"

My voice cracked.

"I don't... I don't know anything."

Lavvy hummed loudly, eyes fixed on me.

"Mmm. Baby, what's weighin' on your spirit?"

Everything.

All of it.

More than I had words for.

Before I could answer, Rusty leaned forward, face red, eyes accusing.

"Well, somebody better talk, because this church is FALLING APART!"

Simone fired back. Pearl gasped. Kyrie typed. Security sighed. The lawyer rubbed his forehead like he was about to quit his job. The accountant whispered about account freezes and IRS audits.

Voices overlapped.

My pulse pounded.

My head rang.

I was drowning in a sea of opinions, accusations, panic, scripture, conspiracy theories, and every ounce of pressure Kingdom Rising had ever put on me.

I gripped the edge of the table.

For the first time in my life—

I understood why my father always said leadership was lonely.

Because in that room full of people...

I was completely alone.

Voices were crashing over each other again—Rusty yelling, Pearl gossiping, Simone strategizing, Kyrie typing like he was live-tweeting the apocalypse. My pulse was pounding so loud I barely heard myself think.

Then Mother Lavvy slapped her fan against the table.

Hard.

"HUSH."

The whole room went still.

Even Rusty froze mid-complaint, mouth open like someone hit pause on him.

Lavvy narrowed her eyes and turned slowly toward the accountant, who was sweating so hard I thought he might slide right out of his chair.

"Baby," she said, voice deadly calm, "what was that little mumblin' you just did?"

He blinked rapidly. "M-Mother Lavvy, I was just—"

She raised one eyebrow.

And it was over for him.

"Don't play with me today," she warned. "Repeat it. Clear. Loud. And with your chest."

Every head in the room swiveled toward him.

His Adam's apple bobbed like he was trying not to choke.

"I... um..." He glanced at the lawyer, who already looked defeated. Then back at me. Then at the table.

Finally, he said it:

"I checked the accounts. All of them."

He inhaled sharply.

"And... they're frozen."

Silence hit first.

Then—

"WHAT?!"

The room detonated.

Pearl screamed like she'd seen the rapture out of order.

Simone clutched her pearls—literal pearls.

Rusty slammed both hands on the table.

Kyrie dropped his laptop.

Security muttered, "Aw hell..." under his breath.

The lawyer closed his eyes like he wanted to be unconscious.

AndLavvy let out a long, dramatic "Mmmm-HMMM!" like her spirit had been trying to warn us all morning.

"They can't be frozen," Simone snapped. "All of them? Every account?"

The accountant nodded miserably.

"Operating fund."

"Building fund."

"Scholarship fund."

27

"Payroll."

"AND Pastor's discretionary fund."

My stomach flipped.

Simone dropped into her chair like her knees gave out.

Rusty kept muttering, "I don't like NONE of this. Not a damn bit."

Pearl clutched her chest dramatically.

"Oh Jesus… the BUILDING fund? Lord, we ain't never gon' build nothin' again."

Then the accountant whispered the death blow:

"Payroll is due Wednesday."

The room went feral.

"Wednesday?!"

"We can't pay NOBODY!"

"The musicians gonna quit!"

"The staff gonna WALK OUT!"

"The IRS gon' come for US too!"

"You can forget about choir practice!"

Lavvy stood up again and pointed at the ceiling.

"Lord, if You don't come down here and FIX IT, we gon' be in the streets holdin' service under a tree like the old days!"

The lawyer pinched the bridge of his nose.

"This is… catastrophic."

Rusty looked at me like this was somehow my fault.

"This is why I didn't want CHANGES! Tradition don't get nobody arrested! If we'd kept things the same—"

Simone spun on him.

"Oh shut up, Rusty! Jeremiah didn't get arrested for CHANGING the bulletin format!"

More yelling.

More panic.

More voices overlapping until I couldn't distinguish one from another.

And all I could think was—

Three hours ago, I was worried about Dad pressuring me into leadership.

Now I was staring at the possibility that the entire church—

every staff member,

every ministry,

every bill,

every plan,

every future Sunday—

was hanging by a thread.

And I didn't know how to hold it together.

The room blurred.

My breath stuttered.

Something cracked in my chest again.

And over the chaos, Lavvy was still hollering,

"I told y'all! I TOLD Y'ALL! That spirit been off ALL MORNING!"

I closed my eyes.

This wasn't just a bad day.

This was the unraveling of Kingdom Rising…

…and the beginning of the unraveling of me.

The shouting in the boardroom swelled again—voices overlapping, chairs scraping, Lavvy breaking into tongues, Simone barking orders, Rusty fussing like the world was ending, the accountant sniffing like he might cry.

My chest tightened so fast I thought someone punched me.

Then the room tilted—just slightly, but enough to make my vision pulse.

I couldn't breathe.

I pushed back from the table without saying a word.

Nobody noticed.

Or maybe they did and didn't care.

My ears rang, drowning out everything except the pounding of my own heartbeat. I stumbled toward the door, blinking hard, trying to stay upright.

When I stepped into the hallway, the glass walls felt like they were closing in around me. Too bright. Too loud. Too open. Too visible.

My throat closed.

I leaned against the wall, palms flat, gasping like my lungs forgot their job. Air wouldn't go in. Wouldn't come out. My vision blurred at the edges.

"Breathe," I whispered to myself.

Nothing.

Just panic clawing at my ribs.

The floor felt unsteady, rolling beneath me like I was standing on a boat instead of carpet.

My father in handcuffs.

The congregation screaming.

The Facebook comments.

The frozen accounts.

Payroll.

Taz's name.

Simone challenging my place.

Lavvy talking in riddles.

Rusty blaming me for everything.

Dad's Bible still open on the pulpit.

"Take care of the church."

"You're next."

My breath hitched sharp and painful.

I slid down the wall, landing on the carpet with my knees pulled in. My hands were shaking so violently I had to sit on them.

Inhale.

Nothing.

Exhale.

Thin and useless.

My chest burned.

My head buzzed.

My vision dimmed.

I pressed my forehead to my knees, trying to trap the panic, hold it still, stop the spiraling.

"Get it together… get it together…" I choked out.

But I couldn't.

Not with the walls closing in.

Not with the board melting down.

Not with Dad in a federal car somewhere.

Not with Taz's name echoing in my skull.

Not with a stranger watching me from the balcony.

Not with everyone expecting me to lead a church hanging by a thread.

I squeezed my eyes shut and dug my nails into my palms.

A broken sob slipped out before I could swallow it.

And then another.

I covered my mouth with both hands, trying to smother the sound— but grief and fear don't listen to pride. It came out anyway, trembling, humiliating, human.

For the first time in my life…

I wished my father hadn't raised me to be the strong one.

I wished someone would just find me sitting on this hallway floor and tell me what to do.

Tell me how to breathe.

Tell me how to lead.

Tell me how to survive this.

But no footsteps came.

No voices.

No comfort.

Just me.

Falling apart where no one could see.

I didn't know how long I sat there—back against the wall, head buried in my knees, breath fighting me like my own lungs were rebelling. The noise from the boardroom still bled through the glass, but out here it was muffled enough to feel lonely.

My heart was thundering so hard it hurt.

I tried to slow it down.

Tried to swallow the panic.

Tried to force myself to be the son my father expected—

But all it did was make the air thinner.

Footsteps approached.

Soft ones.

Not rushed.

Not loud.

Not authoritative like Simone's heels or Rusty's stomp.

Gentle.

Familiar.

"Malik?" Nova's voice traveled down the hallway—quiet, like she already knew something was wrong before she saw me.

I stiffened, wiping my face quickly, though my hands shook too much to hide the evidence. I kept my head down anyway, pretending I could piece myself back together in thirty seconds.

She wasn't fooled.

"Hey…" she said softly as she crouched down beside me. "Look at me."

I didn't.

Couldn't.

The moment I lifted my head, everything I'd been holding back would come pouring out again.

Nova didn't push.

She just shifted closer, her shoulder brushing against mine—light, steady, warm.

"Malik," she murmured, "you're having a panic attack."

"I'm fine," I lied into my knees.

"No, you're not." Her voice didn't waver. "And you don't have to be."

Something in me cracked at that—because no one had said those words to me today. Not once. Not even Dad before everything exploded.

Nova reached out and took one of my hands—slowly, making sure I didn't pull away.

Her thumb pressed softly into the center of my palm, grounding me like she'd done this before.

"Match my breathing," she whispered. "Okay?"

I tried, but my chest still spasmed.

She didn't let go.

"Breathe with me," she repeated, her voice like warm honey poured over a bruise.

"In... one... two..."

Her breath rose slow and steady.

"Out... one... two..."

I tried again.

Air finally moved.

Rough, shaky—but it moved.

Again.

"Good," she whispered, sliding the hair off my forehead like she was tending to one of her little cousins in youth ministry. "You're doing good. Keep going."

My vision started to clear.

The hallway stopped tilting.

My hands stopped trembling as violently.

Nova stayed right beside me, knees on the carpet, fingers still holding mine like she wasn't letting me drift off again.

When I finally breathed without choking, I leaned my head back against the wall and closed my eyes.

"I'm sorry," I managed, voice raw. "I didn't want anyone to see me like this."

She shook her head gently.

"Don't apologize. Malik... your entire world just collapsed in front of a livestream. Nobody expects you to just walk that off."

I swallowed hard, throat tight again—not with panic this time, but with something heavier.

"It's not just that," I whispered. "It's everything. The board. The accounts. Taz's name coming up. My dad telling me to take care of the church. And—"

My breath shuddered.

"—I don't know if I can do this, Nova."

She shifted, turning toward me fully.

"Then don't do it alone."

I opened my eyes, meeting hers for the first time since everything went dark.

There was no judgment.

No pity.

Just clarity.

"You're not your father," she said.

"You're not responsible for his choices."

"And you don't have to carry a ministry on your back by yourself."

Her voice softened even more.

"Let someone carry *you* for a change."

My chest loosened.

Just a little, but enough to breathe.

Nova stood slowly and offered her hand to help me up.

I stared at it for a moment—steady, open, waiting.

And for the first time all day...

I let someone pull me back to my feet.

Nova kept her hand on my arm as we stepped away from the boardroom, walking down the quiet corridor toward the side stairwell. My legs still felt weak, but the panic had mostly settled into something dull and heavy instead of sharp.

She hadn't let go of me yet.

I hadn't asked her to.

We stopped near a small alcove with a bench — a spot the youth ministry used when they wanted someplace quiet to pray. She nodded toward it.

"Sit for a minute," she said softly.

I sank down.

Nova stood instead of joining me, arms folded gently, eyes scanning me like she was reading something written behind my skin.

"Your breathing's better," she murmured.

"Yeah," I said, though my chest still felt tight.

But she didn't sit.

Didn't relax.

Didn't shift into comfort mode again.

Nova stared at me — not with worry — but with something sharper. More focused.

Like she was trying to see past me... or *through* me.

Her brows pinched slightly.

"Malik... something's not right."

I nodded instantly. "I know. The charges. The chaos. The church—"

"No," she cut in gently but firmly. "I mean around *you*."

My breath stalled.

Her gaze didn't drift, didn't waver.

She wasn't being dramatic.

She wasn't trying to scare me.

Nova was discerning something spiritual — something I couldn't name yet.

"I felt it in the sanctuary," she said quietly, voice dropping to a whisper. "Before the agents came in. Before the shouting. Before anything happened."

A chill slid down my spine.

She continued, choosing each word with care.

"It felt like... something cracked open around you. Like something wasn't sitting right in the spirit."

My heart thudded once, hard.

"I thought it was just my nerves," I whispered.

Nova shook her head.

"No. This wasn't panic. It wasn't fear. It felt..." She hesitated, searching for the right phrasing. "It felt like something standing... too close."

I swallowed.

She took a step closer.

"And it wasn't God."

That hit me deeper than anything else that had happened today.

Nova wasn't one to exaggerate spiritual things.

She noticed subtleties — atmospheres, shifts, energies in a room that other people dismissed. Harmony operated the same way, but Nova didn't announce her discernment to everybody.

If she said she sensed something...

It was real.

"What are you saying?" I asked quietly.

She exhaled slowly.

"I don't know exactly. But when I walked into the sanctuary earlier... my spirit felt uneasy. And when I got closer to you? It got worse."

My mouth went dry.

"I—Nova, I'm not—nothing's happening to me. I'm just overwhelmed."

She shook her head again, firmer this time.

"No, Malik. I've known you a long time. I know what overwhelmed looks like on you."

Her eyes softened, but the concern never left.

"This felt... different. Like something was pressing in on you."

A flicker of fear fluttered in my chest.

The man in the balcony.

The feeling of being watched.

The spiritual heaviness that kept tightening around my ribs.

The way the air shifted during Dad's sermon.

The cracking sensation I couldn't shake.

"I don't know what it is," Nova whispered, voice trembling slightly, "but something followed you into that sanctuary today."

My skin prickled.

Nova finally sank onto the bench beside me, her knee brushing mine.

"You're not crazy."

She said it with conviction.

"You're not imagining this. Something is happening around you that we can't see yet."

I looked down at my hands — still trembling faintly.

"I feel it too," I admitted.

Nova breathed in deeply, pressing her palm lightly to my back.

"Then we need to pay attention. Before it gets worse."

Her words landed with a weight I wasn't prepared for.

Because deep down...

I knew she was right.

Something had shifted.

Something had entered my world today.

And whatever it was…

It wasn't finished.

Nova didn't look away. Not once.

Her eyes stayed locked on mine like she was holding the pieces of me together by sheer will.

"Malik…" she said slowly, her voice dropping into that tone she only used when she felt something spiritual pressing on her.

"We're not waiting on this."

I blinked, confused. "On what?"

"To pray."

My breath hitched.

"N—Nova— here?" I glanced down the hallway as if someone might see us. "Right now?"

She nodded once. Firm.

"Right now."

I rubbed my palms over my face. "Nova, I don't… I can't— I don't even know what I'm feeling."

"That's *exactly* when you pray," she said, not missing a beat.

"When you don't know. When something's off. When you're scared. When you feel attacked."

Attacked.

The word landed in my chest like a weight dropped from a height.

Nova didn't wait for my permission.

She stood, stepped in front of me, and took both my hands in hers. Warm. Steady. Anchoring.

"Stand up," she whispered.

My legs wobbled, but I obeyed.

I didn't know why.

Maybe because everything in me was hanging by a thread.

Maybe because Nova was the only person today who'd touched me without wanting something.

Maybe because her voice felt like the closest thing to peace I'd felt in hours.

When I was standing, she moved a little closer, lowering her head.

"Father God," she started, her voice steady but soft, "we come to You right now because something ain't right."

A shiver rippled under my skin.

Nova tightened her grip.

"This young man," she continued, "is carrying weight he wasn't built to carry alone. So we're asking You to put Your hand on his mind, his spirit, and his heart."

Her thumb brushed across the back of my hand, calm and deliberate.

"God, anything dark, anything confusing, anything trying to attach itself to him in this season — we reject it. We cancel it. We shut it down in the name of Jesus."

My chest tightened — not in panic, but in something else.

Recognition.

Release.

Fear.

All tangled together.

Nova kept praying.

"I don't know what's after him, God. I don't know what's been whispering at him or watching him. But I *do* know he is Yours. So surround him. Cover him. Sharpen his discernment. Give him peace where fear is trying to live."

My breath trembled out of me.

I didn't even try to hide it.

Nova squeezed my hands.

"And Lord?" Her voice lowered. "Show him what he needs to see. Warn him of what he needs to know. And don't let anything near him that wasn't sent by You."

39

She paused, breathed, then said gently:

"Protect Malik Cross… from whatever is standing too close."

My knees nearly buckled again — not from panic this time, but from how deeply her words cut.

Nova opened her eyes and looked at me — really looked at me — and I swear for a second she saw something I didn't know how to name.

"You're not crazy," she said softly. "And you're not alone."

I swallowed hard.

"N—Nova…" My voice cracked. "I saw someone."

Her eyes sharpened.

"Where?"

"In the balcony. Watching me. Before everything happened."

She didn't gasp.

She didn't panic.

She didn't dismiss it.

Nova nodded once — slow and chillingly certain.

"Then we need to stay alert. Because something *else* is moving in all this mess."

Her hand stayed on mine.

And for the first time since Dad was taken away…

I didn't feel like I was drowning.

I felt watched.

Still shaken.

Still spiraling.

But not drowning.

"Thank you," I whispered to Nova when she finished praying. My voice was still unsteady, but the fog wasn't choking me anymore.

She gave my hand one last squeeze before letting go.

"Text me if it gets heavy again."

I nodded, breathed deep, and forced myself back toward the

boardroom.

My legs felt like they were moving through water, but I had to face them.

The moment I stepped inside, Simone swooped in like she'd been perched behind the door waiting on me.

"There you are," she said sharply. "We need to talk."

Before I could open my mouth, she herded me into a corner—away from Lavvy, away from Rusty, away from anyone who might soften her edges.

Her perfume smelled like judgment.

"The board needs unity."

Her voice was clipped, precise, weaponized.

"And we need it from you."

I blinked at her.

"Simone—what are you talking about? My father just—"

"Your father," she cut in, "is finished."

The words punched the wind out of me.

"Simone—"

"I'm not being cruel. I'm being practical. Jeremiah is done. There's no coming back from being taken out of the sanctuary by federal agents. *On camera.*"

My mouth went dry.

Pain flared hot in my chest, and I had to swallow before I could breathe again.

"I'm not ready for this," I whispered. "I'm not prepared. I don't know what to do."

Simone tilted her chin up like she was disappointed I hadn't grown a backbone in the last fourteen minutes.

"Whether you feel ready is irrelevant," she said.

"You're the only one clean. You're the only one with credibility. The only one the congregation will trust. Kingdom Rising needs leadership, and it has to be you."

Something inside me recoiled.

"I'm not my father," I said, shaking my head. "I didn't train for this. I didn't want this. I—"

Mother Lavvy suddenly popped up behind Simone, fanning herself like she was cooling down an entire spiritual realm.

"Baby," she said, eyes soft but voice firm, "this mantle fell on you the moment them agents walked in that sanctuary."

I felt my knees wobble again.

Lavvy pressed her hand against my shoulder.

"You didn't choose this," she said. "But God did. And sometimes the call gon' find you whether you ready or not."

Rusty grunted in agreement.

Pearl "mmm-hmm'd."

Simone folded her arms like she'd just presented her case and expected a verdict.

My chest tightened.

My throat burned.

The air felt thick again—

but this time not panic.

Something heavier.

Expectation.

Burden.

Destiny… or maybe destruction.

I couldn't tell the difference.

"I can't talk about this right now," I said suddenly, backing away. "Not tonight. I'm done."

"Malik—" Simone warned.

"No." I raised a hand. "I said I'm done."

The room went silent.

Lavvy nodded slowly.

"Let the boy breathe," she murmured.

I slipped out before anyone could argue.

Kingdom Rising was empty now.

Silent.

Still.

The kind of quiet that sinks into your bones.

I walked down the center aisle slowly, the soles of my shoes echoing against the tile. My father's Bible was still on the pulpit—open to the scripture he never got to finish.

I stepped onto the stage and stared at it.

His handwriting marked the margins.

Arrows.

Notes.

Circles around words he always emphasized.

Restore.

Enemy.

Years.

Steal.

My throat tightened.

I reached out with both hands and picked up the Bible.

It felt heavier than it looked.

I pressed it against my chest.

Hard.

Like I needed something—anything—to keep me from falling apart again.

For a second, I swear I could smell his cologne—

that faint cedar and cinnamon scent he always wore.

"This isn't my life," I whispered.

"I'm not ready. I'm not him. I can't... I can't do this."

The room didn't answer.

God didn't either.

I held the Bible tighter—
like I was holding onto my father
and my childhood
and every expectation
and every fear
and every unraveling truth
all at once.
I didn't know if I was steadying myself
or breaking.
Maybe both.
I gathered Dad's notes, my laptop bag, his watch he'd placed on the podium before preaching, and my jacket.
Then, without looking back, I walked out of the sanctuary.
The night air hit me hard—cold, sharp.
It felt cleaner than the boardroom.
Cleaner than the sanctuary.
Cleaner than anything I'd felt since the agents walked in.
I held Dad's Bible against my chest as I crossed the parking lot, my footsteps hollow in the dark.
My car waited under the streetlight, headlights reflecting faintly off the chrome.
I reached for the door handle.
My hand trembled.
For the first time since the arrest, since the screaming, since the panic attack, since Nova prayed for me—
I let myself whisper the thing I hadn't said aloud:
"I don't think God wants me to lead this church."
My voice shook.
"But maybe… maybe I don't have a choice."
I slid into the driver's seat.
Closed the door.

Exhaled.

The weight of everything — the church, the guilt, the fear, the unknown — settled around me.

I rested Dad's Bible in my lap and laid my forehead against the steering wheel.

And in the shadowed reflection in the windshield...

I could've sworn for a split second that I saw another silhouette standing behind me.

Watching.

But when I jerked around—

No one was there.

Three

NOVA JAMES

⎯⎯✦⎯⎯

Wednesday, *Choir Rehearsal*

By the time I walked into the fellowship hall for Wednesday choir rehearsal, I could feel the tension before I even opened the door. Voices were bouncing off the walls like rubber bullets—loud, frantic, dramatic, and absolutely all over the place.

I paused, closed my eyes, and whispered, "Lord... give me strength," before stepping inside.

It didn't help.

The moment I entered, a wave of noise hit me so hard I flinched.

"I'm telling you right now, if payroll don't hit, I'm NOT singing Sunday!"

"Lord, I knew something was off about Pastor Jeremiah—ain't nobody THAT blessed!"

"My cousin said the church might get shut down—SHUT DOWN, y'all!"

"This is why I tithe in cash!"

"Girl, that's because you don't want nobody tracking you, not 'cause of no scandal."

Winter was standing on a chair yelling for everyone to shut up.

Nobody listened.

Harmony was pacing with her tambourine like she was ready to exorcise somebody.

Deacon Avery peeked in through the double doors and immediately turned back around—coward.

I took a deep breath and clapped my hands.

"Alright, everyone! Let's settle—"

They did not settle.

Instead, Harmony whipped around, tambourine raised like a weapon.

"Nova, before we start," she announced, "I move that we remove all of Pastor Jeremiah's favorite songs off the set list. We don't honor felons."

The choir gasped in fifty different keys.

I almost dropped my clipboard.

"Harmony, we are NOT striking songs—"

"Uh-uh!" she snapped. "He is under FEDERAL investigation. We are not up here singing 'He's a Mighty God' when the pastor might be a mighty criminal!"

From across the room, Winter dragged her so fast it made the sopranos flinch.

"Harmony, GIRL." Winter threw her hands up. "YOUR ex got arrested at a Waffle House for fighting over a pancake. RELAX."

The room exploded.

Laughter.

Shouts.

A few people fell over each other.

Harmony froze like she'd been slapped by the Holy Ghost.

"I rebuke that spirit of disrespect!" she hollered.

"I rebuke your memory!" Winter shot back.

"Oh my God," I muttered behind my hands.

The tenors joined in now:

"So we can't sing Pastor Jay's songs, but we still singing the Bishop's after he ran off with Sister Carla?"

"That was DIFFERENT!" someone yelled.

"How? How was it different, Dario? PLEASE explain!"

I stepped forward again, voice trembling despite me willing it steady.

"Y'all, please—can we *focus*?"

Nobody heard me.

Someone shouted about not getting paid.

Someone else said they were quitting.

Another person said we needed to pray.

Two altos started arguing about who stole whose solo five years ago—completely irrelevant.

I raised my voice louder.

"Everyone, calm down—please!"

Still nobody.

Harmony started speaking in tongues at Winter.

Winter rolled her eyes and said it sounded like expired tongues.

Bass section howled.

The drummer started tapping nervously like he was warming up for a fight.

My pulse quickened.

My throat tightened.

"HEY!" I shouted.

That finally cut through the chaos.

All heads pivoted toward me.

And instantly, I hated that all those eyes were on me.

My voice shook.

My hands felt weak.

I could feel the heaviness hanging over this place—like something spiritual, something unsettled, something we weren't acknowledging.

I swallowed hard.

"Look… I know it's been a rough week," I said, though my voice still trembled. "I know everyone's scared, and confused, and frustrated about payroll—"

"That ain't frustration, Nova!" a tenor shouted. "That's BILLS!"

More murmurs.

More panic rising again.

I shook my head and pushed forward.

"But we can't fall apart like this. Not here. Not tonight. We're supposed to bring *order* into the house, not add to the chaos."

A few people nodded, but it wasn't enough.

Harmony folded her arms.

"Nova, the atmosphere ain't right. And you know it."

And she wasn't wrong.

I *did* know it.

I'd felt it Sunday.

I'd felt it around Malik.

I felt it now—something heavy, something dark, something stirring at the edges of everything.

My voice shook again as I tried to steady it.

"We're going to get through this," I whispered. "But not if we turn on each other."

The choir quieted.

Not calm.

Not peaceful.

But listening.

Barely.

And it was the closest thing to order I could manage while my own faith felt like it was shaking loose inside my chest.

I was just about to start a warm-up—anything to stop the choir from eating each other alive—when the double doors creaked open behind me.

Every head in the room turned.

Every voice fell silent.

Even Harmony's tambourine went still in her hand.

Malik stepped inside.

He looked... better.

Not whole.

Not healed.

But steadier than the shattered man I found in the hallway on Sunday.

His shoulders were squared.

His steps were firm.

His breathing was controlled.

And thank God—his eyes didn't look glassy or lost.

A wave of relief washed over me so strong I almost sagged against the music stand.

Winter whispered behind me, "Oh Lord, Pastor Fine has entered the chat."

I elbowed her without looking back.

Malik offered the choir a small, tired smile. "Hey, everybody."

Half the sopranos clutched their chests like they were seeing Jesus Himself.

Harmony bowed her head like prayer was about to break out.

Even the musicians straightened up.

I stepped forward instinctively.

"Malik, you don't have to be here. Rehearsal is—"

"I know," he said gently. "But I wanted to check on y'all."

The room held its breath.

He looked around at everyone—meeting their eyes one by one—and the panic in the atmosphere loosened just a little.

"I know this week has been rough," he said. "I know you're scared. Confused. Hurt. Angry. All of it is valid."

Harmony sniffed, wiping under her eye.

Winter nodded dramatically.

One of the altos whispered, "You better minister."

Malik continued, voice steady and warm—pastoral without trying to be.

"Payroll will be worked out. I don't have all the answers yet, but I promise you… nobody's getting left behind. We're going to figure this out as a family."

Someone in the tenor section whispered, "Thank you, Pastor Malik," like he'd just saved them from eviction.

The moment the word *pastor* hit the air, Malik flinched—but only slightly.

He masked it well.

But I saw it.

I always saw him.

The choir murmured thanks.

Relief.

Faith trying to stretch itself back open.

Malik glanced my way—and when our eyes met, his smile softened.

Warm.

Grateful.

Quietly leaning on me without touching me.

My chest tightened in a way I prayed no one noticed.

He gave the room one last nod before heading back out the doors.

The second they closed behind him—Winter slid right up to me like she was trying to merge into my skin.

"Soooo…" she sang under her breath, "you wanna explain what

THAT was?"

I frowned. "Winter, what—what are you talking about?"

She popped her gum.

"Don't play with me, Nova. You smiled at him like you just got delivered from depression."

"I did NOT," I whispered harshly.

"You did too!" she whisper-yelled back. "Girl, the whole choir saw it."

I folded my arms. "Winter…"

"Mhm." She leaned in closer. "Everybody knows you still got feelings for your little first love, *Pastor Malik.*"

My heart dropped into my stomach.

Winter wiggled her eyebrows.

"Y'all not slick. I see tension. I see history. I see the way he looked at you like you pulled him back to life."

"Winter—please," I muttered, heat rising in my chest.

She just grinned.

"Mm-hmm. I'm just saying… if the church falling apart, the least God could do is give us a little romance subplot."

I groaned and covered my face.

Lord help me.

The choir was a mess.

The church was a mess.

My heart was a mess.

And Winter was pure chaos wrapped in lip gloss.

Winter was still grinning like she'd uncovered the gospel truth about my life when I grabbed her arm—gently, but firmly—and pulled her away from the rest of the choir.

"Come here," I said through clenched teeth.

Winter let herself be dragged, dramatic as always, stumbling like she had been snatched by the spirit instead of me.

We ducked behind the risers where the sound faded just enough to have a semi-private conversation. Winter popped her gum again, unfazed, waiting for me to speak.

"Winter," I started, lowering my voice, "you've got to stop stirring rumors."

She blinked innocently. "Rumors? Me? Never."

I just stared at her.

She sighed. "Okay, maybe sometimes. But I'm right this time."

"No," I said firmly. "You're messy this time."

Winter scoffed and pressed a hand to her chest. "Messy? ME? Nova, girl, you better fix your tone—"

"I mean it." I leaned in, my voice softer but sharper. "Malik is dealing with the hardest week of his life. His dad is in jail. The church is falling apart. Payroll is frozen. And you're trying to start some Lifetime storyline in the middle of it."

Winter rolled her eyes. "It's not *starting* anything, it's just… stating what everyone can see. Malik looked at you like you hung the moon."

I felt heat crawl up my neck.

"Stop it."

"And YOU looked at him like Jesus just resurrected your self-esteem."

I closed my eyes for a second. "Winter."

She exhaled, finally dropping the theatrics. "Okay, okay. Fine. I'll chill."

"You promise?"

She made a zipping motion across her lips. "Locked."

"And buried too," I muttered.

She snorted. "Girl, you really tellin' me you don't feel nothing for him? Not even a LITTLE spark?"

"Yes," I lied instinctively.

Winter arched a brow.

"Liar."

"Winter!"

She laughed, patting my arm. "Relax. I won't say anything else. But I'm just telling you—if Malik Cross ever decides to shoot his shot again? Baby, you better have your edges laid and a shout ready."

I groaned. "Let's just rehearse, please?"

She snapped her fingers. "Right. Choir. Music. Jesus. Back to business."

We walked back to the choir together, Winter humming like she hadn't just tried to derail my entire emotional life.

People were settling—barely.

Some still whispering.

Some still frustrated about payroll.

Some still traumatized from Sunday.

But at least it was quiet enough to start.

I clapped my hands. "Alright, everyone! Let's warm up."

The pianist hit an unsteady chord—his nerves were showing too.

The tenors groaned.

The altos adjusted their scarves like their throats had been personally attacked by federal agents.

Harmony muttered, "I still say we strike them felon songs, but go off."

I ignored her.

We started vocal runs.

Rough at first—everyone's voice tight, anxious, unfocused.

But gradually the room loosened, the sound rounding, strengthening.

For a brief moment, as the harmonies blended, I felt a flicker of what choir used to be before the scandal:

A place of refuge.

Of unity.

Of breath.

Of worship.

But the air still felt different.

Heavy.

And while my voice guided them, while I held the rehearsal together with a shaky kind of grace...

I couldn't unfeel what I'd sensed around Malik earlier.

Something spiritual was shifting.

Something dark.

Something close.

And as much as I tried to focus on the music...

I couldn't help but wonder:

What exactly had followed him into Kingdom Rising?

Rehearsal had finally started to settle into something that almost resembled order when Winter shrieked loud enough to stop a tenor mid-note.

"OH—NAH! Y'all look at this!" she yelled, waving her phone like she'd won a lawsuit.

Half the choir rushed toward her.

The other half leaned in from afar.

I felt my stomach drop.

Not again.

Winter read the headline out loud:

"ALLEGED INSIDE JOB: Sources Claim Pastor Jeremiah Cross Was Set Up by Someone *Within Kingdom Rising.*"

The choir lost their minds.

"INSIDE THE CHURCH?!"

"Oh, this is JUICY."

"Lord, who snitched? WHO SNITCHED?!"

"I bet it was Pearl Jenkins. She always looked like she carrying secrets."

"Sister Pearl ain't got the RANGE to pull off a federal setup!"

I clapped loudly. "Everyone, please—!"

No chance.

They were already loudly recapping Jeremiah's arrest like it was a new episode of *Real Housewives of Houston.*

Harmony Reese stomped to the center of the room like she was about to host a reunion special.

"Let me make this VERY clear," she announced, placing one hand on her hip. "The ONLY reason the sermon got ruined is because the feds had TERRIBLE timing. Like—who arrests a pastor BEFORE offering?!"

Winter snorted.

"Girl, PLEASE. They was gon' get him regardless. Honestly, I'm shocked they ain't snatch him DURING altar call. Now THAT would've been fireworks."

Half the choir hollered.

I took a deep breath, willing myself not to scream into the void.

"Y'all," I tried again, "can we PLEASE stay focused? We have ministry on Sunday."

Harmony clapped at me like I was a toddler.

"WE? No ma'am. *I'm* not singing until we get clarity. My anointing will NOT be entangled with federal investigations."

Wynter folded her arms.

"Harmony… you ain't anointed. You just loud."

The room erupted.

Harmony gasped, clutching her pearl necklace like she'd been stabbed in the spirit.

"I KNOW you not talking slick with them still-wet baptism waters behind your ears! Girl, you got saved LAST TUESDAY!"

"I BEEN saved two months!" Winter fired back proudly.

"Don't play with me—my holiness is under construction."

Harmony rolled her eyes.

"Under construction? Baby, your holiness is a vacant lot."

"AND YOUR VOCALS AIN'T SAVED EITHER!"

The sopranos screamed.

The altos fell out.

I pinched the bridge of my nose and whispered, "Lord Jesus, please don't let me cuss in a church building..."

Harmony whirled around to face me, pointing dramatically.

"Nova, SEE?! This is why Pastor Malik needs to install a NEW choir director. One with discernment. One with authority. One who can sing lead when necessary."

Winter cackled.

"You mean YOU? Girl, the only thing you can lead is a rumor."

Harmony lunged.

"I WILL lay hands ON YOU and it won't be HOLY—"

"TRY ME!"

I stepped between them, arms spread like I was breaking up disciples at the Last Supper.

"EVERYBODY CALM DOWN!"

Harmony threw her hands up.

"Calm down?! Our pastor got DRAGGED out in handcuffs, the board is a hot mess, payroll is nonexistent, and I BET the livestream hit a MILLION VIEWS already!"

Winter shrugged.

"I'm just saying—the way he got arrested? That's brand-new season energy. Bravo TV needs to CALL US."

"This isn't funn—"

"It's a LITTLE funny," Winter interrupted.

Before I could respond, the door creaked open.

And everything stopped.

Malik walked in again. He must've heard all the commotion.

He looked exhausted.

But composed.

Still calmer than Sunday.

Still hurting, but standing.

Harmony smoothed her hair so fast I heard her edges cry.

Winter spit out her gum into her pocket.

The choir froze like God Himself walked in.

My chest softened automatically.

Malik offered a tired smile.

"I know things feel chaotic right now… but I need your hearts steady. We minister Sunday. And we minister in truth."

Harmony placed her hand over her heart.

"Oh, Pastor Malik… you ain't even appointed yet and you're already blessing my soul."

Winter whispered—loudly, of course—

"He better bless your pitch next."

"HUSH, WINTER!"

Just like that, the choir erupted again.

But Malik smiled—genuinely.

And for the first time since the arrest… it felt a little like church again.

Rehearsal finally dissolved into a messy, exhausted exodus—people grabbing purses, slamming folders shut, muttering prayers, cussing under their breath, and checking their bank apps like it was going to make payroll magically appear.

I stood near the risers, staring blankly at the exit as the last choir member slipped out.

"Y'all be safe," I called quietly.

They didn't look back.

The second the door clicked closed behind them, the room fell silent—too silent.

Sanctuary quiet hits different when your church is falling apart.

When rumors are circulating like vultures.

When you can feel something unseen shifting in the spirit.

I turned off the stage lights one row at a time until the sanctuary glowed only from the house dimmers—soft, warm, hollow.

My feet carried me back to the platform without thinking.

Back to the microphone I didn't bother turning on.

Back to the empty space where worship used to feel safe.

The fear I'd been swallowing all week crawled back up my throat.

Jeremiah was gone.

Malik was rising whether he wanted to or not.

The church was unraveling.

And somewhere in that mess… my own past was waking up in me, hungry and familiar.

I closed my eyes, chest trembling.

When I opened my mouth to sing, the note came out cracked.

I tried again.

Still cracked.

I whispered the first lines anyway, barely audible in the empty sanctuary:

"I've seen darkness fall like rain...
but still You hold the light..."

My voice shook mid-lyric, cracking again, like it couldn't hold the weight sitting on my chest.

"And every shadow, every fear...
will bow to You in time..."

The sanctuary swallowed the sound, leaving nothing but my uneven breathing behind it.

I gripped the edge of the lectern, knuckles white.

This wasn't just grief over the church.

It was *me*.

My secret.

My struggle.

The addiction I'd buried so deep I hoped God forgot about it.

But it had been clawing its way back up lately—

whispering at night,

flaring during stress,

pulling at my body in ways I thought I'd conquered.

And now, with everything spiraling... the urges felt stronger.

Darker.

More insistent.

I squeezed my eyes shut.

"Lord... please," I whispered, voice trembling. "Not again. Not now."

My breathing went shallow.

Fear wrapped around me—not just for myself, but for Malik.

Especially for Malik.

He was walking into fire.

Into leadership he didn't ask for.

Into spiritual warfare he wasn't prepared for.

Into a storm that wanted to swallow him whole.

And I could feel it—

that thing I sensed Sunday

still circling him,

still waiting.

A fresh tear slid down my cheek as I knelt, letting the weight finally push me to the floor.

"God... give him strength," I whispered into my hands. "Please. He doesn't know what's coming."

My throat tightened.

"...and give me strength too. I'm slipping. I feel it. I don't want to fall back into who I was."

Silence stretched across the sanctuary like a blanket too thin to warm anything.

I pressed my forehead against the altar step.

"Cover him," I choked. "Cover me. Cover this church. Because everything feels… wrong."

Another whisper slipped out, broken and honest:

"Help us. Please help us."

The sanctuary didn't answer.

But I stayed there anyway—

kneeling, trembling, praying—

until the fear in my chest calmed just enough to breathe again.

I stayed there longer than I meant to—

kneeling at the altar,

breathing through the fear,

letting the last lines of *Yet* echo in a voice that didn't feel like my own.

The sanctuary was dim and still.

Too still.

I thought I was alone.

I *needed* to be alone.

A quiet sniffle escaped me before I could swallow it back.

Then another one.

And then the kind that shudders out of you when you've reached your limit.

I covered my face with both hands, mortified at how hard I was crumbling.

Which is why I didn't hear the side door open.

Didn't hear the footsteps.

Didn't know anyone was there until a soft, startled voice cut through the silence.

"Nova?"

My whole body jerked.

I spun around so fast I almost lost my balance—and there he was.

Malik.

Standing halfway down the aisle.

Lit by the dim overhead lights.

His father's Bible still in his hand.

Eyes fixed on me with a look that made every part of me go still.

Concern.

Shock.

Something gentler beneath it.

"Nova," he said again, this time quieter.

He stepped closer.

I scrambled to wipe my face, embarrassed.

"I—I didn't know anyone was still here. I thought rehearsal emptied out."

"It did." His voice was low, careful. "I came back for my dad's notes. I didn't mean to interrupt."

I shook my head quickly.

"You're fine. I was just—just praying."

My voice betrayed me, cracking on the last word.

He heard it.

I saw the flicker in his expression—something tightening in his chest.

"You were crying," he said softly, not accusing, just naming what was obvious.

I looked away, swallowing hard.

"Just... a lot on my mind."

He stepped closer, moving slowly like he didn't want to spook me.

"Nova... you don't have to explain anything to me. But you also don't have to sit in here alone falling apart."

My breath caught.

He meant it kindly.

Gently.

But hearing *him* say it—him, who'd been drowning all week—hit someplace tender in me.

"You should be home resting," I whispered. "You've had the longest week of all of us."

"I'm fine," he said.

But he wasn't.

I could see it in the shadows under his eyes.

The tension in his shoulders.

The grief sitting behind his quiet strength.

Still... he was standing.

More than standing.

Leading.

Trying.

And here I was breaking at the altar like God had left me behind.

"I didn't mean to worry you," I said, voice trembling despite my effort to make it steady.

Malik shook his head, his brow furrowed.

"You're allowed to break down too, Nova."

A breath hitched in my throat.

He took two more steps until he was just a few feet away.

Close enough that I could feel the warmth of him.

Close enough that I didn't need to look up to sense the intensity of his gaze.

"Whatever's going on," he said quietly, "you don't have to carry it by yourself."

The sanctuary felt smaller suddenly.

My heart felt louder.

And all I could think was—

if he knew what I was really fighting...

if he knew who I used to be...

if he knew what was clawing back into my life—

He wouldn't look at me like that.

So I straightened, wiped my face again, and forced a small smile.

"I'll be okay," I whispered. "Really."

He didn't look convinced.

But he didn't push.

Instead, he nodded once, slow and soft.

"Then just… don't disappear on me," he murmured. "Not right now."

My breath caught again.

"I won't," I promised, though it tasted like a lie on my tongue.

He held my gaze another beat—steady, warm, painfully gentle—then exhaled and took a step back.

"I'm heading out," he said. "Do you need a walk to your car?"

I shook my head. "No. I'll be fine."

He hesitated.

Then nodded.

"Goodnight, Nova."

And the way he said my name—

like he was anchoring himself with it—

almost unraveled me all over again.

"Goodnight, Malik," I whispered.

He walked out slowly, glancing back once before the door closed behind him.

Leaving me standing in the sanctuary

with a heart beating too hard

and a secret getting harder

and harder

to keep buried.

The moment I closed my apartment door behind me, the silence wrapped around me like a trap instead of a comfort.

This was when it always happened.

Night.

Loneliness.

Emotional exhaustion.

The exact combination that used to send me spiraling.

I dropped my bag on the couch and leaned against the door, breathing through the ache in my chest.

Not tonight, I prayed silently.

Please, God. Not tonight.

But the hunger—the one I hated, the one I thought I'd buried—was already stirring under my skin.

I turned on worship music.

Then turned it off because it made me want to cry again.

I paced.

I drank water.

I tried reading scripture.

Nothing helped.

My phone buzzed.

Just once.

But the vibration slashed through the quiet like a blade.

I froze.

Another vibration.

Then another.

My heart thudded, dread sinking deep.

"No," I whispered, backing up a step. "No, no, no..."

I forced myself to pick up the phone.

A DM request.

From him.

The man I'd fasted over.

Prayed over.

Begged God to break the soul tie with.

The one who knew my weaknesses better than I did.

The one who dragged me into the darkest season of my life.

"God, please…" I whispered, but my fingers were already trembling.

I clicked it open.

"Been thinking about you."

My chest tightened.

Another message appeared instantly.

"You still on my mind… just like old times."

My knees weakened.

Flashbacks slammed into me—

his hands,

his mouth,

nights I shouldn't have survived,

pleasure that felt like drowning,

sin that wrapped around my bones.

I squeezed my eyes shut.

"No. I'm not that person anymore," I whispered.

"I'm not her. I'm not her."

But my fingers hovered over the keyboard anyway.

Just a word.

Just a reply.

Just enough to open the door I'd spent years boarding shut.

My breathing grew shallow.

Another message popped up.

"You still crave me? Because I still crave you."

Heat hit me so fast I had to set the phone down.

My body reacted before my mind could fight it.

Before my spirit could speak.

Before my discipline could catch up.

I paced again.

I prayed again.

I cursed again—quietly, but still.

Then I picked up the phone with trembling hands and scrolled through old pictures I swore I'd deleted.

One tap.

One message back.

That's all it would take to fall again.

"God," I whispered, voice shaking, "help me. Please help me."

My thumb hovered over the reply bar.

My body pulled one way.

My spirit pulled another.

And somewhere deep inside...

that old version of me—the one I'd buried—

stirred awake.

My thumb hovered over the reply bar—

just one tap

one slip

one moment of weakness

one doorway back into the life I swore I'd never touch again.

My heartbeat pounded so loud I felt it in my throat.

The DM notification from him glowed at the top of the screen:

"You still crave me?"

My breath shook.

I knew better.

I *knew* better.

But my body didn't care.

My loneliness didn't care.

My fear didn't care.

And I was so, so tired of being strong.

I exhaled, giving in.

My thumb began to type—

N

Before I could finish the first letter, my phone lit up with a new notification.

A text message.

From Malik.

The screen flashed his name like God Himself slapped the phone out my hand.

I froze.

My heart hit my ribs so hard it hurt.

I swiped to open it, hands trembling uncontrollably.

Malik:

You good?

Just two words.

Simple.

Soft.

Concern bleeding through every pixel of it.

I stared at the message, breath caught somewhere between a sob and a scream.

My body's lust quieted.

My mind snapped back into place.

The fog of old addiction thinned instantly—like shame itself got startled out of me.

I dropped onto the couch, shaking.

Another message came through almost immediately.

Malik:

I left you in the sanctuary looking... heavy. Just wanted to check in.

My throat closed.

He didn't know.

He couldn't know.

But somehow, the timing—

the tenderness—

the *seeing* me even from miles away—

It shattered something in me.

A tear slipped down my cheek.

Then another.

He texted again.

Malik:

If you need anything, even just to talk... I'm here.

I covered my mouth with my hand, fighting a sob.

This was the wrong moment for him to care.

The wrong moment for him to reach into my darkness.

The wrong moment for him to be gentle.

Because it felt too right.

Too intimate.

Too comforting.

Too close to the version of me I wanted to be—

the version I could only be when I wasn't falling apart.

My phone buzzed again—

But this time it was the ex.

"Don't ignore me, baby. I know you feel it too."

Like poison injected straight into my veins.

I flinched.

Malik's messages were still open beneath it, soft and safe.

My thumb hovered between them.

One thread was hell.

One thread was hope.

I sucked in a trembling breath, choosing the only option that didn't make me want to hide from myself.

I clicked back on Malik's text.

My fingers typed slowly—unsteady, honest.

Nova:

Thank you for checking on me. I... needed that more than you know.

I didn't send anything else.

Didn't open the DM again.

Didn't give the enemy another inch tonight.

I turned my phone face-down and pressed it into the couch cushion so I wouldn't see any more notifications.

Then I leaned back, breathing hard, tears drying on my cheeks.

And whispered into the dim silence:

"Thank you.

God… thank you for the interruption."

My pulse was still racing when I picked my phone back up.

Malik's message sat there quietly, like a warm hand on my shoulder.

But beneath it… that DM thread from the man I used to be chained to stained my screen like something unholy.

I refused to let him have access to me again.

I opened the conversation.

My breath hitched as I scanned the messages:

"Been thinking about you."

"You still crave me?"

"Don't ignore me, baby."

A tremor rolled through me.

No more.

Not tonight.

Not ever again.

I held down the thread…

hit **Delete Conversation**…

and felt a strange relief loosen in my chest.

It's gone.

He's gone.

I'm free.

At least for tonight.

I dropped the phone on the coffee table and exhaled hard, trying to shake the leftover ache twisting through my stomach.

I stood, went to the kitchen for water, whispered a shaky prayer, told myself I'd survived the worst of the temptation.

When I came back, the phone lit up again.

A new notification.

I froze.

Instagram DM: 1 New Message from — "Unknown User"

A cold chill slid down my spine.

Slowly—too slowly—I picked up the phone.

My breath caught.

It was the same thread.

The same man.

The same profile picture.

The same username.

But I had deleted it.

I *knew* I deleted it.

I watched it disappear with my own eyes.

My thumb hovered over the notification as dread crawled up my neck.

I opened it.

A single message waited for me.

Sent *seconds* after the thread should have been gone.

"You can delete me... but I'm not gone."

My entire body went still.

The room suddenly felt colder.

Empty and crowded at the same time.

Like someone else was there.

My breath hitched.

A tear slid down my cheek—not from desire this time, but fear.

I whispered, shaking:

"God... please..."

Then my phone buzzed again.

Another DM.

Slow.

Deliberate.

Chilling.

"I still know what you like."

My hands shook so hard I had to set the phone down before I dropped it.

Was it a glitch?

A cached message?

A delayed notification?

Or something... else?

My heart hammered as I backed away from the couch.

Every instinct in me screamed that I wasn't fighting just flesh tonight.

Something darker was pushing against the cracks in me.

And whatever I'd seen in the church hallway earlier?

The figure I thought was Malik?

A sickening realization slid into my mind:

What if it wasn't only Malik being watched?

What if *I* was too?

My phone buzzed again on the coffee table.

I jumped.

The apartment felt too quiet.

Too dark.

Too... watched.

I swallowed hard, forcing my feet to move as I picked the phone up with shaking hands.

Messages stared back at me.

"You can delete me... but I'm not gone."

"I still know what you like."

My heart thudded painfully against my ribs.

"This is tech stuff. A glitch. It's nothing," I lied to myself, breath trembling out of me.

I opened his profile.

Three dots in the corner.

Block.

My finger hovered—God, I didn't want to see his face again. His profile picture alone was enough to yank me back into memories I'd been fasting three weeks to drown.

I hit **Block.**

A confirmation popped up.

User Blocked.

My knees weakened with relief.

I exhaled and tossed my phone onto the couch like distance alone could keep him out of my spirit.

I walked to the kitchen again—

paced,

prayed under my breath,

sipped water,

paced more.

But something felt… off.

Like the air wasn't clearing.

Like the temptation wasn't retreating.

Like the room still held him.

No. No. I blocked him. I deleted the thread. It's over. It's done.

I forced myself toward the couch again.

My phone buzzed.

I froze mid-step.

One buzz.

Then another.

Then three in rapid succession.

My legs stopped working.

Very slowly, I reached for the phone.

The lock screen lit up.

Instagram DM: 3 New Messages — "Unknown User"

My stomach dropped.

No.

No.

I blocked him.

I *blocked* him.

I opened the app with trembling fingers.

My head swam.

The DM thread was back—

fully restored—

like it had never been deleted.

Like I had imagined doing it.

My breath hitched.

He'd sent more messages.

"Blocking me? Cute."

"You always come back."

"We both know what your body needs."

My throat tightened with nausea.

I hit **Block** again.

It worked.

For two seconds.

A notification popped up instantly.

"User Followed You."

I nearly dropped the phone.

He was back.

Unblocked.

Following me.

Messaging again.

A chilling thought slid through me:

This wasn't him.

Not really.

This was spiritual.

This was familiar.

This was the same oppressive pull I used to feel when I was in the darkest part of that relationship—

like something had attached itself to me back then

and tonight it found its way back in.

I backed away from the couch, shaking my head.

"No. No, God, I'm not going through this again. I can't—please—I can't."

The phone buzzed one more time.

One message.

Just one.

I didn't want to look but my eyes dropped anyway.

"Look out your window."

My blood ran cold.

My entire body stiffened.

The apartment suddenly felt too open, too exposed, too vulnerable.

Hands shaking, heart pounding, I slowly turned toward the blinds.

Everything in me screamed **DON'T**—

But something darker whispered **LOOK.**

And before I could talk myself out of it…

I lifted a single slat.

And saw a shadow standing under the streetlight.

Still.

Tall.

Watching my building.

Watching *me.*

My breath stopped—

And for one horrifying second…

I didn't know if it was my ex.

Or if it was the man I thought I saw in the church hallway.

My fingertip barely lifted the blind.

Just enough to see through.

Just enough to regret it.

A figure stood under the streetlight across from my building—

tall, still, unmoving,

like he'd been carved out of darkness and left there to watch me breathe.

I couldn't see his face.

I couldn't make out his features.

But I knew—

I *knew*—

he was looking at me.

My breath hitched sharp in my throat.

I stumbled backward so fast the blind snapped shut.

"Oh God… oh God, no—"

My heart hammered against my ribs so violently I pressed a hand to my chest, terrified it might break out.

"No. No, I didn't just see that. I didn't—"

But I had.

I forced myself to look again.

Slowly.

Terrified.

One finger lifting the blind slat by slat—

The streetlight buzzed softly.

The sidewalk glowed gold.

And the figure was—

gone.

Not walking away.

Not fading into the dark.

Not stepping behind something.

Gone. As if he'd never been there at all.

My knees nearly buckled.

I backed away from the window until my spine hit the far wall.

"No..." My voice shook. "No, no, no—he was there. I saw him. I *saw* him."

My phone buzzed again on the couch.

I jumped like someone fired a gun in the apartment.

Another DM notification lit up the screen.

My stomach flipped.

I forced myself forward, each step trembling, then snatched the phone up with shaking hands.

New message.

But this one was different.

It was shorter.

Colder.

More deliberate.

"Missing me already?"

My breath left me in a rush.

My vision swam.

It wasn't possible.

I deleted the thread.

Blocked him.

I *blocked him twice.*

And he wasn't anywhere near my building last I knew.

This wasn't him.

This wasn't normal.

This felt... targeted.

Spiritual.

Dark.

Like something—

or someone—

was pushing in on my life from every angle.

"God," I whispered, tears rising again, "please help me. Please...

please don't let me slip."

I shut off the phone entirely and sank onto the couch, hands on my knees, heart pounding so hard it shook my whole body.

My mind replayed the hallway at the church.

The figure I thought was Malik.

How he didn't turn when I called his name.

Maybe he wasn't supposed to.

A cold realization crawled down my spine:

Something was following me.

And it wasn't my ex.

I sat frozen on the couch, the apartment too dark, my heart too loud, the silence too heavy to breathe through.

I kept staring at the blank TV screen like it might suddenly switch on and tell me what was happening to me.

What was following me.

What had found me.

My phone—powered off—felt like a grenade in my lap.

I didn't want to turn it back on.

Didn't want to see another message.

Didn't want to risk another shadow.

I took one slow breath.

Then another.

"Okay," I whispered shakily. "Just… breathe. You're safe. You're home. Lock the doors. Pray. Breathe."

I reached for the phone and held the power button.

The screen glowed to life.

Before I could even unlock it, notifications flooded in like the phone had been waiting for me.

1 Missed Text — Malik Cross

My heart jerked.

I swiped it open so fast I almost dropped the phone.

His message sat there alone on the screen.

Malik:

You okay? I just felt something shift.

My breath left me in one violent exhale.

He felt it.

He wasn't here.

He didn't know about the shadow.

He didn't know about the DM that resurrected itself.

He didn't know I was trembling in the dark of my apartment like prey.

But he *felt* something.

The message wasn't casual.

It wasn't small.

It wasn't coincidental.

It read like a warning his spirit picked up before mine could even form the words.

A tear slipped down my cheek.

I typed nothing.

My fingers hovered uselessly over the phone.

What was I supposed to say?

"No, I'm actually being spiritually stalked by something wearing my past like perfume"?

I swallowed hard and typed slowly:

Nova:

What do you mean... shift?

Three dots appeared immediately.

He was still awake.

Still nearby.

Still connected to something bigger than either of us.

Then his reply came through:

Malik:

I don't know. Just felt this heavy pressure a few minutes ago. Like something wrong just happened. It hit outta nowhere.

I covered my mouth to muffle a quiet cry.

Pressure.

Wrong.

A shift.

Exactly what I'd felt.

Exactly when the shadow vanished.

Exactly when the DM resurrected itself like something refusing to release me.

I wiped my eyes with the sleeve of my hoodie and typed back, fingers trembling:

Nova:

I'm okay... just a hard night.

It was a lie.

But I wasn't ready for him to know the truth.

Another message came through.

Malik:

You sure? Because I don't usually feel things like this. It was strong. Felt like... fear. Or danger.

A chill spread through me so cold I shook.

He wasn't guessing.

He wasn't exaggerating.

He felt the same thing that had crawled up my spine and stared through my window.

I stared at his message for a long time, trying to swallow the terror rising in my throat.

Then I forced a response.

Nova:

Thank you for checking on me. I mean it. I'm okay now.

This time, the three dots didn't appear.

He hesitated.

Then finally, his reply blinked onto the screen:

Malik:

If anything happens... anything at all... call me. I'm not kidding.

I closed my eyes, clutching the phone to my chest, a shaky breath escaping me.

He didn't know what he was sensing.

He didn't know who was watching me.

He didn't know what darkness was moving through Kingdom Rising.

But he felt it

like a warning

God whispered directly into his spirit.

And that terrified me more than the shadow itself.

Because whatever was coming for me...

It wasn't mine alone.

It was coming for Malik too.

Four

TAZ MORENO

I watched Jeremiah Cross get dragged out of his own sanctuary on three different screens.

Three angles.

Three humiliations.

All synced perfectly like God Himself hit "play" on the downfall.

Federal jackets everywhere.

Congregation screaming.

Jeremiah's face twisted up in confusion like he didn't know he'd just set his whole life on fire.

I leaned back in my chair, jaw tightening.

The livestream replay rolled again, and something in me snapped.

"This stupid, spineless, Bible-thumpin' IDIOT—"

I grabbed the nearest glass and launched it at the wall.

It shattered loud enough to make the two guards at the door flinch.

I stood up slowly, pacing behind my desk, watching the loop play again on my largest monitor.

"The idiot was supposed to KEEP THE CHURCH CLEAN!" I roared.

My voice echoed through the club office, bouncing off the concrete and neon.

The whole operation was quiet for a breath—like the building itself knew to stay still.

Jeremiah, on all three screens, was shoved into the back of an unmarked SUV.

My lip curled.

"You had ONE job," I muttered. "One damn job."

My right-hand man, Rico—not the bartender, another Rico entirely—stepped forward cautiously.

"Boss... there's more."

I glared at him.

He swallowed.

"Speak."

He held up a tablet showing financial reports.

"As of Sunday, the feds froze the church accounts. All of 'em." He tapped a number that made my blood pressure spike.

"Two point seven mil. Gone."

I stopped pacing.

"Frozen?" My voice dropped to something cold. "Frozen?"

Rico nodded hard.

"Yes, sir."

I looked back at Jeremiah on the monitor.

Being shoved into custody.

Screaming members behind him.

Choir robes fluttering like flags at a funeral.

Two point seven million dollars.

I inhaled slow through my nose.

"That money," I said, "was not his. That money was not THEIRS. It was *mine*."

Rico shifted. "We already reached out to the accountant on our end, he say—"

I cut him a look sharp enough to slice him open mid-sentence.

"Don't bring me PROBLEMS," I said, voice low, "unless you're prepared to bring SOLUTIONS."

Rico shut up instantly.

I turned back to the screens.

Jeremiah, sitting in the back of the SUV, head hanging.

Pathetic.

Weak.

The church had been a clean front.

A legal wash.

A respectable mask.

And now?

Burning.

I exhaled, long and slow, letting the rage settle into something deliberate.

"Fine," I murmured. "Let the old man rot."

Rico blinked.

"So… what now?"

A smile slid onto my face—slow, vicious, familiar.

"We make his son responsible."

Rico stiffened.

"You mean Malik?"

I nodded once.

"He's the new Cross on the pulpit. He inherits the mess… and the debt."

Rico hesitated. "He ain't built like Jeremiah. He's softer."

"That's what makes him controllable," I said.

I turned off two of the monitors, leaving only the main feed playing the arrest on loop.

"And besides…"

I leaned back in my chair, fingers tapping the armrest.

"It'll be like old times."

Rico swallowed.

"I didn't know you and Malik were cool like that."

I smirked.

"Not Malik."

I sat forward, eyes narrowing in satisfaction.

"Marcus."

Recognition flickered across Rico's face.

Marcus Cross.

Jeremiah's black sheep.

The boy who ran from home at fourteen.

The boy I took in.

The boy who became one hell of an earner... until he betrayed me.

"Didn't know Pastor Jeremiah had another son," Rico muttered.

"Most people don't."

I stood, stretching my shoulders, feeling the crack of tension pop down my spine.

"Marcus used to work for me. Smart kid. Loyal... until he wasn't."

I smiled dark.

"But that's alright."

I turned the monitor off.

"Time for a family reunion."

Rico looked uneasy. "And Malik? What you want with him?"

I grabbed my coat.

"I'm going to make him pay back what his daddy lost."

Rico nodded.

"And what if he says no?"

I headed for the door.

"He won't."

Rico frowned. "How you know?"

I smirked without looking back.

"Because I knew his brother. They can't be too different."

By the time I walked out of the club office, the anger had settled into something clearer. Deadlier. Purposeful.

Chaos never frightened me.

But betrayal stirred something ancient in my blood.

I headed into the back corridor where my men stayed posted. Neon lights flickered against their jackets as they straightened when I approached.

"Gear up," I said. "We move now."

Rico jogged behind me.

"Boss, where we posting up?"

I didn't slow.

"Both spots."

He blinked.

"Both...?"

"Malik's house," I said, grabbing my coat from the hook. "And Kingdom Rising Church."

Rico's eyebrows jumped.

"You want both covered?"

"I want him surrounded," I replied. "I want eyes on him the moment he steps out the door or breathes too close to a window."

We pushed through the back exit where three SUVs waited, engines rumbling, windows tinted pitch-black.

My men looked sharp—

cold, quiet, loyal.

Exactly what I needed.

I scanned them, nodding once.

"Here's the play," I said. "I want someone outside his home. Someone outside the church. Someone ready to follow him wherever he goes."

One of the men, Diesel, cracked his knuckles.

"And when we find him, boss? What you want done?"

I smiled.

He didn't blink.

"Nothing yet," I said. "No contact. No threats. No movement."

Diesel frowned.

"Then what we do?"

"You sit," I answered.

"You watch."

"You wait."

Rico stuffed his hands in his pockets, nervous.

"And when we got eyes on him?"

"Call me."

He swallowed. "Just call?"

"Just call."

I stepped closer to him, voice dropping.

"Because I'm delivering this message *myself*."

A slow grin crept onto my face.

"And I want Cross Junior to meet me the right way—face-to-face. Man-to-man."

Diesel nodded. "You want him scared?"

I barked a laugh.

"No. Fear don't work on church boys."

I leaned against the SUV door.

"But confusion?"

A smile spread across my lips.

"Confusion ruins men like Malik Cross."

The men exchanged glances—they knew that tone.

"And when he meets me," I continued, "he won't know why I look so familiar. Why my name sounds familiar. Why my presence feels familiar."

Their expressions darkened.

"So he'll think we met before?" Diesel asked.

"We have," I said.

Not him.

But his twin.

Marcus had once stood where Malik stood now—

on the edge of becoming something dark, twisted, useful.

And now?

Now the second brother would learn exactly how deep his family's sins ran.

I tapped the side of the SUV twice.

"Get in position. Text me when you see him."

My men split into the vehicles, engines roaring to life.

But I stayed back a moment, watching them pull out into the night, splitting directions like wolves on the scent.

Rico looked back at me.

"You really think he'll cooperate? Malik don't seem like his brother."

I smirked.

"That's exactly why I want to meet him."

Rico hesitated.

"And if he don't want the meeting?"

I opened my own car door, sliding inside.

"Oh, he'll want it," I said.

"He just won't know why yet."

I closed the door, engine humming beneath me.

As I pulled off, I murmured to myself—

"Welcome to the family business, Malik Cross."

* * *

My phone buzzed once.

Then again.

Then again.

Three calls back-to-back.

My instincts bristled.

Either my men found Malik Cross... or they were about to piss me off.

I put my cigar out in the ashtray and answered the first call.

"Talk."

Diesel's voice came through, low and steady.

"Boss, we got eyes. Malik just pulled up to his house. Alone."

Good.

"Stay parked," I said. "Don't make contact till I get there."

"Yes, sir."

Before I could hang up, the second phone started ringing—the one I gave the church surveillance crew.

I switched lines.

"This better be good."

A nervous breath crackled through the speaker.

"Boss... uh, we got eyes."

I paused.

"...on who?"

"On Malik."

I sat up straighter, spine tight.

"Say that again."

"Malik, boss. He came out the side door a few minutes ago. Hoodie up. Head down. Looked right at us. Then slipped into the alley like he knew he was bein' watched."

My jaw flexed.

Slowly.

Deliberately.

Then I barked into the phone:

"HE CAN'T BE IN TWO PLACES AT ONE TIME!"

Silence.

All I heard was the crew breathing like they were about to pass out.

I pressed my fist against my forehead, breathing through my teeth.

"Tell me EXACTLY what you saw."

"Uh—he had the build. Tall, slim. Same beard. Same skin tone. Same everything. We thought—"

"You *thought?*" I snapped. "You THINKING now? Since when do I pay you to THINK?"

The man stuttered. "Boss, he looked like him. We swear—"

"Was it him or not?"

A long pause.

"...We don't know."

I slammed my palm against the steering wheel.

"IDIOTS!"

The word blasted out of me in a roar, vibrating through the car.

"You telling me I'm wasting time because y'all can't tell MALIK CROSS apart from some random fool in an alley?!"

"No, boss, we—"

"Shut up. Shut your mouth. I don't want excuses."

A beat.

Then I snapped:

"He looked at you?"

"Yes—yes, boss. Soon as we spotted him. He dipped into the alley the second he felt eyes on him."

I cursed under my breath.

That wasn't Malik.

Malik didn't move like that.

Didn't sense danger like that.

Didn't have the instincts of a street son.

But someone else did.

Someone who shared his blood.

I forced myself to breathe.

"You wasted my damn time," I growled.

"Sorry, boss—"

"I SAID SHUT UP."

He shut up.

I switched back to Diesel's line, voice sharp.

"You still got visual on Malik at his house?"

"Yes, boss. Lights just came on upstairs."

So the one slipping into alleys at the church wasn't Malik.

It was him.

Marcus.

Back from the dead and already playing games.

I clenched my jaw so hard it pulsed.

"Alright," I said, breath cold and controlled now. "Listen up. I'm heading to Malik's house."

Diesel asked, "You want us to stay put?"

"You better," I snapped. "And if Malik leaves—if he so much as breathes in a different direction—you call me immediately."

"Yes, sir."

"And the team at the church?"

I switched back to the other line.

"You stay put too. If that alley ghost shows his face—DON'T move. Don't chase. Don't blink without telling me."

"Yes, boss."

I ended both calls.

Gripping the wheel.

Heart pounding in a way I hadn't felt in years.

"It ain't possible," I muttered to myself. "He gone. He's been gone."

But the streets had a way of resurrecting the dead.

I started the engine.

"Alright, Marcus," I said into the empty car.

"You wanna slither back into my city?"

A slow, dark smile crept across my face.

"Let's welcome your brother to the party first."

I hit the gas and peeled into the night toward Malik's house.

By the time I turned onto Malik Cross's street, the whole block looked too clean.

Too quiet.

Too peaceful for what I came to bring.

Diesel's SUV headlights flashed once — the signal.

I pulled in behind them, killed the engine, and stepped out into the cool night air.

Diesel met me halfway down the sidewalk.

"He's inside," he murmured. "Living room light is on. Been pacing a little. Looks shook, boss."

"Good," I grunted. "Fear makes men honest."

Diesel nodded, but he kept glancing toward the house with a strange tension in his jaw.

I paused.

"What?"

He exhaled through his nose.

"Feels… off."

"Off how?" I snapped.

Diesel wasn't superstitious. He wasn't easily rattled.

He rubbed his forearm like something crawled across it.

"Like someone else is here," he muttered. "Or was."

I narrowed my eyes.

Marcus.

Even dead men left traces if their ghosts were awake.

I walked past Diesel, heading for Malik's front door, coat shifting behind me like wings. My footsteps were heavy but controlled — the kind meant to announce authority, not to hide it.

This wasn't a warning mission.

This was an introduction.

I made it three steps up the walkway before Diesel hissed behind me:

"Boss—movement!"

I spun slightly, catching the motion in my periphery.

Not from Malik's house.

Across the street.

Someone slipped between two parked cars and disappeared into a hedge line with the smoothness of a man who knew how to stay alive.

Too quick for Diesel's men to catch.

Too familiar a gait to mistake.

My blood went cold.

Marcus.

My jaw tightened, teeth grinding.

He was playing games.

Testing me.

Testing Malik.

Testing the old wounds he left behind.

"Which one of you IDIOTS said he looked confused?" I barked without turning.

Diesel bristled. "Boss, it was dark. Could've been anybody."

"Except anybody don't move like *that*," I snapped. "That's Marcus."

Diesel's eyes widened. "But… you said he was dead."

"He was," I muttered. "Until he wasn't."

I forced my hands to relax. My knuckles had gone white.

Marcus watching from the shadows meant one thing:

He wanted Malik scared.

Unsteady.

Off-balance.

He wanted to soften the ground before I arrived.

Smart.

Calculated.

Cowardly.

I turned fully toward the house.

"Aight," I muttered under my breath. "Enough games."

I stepped up the walkway again — slow, intentional, heavy—
the kind of walk a man remembers for the rest of his life.

Diesel whispered behind me, "You want us on standby?"

"Stay put," I said. "If Malik walks out this door, let me handle him
first."

My palm hovered over the doorbell.

But before I touched it…

The house lights flicked off.

All of them.

Like someone pulled the plug from inside.

Diesel stiffened.

"What the—?"

A beat of silence hit the air.

Then another.

My pulse kicked hard.

"Boss," Diesel whispered, "you think he knows we're here?"

I didn't answer.

Because I wasn't looking at the door anymore.

I was looking at the hedge line across the street.

Where a silhouette stood just for a second —

just long enough to be seen —

before slipping away again.

The same height as Malik.

The same build.

But the posture…

the arrogance in the stance…

the way he stared straight at me without fear?

Marcus.

Alive.

Messy.

Unpredictable.

And after two years confirmed dead, bold enough to taunt me on my own turf.

I inhaled slow.

"This ain't about Malik no more," I muttered.

Diesel swallowed. "Then… what now?"

I pressed the doorbell, letting the chime echo through the dark house.

"We knock," I said.

"And we see how many Cross men answer."

I expected Malik Cross to answer the door soft.

Most church boys were.

Polite.

Respectful.

Unaware of the wolves walking right up to their porch.

But I wasn't prepared for how much it would shake me to see Marcus's face staring back at me.

Not identical.

Not twins-on-TV identical.

But close enough that the memory hit the back of my throat.

Marcus at fourteen.

Marcus running errands.

Marcus with blood on his knuckles trying to prove something.

Marcus looking for a father in every place except his own damn house.

And now here stood Malik.

Cleaner.
Brighter.
Lighter.
But still a Cross.
Still mine to deal with.
He cracked the door, cautious, eyes wide but not stupid.
Good.
Fear without panic was workable.
"Evening," I said, voice low.
He nodded, gripping the edge of the door like he planned to slam it if I breathed wrong.
"Can I… help you?" he asked.
There it was—
respect.
Worry.
Curiosity.
"You Malik Cross?" I asked, though I already knew.
"Yes, sir. Who's asking?"
"I am."
His brows pulled tight for half a second.
I recognized the expression—
Marcus used to do the same thing when he tried to place a threat he didn't fully understand yet.
I stepped forward an inch.
"Your father and I had business."
He stiffened.
"My father is—"
"Arrested," I finished for him. "I saw."
His eyes darted down, then back up.
Good.
He was rattled but not broken.

Perfect for molding.

He asked for my name.

I ignored the question.

"We now have business," I said instead.

Because we did.

Sooner than he wanted.

He tried to hold ground.

"I don't want trouble."

"Oh, good," I replied. "Then you and me gon' get along fine."

The lie tasted clean on my tongue.

He looked at me differently after that—

like something inside him whispered that danger had stepped into his world and smiled politely.

He said he didn't know anything about his father's dealings.

I already knew that.

His father hid everything.

Jeremiah always did.

Which was why Malik was the perfect pressure point.

"I'm not here about Jeremiah," I said, letting my tone fall flat.

"I'm here about you."

That's when fear hit him.

Real fear.

Not the polite tension from before.

The kind of fear men felt when a world they never stepped into suddenly knew their name.

"I'm not part of anything illegal," he said quickly.

"I didn't say you were."

I let my gaze drag over him slow.

"But you share his blood. That's enough."

He swallowed so hard I saw his throat jump.

Then—

I played my trump card.

"Marcus used to say that too."

His whole face changed.

Shock.

Confusion.

A flash of a wound only family could cause.

He whispered Marcus's name like it hurt to say it.

I kept my face smooth.

Controlled.

Deadly calm.

"We go way back."

And in the porch light, I saw the exact moment Malik realized he didn't know half the story of the man he shared a womb with.

I stepped off his porch, giving him space but not giving him peace.

"We gon' talk real soon, Malik Cross."

I tapped two fingers to my temple in a mock salute.

"Tell your brother I said hello."

His breath caught.

He stared like I cracked open a grave at his feet.

Good.

Confusion softened men.

Made them pliable.

Made them desperate for answers.

And answers were the leash I planned to use.

As I walked back to the SUV, Diesel opened the passenger door.

"You think he bought it?" he asked.

"He ain't got a choice," I said.

Diesel nodded. "He looked scared."

"He should be."

I glanced once more at Malik's darkened house.

"But that wasn't fear of me."

Diesel frowned. "Then what was it?"

I smirked.

"He's afraid of doing wrong."

I shut the door and leaned back as the engine rumbled to life.

"And he ain't even met the man that Marcus became."

Back at the club, I shut myself in my office, the bass from the main room thumping through the walls like a heartbeat I didn't trust anymore.

I poured myself a drink — neat, no ice — and didn't taste a thing.

My mind kept replaying Malik's face on the porch.

Not because of Malik.

Because of Marcus.

The way Malik's eyes flashed confusion, then fear, then something deeper — something only people with ghosts feel — cracked open a memory I'd buried.

I sank into my leather chair, staring at nothing, letting the past claw its way back up to the last night I saw Marcus.

He was fourteen.

Skinny but sharp.

A shadow of anger wrapped in a boy's body.

He stood in the alley behind my club, jaw swollen from a fight he wouldn't explain, eyes lit up with something reckless.

"You sure you want this life?" I asked him.

He nodded without hesitation.

"Then don't ever stop running toward it," I told him.

And Marcus didn't.

He ran headfirst —

into business he was too young for,

into loyalty he didn't deserve,

into violence he learned too fast.

He made me money.

He made me laugh.

He annoyed the hell outta me sometimes.

But he was mine.

And then one night... he wasn't.

He came to me with a bag of cash and a busted lip.

"Gotta disappear," he said.

"Heat's on me."

I remember staring at him too long, feeling it.

Not fear.

Not regret.

Intent.

"Disappear where?" I asked slowly.

He smirked — that same half-arrogant, half-sad smile he used when he thought I couldn't read him.

"You'll see."

He left.

Two days later, a body turned up.

Burned.

Unrecognizable.

Dental records matched to Marcus.

Or so they claimed.

I poured money into that funeral.

Closed casket.

Lot of whispers.

But nobody questioned it.

Nobody.

Not even me.

Because Marcus was the kind of kid trouble found —
or the kind who found trouble first.

I took it at face value.

He's dead.

He's gone.

End of story.

But tonight — watching that shadow duck into the alley outside the church —

watching Malik's face twist when I said his brother's name —

everything in me snapped awake.

I leaned back in my chair, the leather creaking under the weight of the truth.

"That wasn't Malik," I muttered.

Diesel had asked earlier what "off" felt like.

I knew now.

It felt like Marcus.

It felt like betrayal with a pulse.

It felt like a boy who learned how to disappear...

and came back a man who knew how to blend in.

"He planned this," I whispered.

The words hit the room heavy.

Marcus didn't run because he was scared.

He didn't fake his death because he was sloppy.

He didn't let Jeremiah bury a stranger by accident.

No.

Marcus dug his own grave and climbed out of it with a smile.

This wasn't survival.

This was strategy.

I stood, pacing in front of my desk, piecing the puzzle with a clarity I hadn't felt in years.

"He set Jeremiah up," I muttered.

"He dumped the heat on the church."

"He waited."

"He watched."

"And now—"

I slammed my hand against the desk, breath sharp.

"He wants Malik to take the fall next."

All those years of mentoring that kid…

all those nights teaching him how to move, how to think, how to disappear…

he'd used every lesson.

Against me.

Against his father.

Against his brother.

I laughed once — low, humorless, full of disbelief.

"Marcus Cross, you magnificent little bastard."

I grabbed my phone and started dialing.

Diesel answered immediately.

"Yes, boss?"

I stared at my reflection in the dark window —

older, sharper, and more dangerous than the man who raised Marcus.

"Marcus is alive," I said.

Diesel's breath hitched.

"You sure?"

I downed the rest of my drink.

"I'm positive."

A slow chill crawled across the room.

Diesel's voice came through tense, ready.

"What now, boss?"

I smiled — the kind that meant someone's world was about to crack.

"We change the plan."

I picked up my coat.

"This ain't about collecting money no more."

I walked toward the door, darkness pulling tight behind me.

"This is a hunt."

The club was loud, but my office felt too quiet.

The kind of quiet that comes right before a storm hits the block.

I stood there staring at the blank monitors, adrenaline burning slow through my veins.

Two years.

Two years I'd believed Marcus Cross was dead.

And now he was slipping through alleys, watching me confront his twin like it was entertainment.

Enough was enough.

I grabbed my phone, hit the encrypted speed dial, and waited.

Diesel picked up in one ring.

"Boss?"

"Get everybody," I said. "Right-hand men, shooters, runners—everyone loyal. Ten minutes. My office."

Diesel didn't ask questions.

"On it."

I hung up and waited, pacing, replaying every memory I had of Marcus.

The kid was clever.

Too clever.

Always playing three steps ahead but pretending to be two steps behind.

He didn't vanish by accident.

He didn't get "killed" by mistake.

He didn't leave a burnt body because he had no choice.

He crafted an exit.

A perfect little magic trick.

And now he was back.

By the time my crew filed into the room, I'd already made up my mind.

Diesel shut the door behind him.

Twelve men stood waiting—some nervous, some eager, all armed.

I let the silence stretch.

Then—

"Marcus Cross is alive."

Half the room stiffened.

Diesel blinked, jaw tight. "You sure?"

"He watched y'all outside the church tonight," I said. "Slipped into an alley like a ghost soon as you spotted him."

A murmur rippled through the room.

"Thought he was burned up."

"That funeral was real—"

"We watched his casket go in the—"

I raised my hand.

Silence snapped into place.

"That wasn't Marcus in that casket," I said. "It was whoever he needed the world to believe was him."

I stepped forward, voice low.

"He planned his death. He set Jeremiah up. And now he's moving pieces we can't see yet. He stole my money. He's the one we put me on his dad. Assured me he'd jump at the opportunity to launder my money."

Diesel asked, "What you want done, boss?"

I didn't hesitate.

"Find Marcus," I said.

I let the words hit them one by one.

Slow.

Heavy.

"Find him ALIVE."

Silence followed—sharp, stunned.

Then the questions started.

"Alive? Why alive?"

"What you need him for?"

"Boss… Marcus ain't gonna come in quiet."

I cut them off with a look.

"I didn't ask for quiet."

I leaned on the desk, eyes locked on every man in that room.

"Marcus Cross is dangerous. Smart. Strategic. He thinks he's untouchable because he fooled the world once."

A slow grin pulled at my mouth.

"But he ain't fooling me again."

I pointed toward the door.

"I want eyes on Malik. Eyes on Nova. Eyes on that damn church. If Marcus shows his face, you don't shoot. You don't chase. You don't blink."

I straightened.

"You call me."

Rico frowned. "Why keep him alive?"

I smirked darkly.

"Because I'm the only man he's ever feared," I said. "And when I'm done with him—"

I exhaled slow, steady, lethal.

"—he's gonna remember why."

Diesel nodded once and moved to open the door.

"Move," I ordered.

The men filed out fast, tension crackling around them.

When the door shut, I rested my hands on the back of my chair, eyes burning on the empty monitors.

Marcus wasn't dead.

He wasn't lost.

He wasn't gone.

He was hunting.

And now?

So was I.

Five

MALIK

S leep didn't exist anymore.

Not since Taz Moreno showed up on my doorstep like he owned the night...

and my father's downfall...

and somehow—

my brother's memory.

Marcus.

Even thinking his name felt like reopening a wound I'd worked two years to scar over.

Taz talking about him like he was still alive?

Still out there?

Still part of something?

It made me sick.

Taz was the reason Marcus broke.

The reason Marcus left.

The reason the darkness in him grew faster than the light in him ever had a chance to.

He didn't get to say my brother's name like a greeting.

He didn't get to act like they were old friends.

I rubbed both hands over my face and stared at the clock.

4:32 AM.

Three hours until I had to preach my first sermon as interim pastor of Kingdom Rising.

Three hours until I had to stand in the pulpit my father built

and my brother rejected

and pretend like the ground under my feet wasn't splitting open.

All week I'd shut myself off —

ignoring calls, ignoring texts, ignoring Simone's seventeen messages about service structure.

"Rest," Nova had texted.

"I'm praying for you."

I didn't answer her either.

I couldn't answer anybody.

There wasn't enough of me to go around.

I hadn't spoken to my father since the arrest.

I hadn't been allowed to see him.

His lawyer kept saying "be patient," but patience felt like choking.

I got up from the bed and stood there a moment, palms braced on my knees, breathing slow.

"I cannot fall apart today," I muttered.

But it felt possible.

Too possible.

I walked to the dresser and looked at the suit hanging on the door — black, pressed, ready.

It didn't look like mine.

It looked like Jeremiah's.

Like something he'd wear while preaching a sermon titled *Hold On to Your Hope.*

Except hope felt thin right now.

A vibration buzzed my phone.

Not a message—

a voicemail.

From the jail.

My heart tripped hard in my chest.

I played it.

My father's voice came through fractured, rushed, strained:

"Malik... son... listen... everything is—don't trust—don't let—"

Static swallowed his words.

Then the call disconnected.

I stood still, the phone warm against my hand.

No fear.

No panic.

Just clarity.

Whatever this was, whatever storm had swallowed my family, whatever secrets were clawing their way up from the past—

I had to preach anyway.

I had to lead anyway.

I had to walk into that sanctuary with my father gone, the board in chaos, the congregation whispering, payroll overdue, and my brother's ghost stirring up trouble he didn't even cause.

I straightened my back.

I inhaled slow.

Then I whispered to myself—

"Marcus, whatever mess you left... I'm not letting it take us out."

I grabbed my suit.

I got dressed.

And I headed to Kingdom Rising.

Just a man carrying more than he ever asked for.

I pulled into the church parking lot before sunrise.

The sky was still that deep bruised blue, the kind that made the cross on top of Kingdom Rising look like it was floating.

This early, the lot should've been empty.

It wasn't.

Three cars sat crooked near the main entrance.

Lights were on in the administrative wing.

Shadows moved behind the glass.

My stomach tightened.

They were already here.

And not just here—gathered.

I stepped out of my car, the morning air cold enough to bite.

As soon as my shoes hit the pavement, the door to the admin hallway opened, and Elder Simone stepped out like she'd been waiting for me.

She was dressed head to toe in navy blue, glasses dangling from a beaded chain, her Bible tucked under her arm with the authority of someone who believed she'd been chosen, not elected.

"Pastor Malik," she said.

I flinched at the title.

"Good morning, Elder," I replied.

"Morning?" She checked her watch. "Barely. We've been here since five."

"We?"

The door swung wider, and the others stepped out behind her.

Rusty Hargrove.

Pearl Jenkins.

Church treasurer Kendra Mills.

And Mother Lavvy, fanning herself with a bulletin already like it was a holy artifact.

All of them looking at me.

Some desperate.

Some annoyed.

Some sizing me up like a student who just got called to the board.

Rusty grunted.

"You're late."

"It's 5:50 AM," I said quietly.

Rusty shrugged. "Timing is everything."

Simone stepped forward.

"We didn't know if you were coming today," she said. "You've been...
unavailable."

I inhaled through my nose.

She wasn't wrong.

But I wasn't in the mood for a lecture.

"What's going on?" I asked.

Simone clasped her hands together.

"We need clarity before service."

Lavvy cut in, dramatic as only she could manage:

"They're panicked, baby," she said. "They been pacing like the rapture
on a countdown timer. Half the congregation think you gon' resign.
The other half think you gon' get arrested next."

"LAVVY!" Simone hissed.

"What?" Lavvy blinked innocently. "We supposed to tell the truth in
the house of the Lord."

Rusty stepped closer, jaw tight.

"Malik, we gotta talk money. Payroll. Messaging. Optics. The
livestream comments are out of hand. Folks digging through
Jeremiah's old sermons like they're evidence. We need—"

"I know," I said, more sharply than intended.

They all paused.

Kendra spoke up, voice softer.

"We're not the enemy, Malik. We just... don't know what happens
today. The congregation is confused. Scared. We need leadership
from you."

Leadership.

The word sat heavy on my chest.

"I'm working on my sermon," I said. "I'll be ready."

Simone studied me too long.

"You don't look ready."

I locked eyes with her.

"I said I'll be ready."

The tension between us crackled like static.

Mother Lavvy stepped forward suddenly, pressing a hand to my cheek like I was still five years old.

"Baby," she whispered, "your spirit looks tired."

My throat tightened.

It was the gentlest sentence anyone had said to me all week.

Before I could answer, Pearl Jenkins chimed in with her signature brand of chaos:

"Well, if he tired now, he better wake up by 10 AM because saints don't play about start times. Service delayed ONE minute and they'll start calling Jesus directly."

"Pearl—PLEASE," Simone snapped.

Pearl held up her hands. "I'm just saying!"

The group erupted again—talking over each other, debating, worrying, fussing.

And I stood in the middle of them, stunned by how loud it all was.

How heavy it all felt.

How much responsibility had shifted onto my shoulders in less than a week.

Finally, I lifted both hands.

"STOP."

They fell silent.

All eyes on me.

"This morning is about God," I said slowly. "Not optics. Not rumors.

Not panic."

They waited.

I swallowed.

"And I'm going to preach. I promise you that."

Simone nodded, even if she didn't look fully convinced.

Rusty grunted in agreement.

Lavvy touched my arm.

"You ain't alone, baby," she said softly. "God got you."

I wished I believed that as much as she did.

But I nodded anyway.

"Thank you," I murmured.

I turned toward the sanctuary doors.

"Let me get ready."

They stepped aside, watching me walk in.

Watching me become something I never asked to be.

Something I wasn't sure I was built to handle.

Interim pastor.

Leader.

The Cross still standing.

I cut through the sanctuary, the early morning light spilling through the stained-glass windows in fractured blues and reds. The room was empty, quiet, too still for everything churning inside me.

Jeremiah's office sat behind the pulpit hallway — a door I hadn't walked through alone since I was a teenager. The air always smelled like polished wood, expensive cologne, and secrets.

I opened the door slowly.

The scent hit first.

Warm.

Heavy.

Lavish.

Exactly like him.

I stepped inside.

The opulence made my stomach twist immediately.

Gold plaques lined the wall — "Pastor of the Year," "Community Impact Award," framed certificates Jeremiah made sure everyone saw but never talked about earning.

Designer suits filled an open wardrobe — deep navy, charcoal gray, royal purple, expensive fabrics that looked like they belonged to politicians more than a man of God.

Beneath the bookshelf, barely hidden if you knew where to look, sat two bottles of liquor behind a sliding wooden panel.

He thought we didn't know.

I sat in his oversized leather chair and immediately felt swallowed.

I didn't belong here.

The room didn't fit me.

The legacy didn't fit me.

I felt like a child pretending to wear a king's robe.

I opened my notebook — blank pages staring back at me like they were waiting for someone else's handwriting.

I hadn't written my sermon yet.

I hadn't written anything.

My throat tightened.

"I'm an imposter," I whispered to no one.

Jeremiah would never have admitted fear.

Marcus would've mocked it.

The board expected greatness.

The congregation wanted comfort.

Nova prayed for me.

Rusty doubted me.

Simone pushed me.

And I just wanted to breathe.

I closed my eyes and prayed — or tried to.

"Lord… I don't know what I'm doing. I don't know what You want me to say. I don't even know if I'm supposed to be here."

Silence.

Thick.

Quiet.

Suffocating.

I tried again.

"God, please. I need direction. Something. Anything."

Nothing.

No warmth.

No answer.

No whisper.

Just the hum of the office lights and my own pulse pounding in the stillness.

I leaned forward, elbows on my knees, fingers interlocked.

"This isn't my calling," I murmured. "It's his. I'm just the one left standing."

I looked at the plaques again — reminders of everything Jeremiah built.

Then at the hidden liquor — reminders of everything he hid.

Then at the door Marcus once slammed on his way out when he said he was done pretending.

Two brothers.

Two sons.

One dead, one left.

And now me, sitting in the seat of a man who built a kingdom on charisma and cracks I was only just now noticing.

Tears pricked the corners of my eyes, hot and unwanted.

"I can't preach hope when I can't feel it," I whispered.

I bowed my head, but the prayer didn't rise.

It stayed stuck in my chest, heavy and aching.

The silence didn't break.

Not for me.

Not this morning.

I wiped my face, straightened my back, and forced myself to stand.

If God wasn't speaking, then I would have to walk anyway.

Not because I was ready.

But because everyone expected me to.

I grabbed my notebook and walked out of Jeremiah's office — the legacy he built, the secrets he hid, the mess he left and headed toward the pulpit he would not be standing in today.

I left my father's office feeling hollowed out, the silence still clinging to my skin.

My sermon notes were nothing but blank lines and anxiety.

I reminded myself to breathe as I headed down the hallway toward the sanctuary.

That's when I saw it.

A folded piece of paper slipped under the door of my private study— the room the choir used for prayer, the one only staff had access to.

I frowned and picked it up.

No envelope.

No name.

Just a message scribbled in jagged handwriting: "**You owe us. Meet tonight.**"

My stomach dropped so fast it made me dizzy.

I read it again.

You owe us.

Owe who?

My hands went cold.

This wasn't a prank.

This wasn't a board issue.

This wasn't a congregation rumor.

This was connected to whatever world my father had fallen into…
and whatever world Taz thought I belonged to.

My pulse kicked, sharp and panicked.

I flipped the note over — a number was written on the back.

No name.

No instructions.

Just ten digits and expectation.

I dialed immediately, hand shaking.

The call rang once.

Twice.

Then: **"This number has been disconnected."**

Disconnected.

Right after leaving the note?

Right before service?

The timing made my chest tighten.

I stared at my phone, breath short, willing the number to work again
even though I knew it wouldn't.

I deleted it from my recent calls on instinct.

That's when footsteps echoed behind me.

"Kyrie" I called out before he even turned the corner.

He stopped mid-step.

His camera bag hung off one shoulder, his curls were tied back,
and his expression said he'd been up all night watching the internet
combust around us.

"Pastor." He gave a small nod, then winced. "Sorry—Malik. Habit."

I tried to gather myself.

"What's up?"

He opened his mouth.

Hesitated.

Closed it again.

I watched his eyes. They weren't just tired—they were worried.

"Something you need to tell me?" I asked quietly.

He shook his head too fast.

"No—no, it's… never mind."

"Kyrie."

He took a small step back.

"I shouldn't… it's probably nothing," he whispered.

Fear flickered in his eyes before he forced a smile that didn't reach his face.

"If you need me, I'll be in the media booth. Livestream's a mess today."

He started to walk off.

"Kyrie," I said again, louder.

He stopped but didn't turn around.

"Are you okay?" I asked.

A long pause.

Then—

"Ask me that after service," he murmured.

And he kept walking.

I watched him go, the note burning a hole in my pocket, the disconnected number echoing in my ears, the weight of the entire church pressing on my chest.

Whatever was happening—

It wasn't just about money.

Or reputation.

Or my father.

Something bigger was moving.

And now it had reached me.

The sanctuary felt unfamiliar when I stepped onto the pulpit.

Thin crowd.

Sparse amens.

A room that once overflowed with bodies now scattered with

hesitation and folded arms.

Scandals always split congregations.

Some came to pray.

Some came to gossip.

Some came to see if I would crack.

I almost did.

My hands trembled as I set Jeremiah's Bible on the pulpit.

My breath felt shallow.

My chest tight.

Lord... I don't have it today.

I cleared my throat.

"Good morning," I started softly.

A few murmured responses echoed back.

I swallowed hard and forced myself to continue.

"I know... things feel broken right now."

The sanctuary quieted.

People leaned in.

"I know our hearts are heavy, our leadership is shaken, and the future feels uncertain."

My voice wavered, but I didn't hide it.

"I'm not here to pretend I have all the answers. I'm not here to fill my father's shoes. I'm... I'm just a man trying to stand where God put him. Even if I don't fully understand why."

Someone sniffed.

Another whispered, "Help him, Lord."

My throat tightened.

Behind me, Nova's soft alto rose in a hum—steady, gentle, anchoring the room the way she always did.

Her voice carried something mine couldn't yet.

Strength.

Permission.

Peace.

I opened the Bible, hands steadier now.

"My scripture this morning comes from *Psalm 34:18:*

'The Lord is close to the brokenhearted and saves those who are crushed in spirit.'"

A ripple moved through the sanctuary.

"That's where we are today," I said. "Brokenhearted. Crushed. Confused."

I pressed my hand to the pulpit.

"But God does His best work in ruins."

A quiet amen rose.

"God does His best work when the stage is empty, when the crowds are thin, when the leaders fall, when the plans collapse. Because that's when we stop trusting the structure..."

My voice grew stronger.

"...and start trusting the Savior."

Now the room was with me.

People sat up straighter.

Heads nodded.

Hands lifted.

"The enemy loves scandal. Loves division. Loves when the church is wounded. But he forgets—God can resurrect anything."

A wave of *yes, Lord* washed across the sanctuary.

Nova's hum grew fuller, pushing courage into my lungs.

"And maybe—just maybe—this isn't the end of Kingdom Rising."

Silence.

Then—

"Amen!"

"Maybe this is God stripping away what was never His in the first place."

The crowd stirred.

"And rebuilding something better."

Hands clapped.

Voices rose.

The anointing hit me like warm oil poured over my shoulders — heavy, real, unmistakable.

Words I hadn't planned, hadn't written, hadn't rehearsed poured out like they'd been waiting for this exact moment to breathe.

"The Cross family may be broken— but so is every family God ever used."

People stood.

"Yes, Pastor!"

"My father may be in chains— but God specializes in freeing what looks finished."

Applause.

Sobs.

The sound of faith crawling its way back into the room.

I felt alive.

Present.

Led.

I lifted my eyes to emphasize my next point and froze.

A man stood in the back doorway.

Tall.

Slim.

Head slightly tilted.

My face.

My height.

My build.

Me.

I blinked hard, breath catching.

He didn't move.

He just watched me.

Expression unreadable.

Like he knew I would see him.

Like he *wanted* me to.

My pulse crashed in my ears.

I stepped slightly forward, squinting and in the space of a single exhale he was gone.

Not faded.

Not walked away.

Gone.

The doorway was empty.

The hall behind it still.

A cold prickle crawled up my spine, but I forced myself back into the sermon, voice steady even as my insides twisted.

"Church..." I said, gripping the pulpit, "God sees what's hidden. And He reveals what's been buried."

The congregation hollered.

They thought I meant Jeremiah.

Or sin.

Or spiritual warfare.

But my hands trembled because I knew—

I hadn't preached that line.

It came out of me the moment I saw the face that matched mine.

Marcus.

Alive.

And closer than I thought.

The moment I stepped down from the pulpit, the sanctuary was still buzzing.

People hugging.

Crying.

Lifting their hands.

Telling each other, *"Maybe God ain't done with us yet."*

For a split second, I let myself breathe.

But peace never lasts long around here.

Before I even made it to the hallway, Elder Simone was already marching toward me, heels clicking like spiritual gunfire.

She grabbed my elbows firmly — too firmly.

"That," she said through a tight smile, "was the sermon Kingdom Rising needed."

I nodded, but her grip didn't loosen.

"And it was the sermon we needed," she added more quietly.

Her eyes flashed with something I couldn't name — part approval, part calculation.

Before I could respond, Rusty Hargrove came barreling up behind her.

Rusty didn't do quiet.

His voice hit the hallway like a bass drum.

"It was… fine."

Simone shot him a glare.

"Rusty."

"What?" he shrugged. "Man did good for a first sermon, but let's not act like the boy turned water to wine."

I exhaled slowly.

"Thank you, Deacon."

"I ain't complimented you," Rusty muttered. "I just ain't insulted you."

Simone elbowed him sharply.

He grunted.

Mother Lavvy swooped in next, fanning herself hard enough to create a personal climate.

"BABY!" she declared, grabbing my hands. "You preached that word like angels was standing behind you feeding you bullet points."

I couldn't help smiling.

"Thank you, Mother Lavvy."

"I felt the anointing all in my left hip! The Holy Ghost hasn't hit that hip since '03!"

"Lavvy..." Simone groaned.

But Lavvy ignored her, pulling me into a head-patting hug.

"Don't you let nobody tell you God ain't called you for a time such as this," she whispered fiercely.

Over her shoulder, I caught sight of Pearl Jenkins, arms folded, face scrunched, clearly contemplating whether the message was enough to cancel the church group chat meltdown she orchestrated every week.

She spoke up finally.

"I give it a B minus," Pearl said. "Good content, shaky delivery. And you sweat too much."

Simone nearly choked.

Rusty barked a laugh.

Lavvy smacked Pearl's arm.

"What?!" Pearl snapped. "We need excellence in the Lord's house!"

I pinched the bridge of my nose, already exhausted again.

Then Kendra, our treasurer, approached hesitantly.

Her voice was soft, almost timid.

"Malik... that was beautiful," she said. "I... I needed that."

There was sincerity there — real, unpolished sincerity — and it steadied something in me.

But the moment passed quickly.

Because Simone stepped forward again, posture straight, tone cool.

"We'll need to meet this week," she said. "Payroll. Budget freeze. Public statement. And... optics."

"Optics?" I repeated.

She nodded.

"The sermon was excellent, Malik. Truly. But revival is emotional. Recovery is administrative. The board wants to move quickly."

Rusty chimed in.

"We gotta talk numbers, Malik. Bills don't care about the anointing."

Simone shot him another glare, but he wasn't wrong.

Pearl folded her arms tighter.

"And we need to figure out who left during the sermon. I counted at least fourteen people who slipped out. Including Sister Thelma who owes *me* twenty dollars."

Lavvy gasped.

"That woman ain't paid a debt since Reagan!"

Rusty threw up his hands. "For the love of God, will everybody shut—"

"ENOUGH," Simone barked.

Silence fell instantly.

Then all eyes returned to me.

It felt like the weight of the whole ministry sat on their stares.

Simone stepped closer, voice dropping.

"Malik," she said, "today proved you can lead. Whether you feel ready or not. Don't waste this momentum."

Her tone wasn't encouragement.

It was direction.

Expectation.

Pressure wrapped in professionalism.

Then Rusty slapped my shoulder — hard enough to sting.

"You held it down, kid," he grunted. "But preaching is the easy part. Leading? That's the storm."

Pearl nodded, lips pursed.

"We're watching you."

Lavvy elbowed her again.

"Watching him for what? You want him to part the Red Sea?"

Pearl shrugged.

"If he can fix payroll by Wednesday, I'll settle for that."

Simone lifted her chin.

"We'll see you in the boardroom tomorrow morning at nine."

It wasn't a question.

Kendra gave me one last reassuring smile, then followed the others down the hall.

And like that—

the applause faded,

the encouragement evaporated,

and I was just Malik again.

A man with too much on his plate

and too little guidance.

I leaned back against the wall, exhaling hard.

For a moment, the sermon felt like breakthrough.

But now it felt like the beginning of a storm I wasn't prepared for.

The hallway finally emptied.

Simone's perfume faded in the air.

Lavvy's fan clicks softened behind a closing door.

Rusty's voice echoed somewhere complaining about the thermostat.

I leaned against the wall and closed my eyes.

I needed five minutes.

Just five minutes to breathe without somebody asking me for leadership, money, a plan, a miracle—

"Malik."

I opened my eyes.

Kyrie stood at the end of the hall, half in shadow, camera strap twisted in his hands. He looked nervous—more nervous than he did when the livestream crashed during Easter service last year.

I straightened.

"You good?" I asked.

He swallowed hard.

"We need to talk. Now."

The tone made my stomach drop.

I nodded and followed him into a small side room near the media booth. He shut the door behind us and lowered his voice.

"I didn't want to say anything earlier because... honestly, I didn't want it to be true."

My pulse kicked.

"Kyrie... what's going on?"

He looked up at me — wide-eyed, tired, scared.

"During your sermon," he said slowly, "I saw someone in the back hallway."

My chest tightened.

"A man?" I asked.

He nodded.

"Tall. Slim. Same haircut as you. Same build. Same beard shape. I—I thought it *was* you at first."

My mouth went dry.

Kyrie continued, voice thin:

"He was standing in the doorway watching you preach. But when I turned to check again, he was gone."

Every hair on my arms stood up.

Kyrie swallowed, then whispered:

"Malik... it looked like Marcus."

My breath caught so sharply it hurt.

Kyrie kept going before I could react.

"I know he's gone. I know what happened. I know we buried him. But—"

He shook his head.

"I've been seeing that same silhouette around campus all week. I thought I was tripping. But today? The way he watched you? Malik... I think someone is pretending to be him. Or—"

"No," I said, too fast.

My voice cracked.

"No, Kyrie."

He stared at me.

"You saw him too," he said quietly. "Didn't you?"

I didn't answer.

I didn't have to.

The look on my face told him everything.

Kyrie stepped closer.

"Malik… what if Marcus is alive?"

My hands trembled.

"Don't," I whispered. "Don't say that."

Kyrie didn't back down.

"You asked what I was gonna tell you earlier."

He hesitated.

"I saw him Thursday too. Outside the youth wing. He looked right at me."

A cold rush slid through me.

"Kyrie… Marcus is dead."

Kyrie ran a hand through his curls.

"Then who the hell was that?"

I stared at him, heart pounding.

Whoever it was… he moved like Marcus.

He watched like Marcus.

He stood in the shadows like Marcus.

But Marcus was buried.

Right?

Right?

Before I could respond, someone knocked on the door.

Soft.

Concerned.

"Malik?"

Nova's voice.

Kyrie and I exchanged a glance.

He exhaled hard.

"Talk to her," he murmured. "You look like you're about to fall over."

He slipped out through the side door before Nova entered.

Nova stepped in gently, eyes scanning my face with worry.

"You okay?" she asked softly.

Something in me cracked.

I didn't have the strength to fake it.

"No," I whispered.

Her expression softened even more.

She stepped closer but didn't touch me—not until I gave her permission with my silence.

She placed a steady hand on my arm.

"You preached beautifully," she said. "But the moment you stepped down… something shifted in you."

Her voice was calm, warm, grounding.

"What's going on?" she asked.

I opened my mouth—

And for the first time since this nightmare started,

I almost said it:

I saw Marcus.

Alive.

And I don't know what that means.

I don't know what's coming.

I don't know what to do.

But the words stuck.

Because if I said them out loud,

I'd have to face the truth:

My brother might not be dead.

And whatever he was doing back here…

It wasn't for reconciliation.

It was for destruction.

Nova squeezed my arm gently, pulling me back into my body.

"I'm here," she whispered. "Just tell me what you need."

I breathed hard, trying to steady myself.

But nothing felt steady anymore.

Not my spirit.

Not my memory.

Not my reality.

Because if Marcus was alive…

Why the hell had he come back?

Nova didn't push me.

She didn't rush me.

She just stood there—soft, steady, patient—like she knew forcing words out of me would break something I couldn't put back together.

"Malik…" she murmured, "let me pray with you."

I nodded because that's what I was supposed to do.

Because I was the pastor-on-deck.

Because she was trying to help.

Because saying no felt like failing at something else today.

But inside?

My mind was far from here.

Nova took my hands gently—warm fingers wrapping around mine—and bowed her head.

I bowed mine too, but my jaw was clenched so tight it hurt.

She started praying.

"Father, strengthen Malik right now. Give him peace in every place that feels shaken. Remind him he's not walking into this alone. Cover his mind. Cover his heart. Cover the weight he's carrying—"

Her words should've comforted me.

Normally they would've.

But all I could see was the man in the doorway.

My face.

My height.

My shadow.

Marcus.

Alive.

How?

Why?

What did he want?

What was he planning?

Nova squeezed my hands, mistaking my silence for humility instead of panic.

"Lord, remind him that You have not given him the spirit of fear—"

Marcus's eyes.

Marcus's stance.

Marcus watching me preach like he was measuring the distance between my life and his revenge.

"—but of power, love, and a sound mind."

A sound mind.

Mine didn't feel sound at all.

I blinked, and suddenly the memory played sharp:

Marcus at fifteen, leaning in a doorway watching me practice a sermon for youth night—same posture, same tilt of the head, same smug little smirk.

"Your delivery sucked," he'd said back then. "But you got potential."

And now he was back?

Watching me again?

Judging me again?

Or stalking me?

Or setting me up?

Nova's voice softened even deeper.

"God, settle his spirit..."

She didn't know my spirit wasn't unsettled.

It was unraveling.

I felt my breath stutter, too shallow, too fast.

Her thumbs brushed my knuckles as she kept praying—

"...give him clarity about anything causing confusion or fear..."

I swallowed hard.

If I told her what I saw...

If I told her Kyrie saw it too...

If I said out loud that Marcus wasn't dead...

Would she believe me?

Would she panic?

Would she run?

Would she pray harder?

Or worst—would she think I was losing my mind?

When Nova finally whispered "Amen," I didn't realize I'd been staring at the floor the whole time.

She lifted her head, her eyes soft with concern.

"Malik... you weren't with me at all."

The truth hit too fast to dodge.

I tried pulling away but she held my hand tighter.

"What's going on?" she whispered.

My throat felt too tight to answer.

She stepped closer, her voice barely above breath.

"Whatever it is—you don't have to hold it alone."

But I *was* alone.

Because how did I explain that the brother I buried might have been standing in the church watching me preach?

I let out a shaking breath.

"...Nova, I'm not okay."

It was the closest I could get to the truth.

Her eyes softened—sad, tender, deep.

"Then let me carry some of it with you," she said.

I almost broke right there.

But before I could say another word, footsteps echoed from the sanctuary—

board members returning, people gathering, someone calling my name, chaos approaching.

Nova released one hand but not the other.

"Later," she whispered. "Tell me later. Please."

I nodded.

But later already felt too late.

Because if Marcus was alive...

He was already five steps ahead of all of us.

* * *

After the service, after the praise, after the board's demands and Nova's prayers and Kyrie's confession, I thought the worst part of the day was over.

I was wrong.

I had just stepped out of my car in my driveway when headlights washed over me from behind.

A black sedan.

Tinted windows.

Engine humming too smooth to belong to anyone I knew.

Before I could react, a man stepped out — tall, built like a wall, no expression.

"Malik Cross?" he asked.

I froze.

"...Yeah?"

"Boss wants to see you."

I didn't need to ask which boss.

He opened the back door.

"Now."

My throat dried.

I tried to pull one step back, just one, but another man appeared behind me, blocking retreat.

I got in the car.

The ride was silent.

No radio.

No conversation.

Just the sound of my breath getting tighter by the minute.

We didn't pull into the front of the club — of course not.

They took me around the back where deals happened, fights started, and bodies disappeared.

The henchman escorted me through a steel door into a dim hallway that smelled like liquor, smoke, and danger.

Every step made my pulse thud harder.

When Taz finally turned around from where he stood at the bar, it felt like the room shifted.

He smiled like he'd been expecting me all night.

"Pastor Cross."

My title sounded like mockery.

He gestured toward a leather chair.

"Sit."

I didn't move.

"I said sit."

I sat.

He leaned against the counter, arms crossed, studying me like a problem he enjoyed solving.

"You know why you're here."

I forced myself to speak.

"I don't belong in this world, Taz. Whatever business you had with my father—"

"Two point seven million," he interrupted. "That's the business."

My breath hitched.

"That money's gone," I said quietly. "Frozen. The church is in shambles. I can't—there's no way I can come up with that."

"Yes," Taz said, "you can."

He moved closer, slow and deliberate, like a wolf circling prey.

"You Cross boys always find a way when your backs are against the wall."

"My father hid things from me," I said. "I don't know anything about money laundering or fronts or whatever he was mixed up in. I didn't ask for this."

Taz shrugged.

"And I didn't ask to lose $2.7 million. Yet here we are."

My hands clenched against my knees.

"Taz, please—"

He cut me off with a raised hand.

"I don't want your prayers, Malik. I want my money."

"I can't give you what I don't have," I said, voice cracking.

He sighed like I was inconveniencing him.

"Well... figure it out."

"Taz—"

He grabbed my jaw suddenly, forcing me to look him in the eyes.

"You think Jeremiah's scandal broke you?" he growled. "You think preaching one sermon makes you a man? Let me teach you something nobody told you while you were growing up in that pew."

He leaned in, breath cold.

"Strength don't come from titles. It comes from pressure."

He released my face.

"And I'm about to apply a lot of pressure."

My stomach flipped.

"I'm not my father," I whispered.

"No," he agreed. "You're softer."

Then he smiled — that same vicious smile from my porch.

"But maybe Marcus can help toughen you up."

My heart stopped.

"What did you say?"

Taz tilted his head.

"You heard me."

My pulse roared in my ears.

"No," I stammered. "That's—that's impossible."

"Is it?"

"He's dead."

Taz laughed.

Actually laughed.

"Oh, Malik," he said. "You're smart, but you're naïve."

My legs trembled, breath uneven.

"Where is he?" I whispered.

Taz shrugged.

"Somewhere close. Closer than you think."

My body went cold.

"Why didn't he come to me?"

My voice shook.

"Why didn't he check on our father? Why didn't he—?"

I swallowed hard.

"Why would he let everyone think he was dead?"

Taz stepped back, eyes narrowing.

"Malik... you ever consider he wanted it that way?"

My heart sank into my stomach.

"You're lying," I whispered.

"Am I?" Taz shrugged. "Or did your brother fake his death, disappear, set up your father, and now wants to watch you crumble too?"

My legs buckled.

Literally.

I fell to my knees, hands catching the floor, breath choking out of me.

Taz watched, expression unreadable.

"Get up, Cross."

I couldn't.

Everything in me shattered.

Marcus alive.

Marcus watching me.

Marcus letting me mourn him.

Marcus letting our father rot.

Marcus starting something he wasn't finished with.

"Why... why would he do this?" I whispered, voice breaking.

Taz crouched in front of me, gripping my chin again, forcing eye contact.

"Because the Marcus you mourned?" he said softly.

"That wasn't the real Marcus."

I froze.

"The real one," Taz continued, "has a plan. And you? You're in it."

My breath stuttered, sharp and painful.

"Welcome to the family business," Taz whispered.

"And pray your brother shows mercy."

Six

MARCUS CROSS

I watched from the rooftop across the street.
Not hiding.
Not rushing.
Not nervous.

Just watching.

The black sedan pulled into the alley behind Taz's club, headlights slicing through the dark. One of Taz's men stepped out, opened the back door, and pulled Malik out by the arm.

My brother stumbled, confused, scared, trying to keep his dignity even though he had none left to cling to.

They walked him through the back entrance.

I didn't blink.

Didn't flinch.

Didn't feel anything at all.

You'd think watching your twin get dragged into a place that almost killed you would stir something — fear, anger, sympathy.

It didn't.

Malik always looked like that:
slightly overwhelmed,
slightly breathless,
slightly out of place.
He was built for pulpits.
For soft words and soft hands.
For a life that assumed safety.
I wasn't.
And the world never let you forget which brother it preferred to keep.
I leaned on the railing, hands loose in my pockets, the city buzzing beneath me.
The henchman nudged Malik forward again.
He tripped this time.
I exhaled a small laugh.
Still clumsy.
Still predictable.
Still fragile.
Taz pulled him inside and the door slammed shut.
Good.
Let him learn.
Let him sweat.
Let him realize the Cross name isn't a shield anymore.
It's a target.
I shifted my weight and watched a few seconds longer, just to see if Malik would try to run. He didn't. He never did. Even as a kid, he froze under pressure. I was the one who fought back.
I was the one who learned to disappear.
I was the one who understood the world wasn't built to be fair.
Malik waited for life to hand him the next step.
I took mine by force.

I checked my watch.

Taz wouldn't kill him — not yet.

He needed Malik scared, not buried.

And fear was Malik's native language even if he didn't admit it.

A door creaked near me; the rooftop access.

I didn't turn.

Didn't need to.

The footsteps were too quiet for an enemy, too familiar to be new.

"You showed yourself today," a voice said beside me.

I smirked slightly.

"Just enough."

"Dangerous move."

"Only if someone catches me," I said.

I didn't look at him.

Didn't need approval, didn't need advice.

I watched the alley instead, watched the shadows settle as if nothing had happened.

"Why now?" he asked. "Why reveal yourself now?"

I finally looked over.

My eyes were calm.

Empty.

"Because the Cross family owes me," I said. "And debt always comes due."

I returned my gaze to the alley door.

"And Malik?" he asked.

A pause.

A thin smile crept across my lips — not cruel, not warm.

Just... inevitable.

"Malik is step one."

I straightened, dusted off my jacket, and headed toward the exit door.

Tomorrow, the real work begins.

And the beautiful part?

Malik still doesn't realize:

I faked my death for a reason.

I stayed gone for a reason.

And I came back for a reason.

A reason he's not ready for.

A reason I don't intend to explain until it's too late.

I left the rooftop without a backward glance.

Because watching Malik break did nothing to me.

Absolutely nothing.

Only one vision in my mind. The night I disappeared for good.

Fire.

Smoke.

A body burned beyond recognition.

Dental records swapped with one of Lysander's victims.

Taz knew, but not all the details.

Jeremiah never questioned it.

Malik definitely never questioned it.

The world bought the story with zero effort from me.

Because here's the truth people don't like to admit:

Nobody looks too closely when a troubled kid dies.

Not even family.

I hid in the shadows.

Watched from a distance.

Waited to see who mourned me.

Who would crumble?

Who would cry?

Who would scream that it wasn't me?

No one.

Not a single damn person.

Jeremiah preached a sermon about "the dangers of rebellion," barely choking up during the altar call.

Malik cried for maybe a week.

Then he tucked himself back into the safety of church walls like nothing ever happened.

Taz?

Business as usual.

Didn't miss a step.

Didn't miss a meal.

Didn't miss me.

The boy he claimed he raised in the streets?

Forgotten.

I watched them all move on while I became a ghost.

And in that silence, something inside me hardened.

If they wanted a ghost, I'd give them one.

If they could live without me, I'd show them how wrong they were.

But Malik... Malik was the key.

He had the face.

The access.

The favor.

Everything people withheld from me.

Everything they robbed me of.

So I studied him.

His posture.

His sermons.

His tone.

His routine.

His walk.

He made it easy.

People are stupid when they like you.

They project whatever they want to see.

And I'm the mirror in his face.

Identical enough to pass.

Different enough to choose when to blend.

A blessing and a curse.

Mostly a weapon.

And now it's time they all learn how much I mattered.

Jeremiah will learn.

Taz will learn.

Malik will learn.

Especially Malik.

I'm not coming back to reclaim my life.

I'm coming back to ruin theirs.

People often assume I vanished because I was afraid of Taz, but that was never the full story. Taz was dangerous, sure, but he wasn't the most dangerous man in the room. There are levels to the underworld, and once you cross a certain threshold, you learn quickly who truly holds power. I didn't disappear because Taz could hurt me. I disappeared because someone far worse could erase me without a trace: Lysander Cole.

The night I stole from him was the night my life split into two versions—before and after. I had skimmed a small amount of cash from a drop, thinking I was being clever, thinking nobody would notice ten thousand dollars on a route that saw hundreds of thousands moving through it. But Lysander noticed everything. When I walked into that warehouse with Taz's payment, Lysander was already waiting. He didn't yell or threaten. He didn't posture. He simply laid out evidence—photographs, timestamps, recordings—that showed he had watched me long before I knew his name.

He told me calmly that men who stole from him didn't get warnings. They got executed. But he also told me I had a skill set he found useful. He said I was quick, observant, and invisible when I needed to be.

Then he gave me a choice that wasn't a choice at all: either I would actually die that night, or I would "die" in a way that benefited him. He instructed me to disappear completely, and he made it clear he wasn't asking. If I was seen again, if anyone discovered I was alive, he would kill me himself.

From that moment forward, I wasn't living. I was serving. Lysander turned me into exactly what he needed—someone who could operate without being recognized or missed. I became a cleaner, wiping down scenes nobody should remember. I became a courier, transporting items that needed hands steady enough not to panic. I became an informant, gathering information in places where people never looked twice at me. And I became a shadow, moving from city to city with no ties, no family, and no future I controlled.

It wasn't courage that kept me alive; it was fear. Lysander had people everywhere. I learned early that running wasn't an option. There was no corner of the world he couldn't reach, no alias I could craft that he couldn't dismantle. The only thing I could do was stay useful and stay quiet, because being useful meant postponing death, and quiet meant staying off the radar of men who specialized in hunting ghosts.

Everything changed on a random Tuesday. I was in another abandoned building, cleaning a mess someone else made, when I overheard one of Lysander's lieutenants whisper that he had been shot. The rumor spread quickly and unevenly—one person claimed it happened during a deal, another swore it was an internal betrayal, and a third insisted it was a federal takedown gone sideways. No matter the truth, the result was the same: Lysander was dead.

His organization unraveled almost immediately. His top men turned on each other, fighting for pieces of an empire none of them were qualified to run. Some were killed in the chaos. Others fled the country. For the first time since my staged death, I realized there was no one left to enforce the threat that kept me locked in the shadows. I didn't celebrate; survival had trained that out of me. But I understood something important—if there was ever a moment to reclaim my life, this was it.

With Lysander gone, I wasn't tethered to servitude anymore. I didn't have to hide behind aliases or watch every doorway for a familiar silhouette. The leash he kept around my neck had snapped, and with it came a clarity I hadn't felt in years. Being dead to the world had become a punishment, but now it became an opportunity. No one had mourned me. No one had questioned the story. My father moved on without guilt. Taz continued business without blinking. Malik returned to his life as if nothing had fractured.

Their indifference lit something in me that even Lysander never managed to extinguish.

Now that I was free, I intended to return—not to pick up where I left off, but to confront the lives that kept going without me. Jeremiah, Taz, and especially Malik would finally understand what it meant to lose what they took for granted. They would finally see the version of me they helped create, even if they never realized it.

And with Lysander gone, there was no one left to stop me.

I needed Kingdom Rising stable before I made my first move. A dying church couldn't serve the purpose I had in mind. That's why, earlier that week, I dropped fifty thousand dollars into the offering basket during Sunday's twelve o'clock service. I stayed out of sight and timed it between usher rotations so no one questioned how the money got there. Panic turned to praise in a matter of seconds, and by Monday morning the board was already whispering that "God" had made a way. They had no idea they were thanking the wrong man.

With that handled, I focused on Tuesday.

Every Tuesday at six, the board held its weekly meeting. Malik always arrived early—five fifty on the dot, sometimes earlier if Nova caught him in a hallway conversation. The staff relied on his predictability, and he offered it freely. That made him easy to study.

For weeks, I'd watched him interact with a woman named Tiffany Monroe, a single mother who came to the church desperate for guidance about her son. She latched onto Malik the way hurting people latch onto anyone who will listen without judgment. He offered her patience, reassurance, prayer—tools I could replicate with minimal effort. And she trusted him. That mattered.

Tiffany also had a habit of arriving early on Tuesdays, hoping to catch Malik before the board meeting. He always made time for her, even when he didn't have it. That consistency made her the perfect entry point.

My plan was simple: arrive before Malik, intercept Tiffany, and establish myself as him—at least for a few minutes.

The opportunity was ideal. Traffic near the church thinned around five thirty. The staff offices were sparsely occupied by then. And most importantly, my old access still worked. My key fob scanned without question, and my old door codes remained active. Because I was presumed dead, no one thought to disable anything. A dead man wasn't a security concern.

I walked the hallway outside Jeremiah's former office—Malik's now, technically—and considered the steps carefully. I wasn't going in blind. I had spent months learning Malik's posture, cadence, tone, the way he softened his voice when he wanted someone to feel safe. I didn't need to imitate him perfectly. People saw what they expected to see, especially when emotions were involved.

If Tiffany believed she had already spoken with him when Malik actually arrived later, that confusion would work in my favor. All I needed was for one person to vouch that Malik had been in the building earlier than he actually was. It would plant the seed that there were moments he didn't remember—or moments people misremembered. Either way, it chipped at the edges of certainty.

The real goal wasn't Tiffany.

It was credibility.

Once someone believed they'd talked to Malik, even briefly, that belief would spread effortlessly. That's how churches worked. One person walked away confident, and ten others accepted their version of events without question.

Tonight would be the first test.

Not an impersonation in full—just a nudge, a proof of concept.

Tuesday was approaching.

The timing needed to be exact.

I wasn't rushing into Malik's life.

I was easing into the cracks he didn't even know he had.

Once he stepped into the building that evening and people swore they'd already seen him...the real game would finally begin.

* * *

I arrived at Kingdom Rising twenty-five minutes before the board meeting, just early enough to avoid drawing attention from the few staff who lingered after hours. The parking lot was mostly empty. A couple of cars belonging to administrative workers sat by the side entrance, but no one was milling around. That worked in my favor.

The key fob unlocked the door with a soft click, the green light flashing like it always had. It was almost insulting how easy it was. They never deactivated anything connected to me. They never imagined I would walk through these doors again.

Inside, the building felt still—more like a museum than a church. The scandal had drained the warmth out of it. Even the smell of old hymnals and polished wood seemed faint.

I moved toward the lobby and positioned myself near the hallway leading to the conference rooms. Tiffany Monroe usually came through this entrance, but always hesitated for a few minutes before stepping fully inside, like she needed to gather herself first. Trauma and exhaustion made people predictable.

Right on time, the side door opened.

She stepped in wearing her usual work uniform, hair pulled back, stress visible even in the way she exhaled. She clutched her purse against her chest like it was armor.

When her eyes landed on me, relief washed across her face.

"Oh—Pastor Malik. I didn't know you came early today."

I nodded with the same gentle expression Malik used when he wanted someone to feel safe.

"It's good to see you, Tiffany. How's your son holding up?"

Her whole posture softened. Just hearing his name steadied her.

"He had a rough night," she said. "He got into another fight at school, and the principal says if it happens again, he may be expelled. I didn't know who else to talk to."

I stepped a little closer, careful not to move with confidence that felt unfamiliar to Malik.

"You're doing the best you can," I said, mirroring Malik's cadence. "And your son isn't beyond help. He just needs someone stable to anchor him right now."

Her eyes filled with tears—exhaustion more than emotion.

"That means a lot," she whispered. "Thank you for always listening."

I nodded. "We'll get him there. One step at a time. I'll talk to him."

She breathed out slowly, believing every word. It didn't take much; people trusted Malik without question. It was effortless to slide into that trust.

"I don't want to keep you," she said, wiping her face. "I know you have that board meeting soon."

"Yes," I said. "But I'll check in on you both this week."

She smiled, grateful. Then she walked down the hallway toward the sanctuary, leaving me exactly where I wanted her: thinking she'd spoken to Malik, believing he'd taken time for her.

I watched her go, then checked my phone. Five minutes until Malik arrived.

Time to disappear.

I moved through the corridor quietly, cutting across the back hallway toward the children's wing—an area with multiple exits and poor lighting. I knew the building better than most; I'd lived in its shadows long before I left home.

Before I reached the door, footsteps echoed faintly near the lobby. Malik's.

He always walked with a soft, uneven rhythm—part hesitation, part humility. A nervous stride he never corrected.

I slipped out the side exit, letting the door close just as his silhouette passed through the glass of the lobby doors. I caught only a brief glimpse of him from behind—the same build, same posture, same frame as mine.

He paused, as if sensing something, but didn't turn around.

Good.

Tiffany stepped out from the hallway a moment later and waved at him.

"Pastor Malik—thank you again for talking with me," she called out.

Malik froze slightly, confusion flickering in his expression even from a distance.

Perfect.

By the time he pieced together what she meant, I was already across the parking lot, blending into the fading daylight and moving toward the street.

This was how it began.

Not with chaos.

Not with theatrics.

But with small fractures in reality.

One person believing she spoke to Malik when she hadn't.

One interaction rewritten.

One moment stolen.

Soon, the line between us would blur for everyone.

Seven

MALIK

iffany's comment stuck in my head long after she walked away.

"Thank you again for talking with me."

When? I'd just made it to the church.

I hadn't spoken to her in over a week. I had barely spoken to anyone. But she looked so sure, so relieved, that I didn't want to embarrass her by asking what she meant. Maybe she'd mistaken someone else. Maybe she'd misunderstood. Maybe I was just exhausted.

I brushed it off and kept moving.

I dropped my things in my father's—no, *my*—office. The room still smelled like his cologne and old leather. I didn't linger. I didn't have the strength. Instead, I walked straight into the conference room.

Everyone was already seated.

Lavvy fanned herself dramatically. Rusty sat with his arms crossed so tight his biceps looked ready to burst through his shirt. Simone had her tablet out. Kyrie looked jumpy. And Pearl Jenkins—Lord help me—was perched at the head of the table like she owned the building.

The moment I stepped in, she clapped her hands.

"Well, since our shepherd is absent-minded today—"

Lavvy didn't even wait.

"Pearl," she snapped, "your spiritual gift is confusion. Sit back down."

Pearl gasped like someone slapped her soul, but she sat. Rusty muttered "thank God" under his breath.

I took my seat slowly.

Simone cleared her throat. "Before we get into the financial agenda, a few of us... experienced some unusual things this week."

"Unusual how?" I asked.

Kyrie shifted. "I, uh... thought I saw you outside Taz Moreno's club last night."

My stomach dropped.

"What? Kyrie, no. I wasn't anywhere near there."

Pearl raised a hand like she was testifying in court. "I saw him too—carrying a brown paper bag out the liquor store on Highway 9."

Everyone turned to stare at me.

"I—what? Pearl, that wasn't me."

Rusty slammed his hand on the table. "Absolutely not. We are *not* doing this again. We will not—WILL NOT—have this church wrapped up in another scandal. Not after Jeremiah's mess."

Lavvy clutched her chest. "Lord, Rusty, sit still! Ain't nobody accusing him of nothing yet!"

Rusty glared at me over his glasses. "Explain it, Malik."

"I can't explain something that didn't happen," I said. "I wasn't at a club. And I wasn't at a liquor store."

Pearl scoffed. "Well somebody who looked exactly like you was! And he had the same walk too. That little pastor shuffle you do."

I closed my eyes briefly.

This wasn't good.

Simone leaned forward. "Malik, we've had multiple sightings. If someone is impersonating you, that needs to be addressed immediately."

Rusty shook his head like he was already fed up. "Or the boy is lying to cover tracks."

My voice tightened. "Pastor Rusty, with all due respect, I'm telling the truth."

He pointed a finger at me. "Truth didn't help your father."

Lavvy fanned herself faster. "Rusty! God ain't through with you yet but He's gon' be tired when He gets done!"

The room erupted—voices overlapping, accusations swirling, confusion thick enough to choke on. Half the board argued about my innocence. The other half argued about security breaches. Pearl started listing every location she thought she'd seen me in the past forty-eight hours, including a Taco Bell drive-thru that I definitely had not visited.

And through all of it, the same cold thought gnawed at the back of my mind.

Kyrie saw someone who looked like me at the club.

Pearl saw someone who looked like me buying liquor.

Tiffany thought she talked to me earlier.

This wasn't exhaustion.

This wasn't coincidence.

Someone was moving in my place.

Someone who looked exactly like me.

Marcus!

The noise in the conference room felt like it was pressing in on me from all sides. Accusations, questions, speculation—everyone talking over everyone else. And underneath it all, a slow rising panic I couldn't let them see.

Because I *knew* exactly who they'd seen.

Marcus.

Alive.

Moving around the city like he had the right to share my skin, my shadow, my life.

But I couldn't say that here.

If I did, the board wouldn't just panic—they'd unravel. People already thought Kingdom Rising was cursed. The last thing we needed was rumors that the pastor's dead twin was suddenly showing up around town like a ghost.

So I forced my breathing to steady and raised my voice.

"Everyone, please—just give me a second."

The room quieted in uneven patches. Rusty still glared at me like he was waiting for a confession. Pearl pursed her lips. Simone watched me closely. Lavvy fanned her chest like the Holy Ghost had one hand on her and indigestion had the other.

I clasped my hands together on the table.

"Look… someone is clearly trying to take advantage of the scandal we're already dealing with. They're using my face to stir confusion."

Rusty scoffed, but I kept going.

"You all know me. Every one of you watched me grow up in this church. Even in my teenage years, I never drank. I never went to clubs. I never did anything to jeopardize our name."

That part wasn't entirely true.

I *had* been at Taz's club—last night, in fact—but that was a detail I planned to take to my grave.

Pearl nodded slowly, buying it. "That is true. He always was the good one."

Lavvy pointed her fan at her. "Hush, Pearl. You ain't finna start no comparison spirit up in here."

I pushed forward before they derailed the meeting again.

"Whoever people are seeing around town—it's not me. We don't need to jump to conclusions. We just need to increase security and pay more attention to who comes in and out of the building."

They seemed to accept that.

A few shoulders relaxed.

Even Rusty's glare softened by a degree.

Lavvy stood abruptly, digging in her purse.

"Well, regardless of who it is, the devil is BUSY. And whenever he busy, I stay busier." She pulled out a small bottle of anointing oil with a label so faded it might've outlived Moses. "Bring your head here, Pastor."

I blinked. "Mother Lavvy, I don't—"

"Boy, don't argue with me when the devil out here wearing your face. Tilt."

She pressed her palm to my forehead before I could protest. The smell of olive oil and eucalyptus filled the room as she prayed with enough force to shift the air. Several board members murmured "amen" under their breath.

By the time she finished, my forehead was shining, and I felt even more exposed than before.

Simone cleared her throat and tapped her tablet. "Well. In other news—something positive. We received a significant donation in the offering on Sunday. Enough to cover payroll from last week and this week, plus utilities."

The room collectively exhaled. Shoulders dropped. Hands unclenched. Exhaustion softened into relief.

"Praise God," someone whispered.

Rusty, of course, didn't share the sentiment.

"That donation is a temporary fix," he said flatly. "A bandaid on a bullet wound. We need a long-term resolution. Clear leadership. Clear financial oversight. And a plan for rebuilding trust."

His gaze landed on me again.

A reminder that the pressure wasn't letting up.

Not for a second.

The relief in the room dissolved as quickly as it came, replaced by the same weight that had been sitting on my chest since Jeremiah's arrest.

I gave a small nod. "I understand. And I'm working on it."

No one needed to know how close I was to falling apart.

How the walls felt like they were tightening.

How Marcus's shadow lingered on the edges of every thought.

They couldn't see that.

Not yet.

The meeting finally broke apart, people scattering in different directions while trying to pretend everything was fine. Simone gathered her tablet. Pearl sniffed dramatically like she'd personally carried the weight of the entire discussion. Lavvy patted my shoulder, leaving another olive-oil fingerprint I didn't have the heart to wipe away.

I adjusted my tie and headed for the hallway, desperate for air, when I heard heavy footsteps behind me.

"Malik. Come here a minute."

Rusty's voice—gravelly, stern, impossible to ignore.

I turned.

He stood in the doorway of the conference room, arms crossed, brows drawn so tight it looked painful. He didn't gesture for privacy, didn't lower his tone. Rusty never hid his opinions.

I walked toward him.

The moment the door closed behind us, he didn't waste time.

"You're losing control, son."

My stomach tightened. "Deacon Rusty—"

"No," he said, holding up a hand. "Don't give me titles right now. I'm talking to you as a man. Not a superior. Not a colleague. A man who's watched you grow up in this ministry."

He leaned against the table, staring at me like he was looking through the version of me I presented.

"You're shaken," he said plainly. "Shaken men make mistakes. And mistakes are the last thing this church can afford."

I swallowed, trying to keep my voice steady. "I'm doing the best I can with everything that's happened."

Rusty shook his head. "Your best ain't the issue. Your honesty is."

I stiffened. "I haven't lied to anyone."

He narrowed his eyes the way only old pastors can—the look that says *I know more than you think I do.*

"You expect me to believe you were at home last night?" he asked quietly.

I froze.

"I wasn't—"

He cut me off again. "Something is off, Malik. You're distracted. You're jumpy. You're not giving clear answers. And people are seeing you in places you claim you haven't been."

My heartbeat quickened.

He stepped closer—not aggressively, but fatherly in a way Jeremiah never was.

"I'm telling you this because I care about the kingdom, and because whether you like it or not, the mantle is falling on you. I won't let this church sink, not again. And I sure won't let you spiral under the weight of something you're clearly not talking about."

My throat tightened.

"Rusty… nothing's happening," I said, but the words sounded weak even to me.

He frowned. "That's the problem. You're trying to hold whatever this is by yourself."

He tapped the table lightly, a steady rhythm.

"You've always been the responsible one. The quiet one. The steady one. But steady don't mean silent. You don't talk, you break."

I opened my mouth but nothing came out.

Rusty exhaled through his nose and adjusted his glasses.

"Get ahead of whatever's going on before it swallows you. And if you can't get ahead of it…" His voice softened slightly. "At least stop pretending nothing's wrong."

He pushed off the table and moved toward the door.

Right before stepping out, he paused.

"And Malik?"

I looked up at him.

"Whoever folks are seeing out there—it better not be you. This church won't survive another scandal."

He walked out, leaving me alone with a truth I couldn't speak and a secret I didn't know how to carry.

Marcus was alive.

People were seeing him.

And I was the one who would take the blame if this spiraled.

I pressed both hands against the table and forced myself to breathe.

Rusty thought I was losing control.

The terrifying part was… he wasn't wrong.

I shut the office door behind me and leaned against it for a moment, trying to steady myself. The room felt too small, too warm, too heavy with everything I didn't want to feel. I went to the desk and sat down, but my thoughts wouldn't settle. They scattered in every direction except the one I needed.

Why would Marcus do this?

Why now?

Why show up at the club, the liquor store, the church—everywhere except where I was? Why mimic me? Why put the church in the line of fire? Why target me of all people?

No matter how hard I thought, there was only one reason that made any sense, a reason old enough to feel biblical.

Jealousy.

It was there from the beginning, even if none of us had the language to name it. While I was uplifted in church, Marcus was corrected. While I was encouraged, Marcus was scolded. Whenever I sang or prayed or quoted scripture, the elders beamed. When Marcus tried, they told him to "calm down" or "stop playing" or "act right."

The difference between us was never subtle. It was carved into our upbringing.

And it wasn't always fair.

I remembered the fights we had growing up—actual fistfights, not the mild arguments people think Christian kids have. We went after each other. Hard. And every time Jeremiah walked into the room and saw raised voices or bruised cheeks, he looked straight at Marcus.

"What did you do now?"

Marcus never had a chance to defend himself. The verdict always came before the evidence. And the worst part was, I let it happen. I didn't correct my father. I didn't set the record straight. I didn't admit the truth:

I started just as many fights as Marcus did.

Sometimes more.

I pushed his buttons. I picked at his insecurities. I took advantage of how quickly he got angry and how fast he reacted. And when he reacted, that was the moment Jeremiah stepped in—never to ask questions, only to punish.

If Marcus was the Esau in our story, the one losing ground before he even understood the rules, I was Jacob—the one favored, the one chosen, the one who didn't always deserve it.

Marcus carried the blame.

I carried the praise.

And deep down, even as kids, we both knew it.

I rubbed my forehead, trying to push away the sting building behind my eyes. Maybe Marcus wasn't sabotaging the church itself. Maybe this wasn't about Kingdom Rising or its scandal or its money. Maybe it wasn't even about Jeremiah.

Maybe it was about me.

Maybe he was doing the one thing Esau never got to do—claiming a birthright he believed was stolen from him. Not the church leadership, not the ministry, but something more personal:

Identity.

Worth.

The place he never got to stand in.

I sat back in the chair, the leather groaning softly under me. The idea that Marcus felt overshadowed by me wasn't new. I'd sensed it my entire life. But the idea that he would return from the dead—literally or figuratively—to take my life apart piece by piece?

That part I wasn't prepared for.

Because beneath all the jealousy, all the resentment, all the distance between us...

I still loved him.

Even now.

Even after everything.

Which made the question even harder:

How do you fight someone who shares your face, your history, your childhood—and believes the world owes him the years he lost?

I didn't know the answer.

And admitting that scared me more than anything else tonight.

I stayed in my office longer than I meant to, staring at the wall, hoping the knot in my chest would loosen on its own. It didn't. No amount of logic or distraction could quiet the storm building inside me, and finally, when I couldn't hold it anymore, I pushed myself to my feet and walked out.

The sanctuary was dark except for the faint glow from the exit signs. It made the room feel larger than usual, almost hollow. The kind of silence that forces you to hear your own heartbeat.

I walked down the aisle slowly, running my hand along the back of a pew the way I used to when I was a kid waiting for service to start. Back then, this place felt like home. Tonight, it felt like a question I didn't know how to answer.

I stopped at the altar.

I didn't kneel at first. I just stood there, unsure of how to begin. I'd prayed for guidance before. I'd prayed for peace during storms. But I had never prayed for clarity about a brother I buried.

After a long moment, I lowered myself to my knees.

"God... I don't even know what I'm asking for right now."

My voice sounded rough in the empty room.

I clasped my hands but couldn't keep them still. They shook—not from fear of Marcus, but from the weight of everything I couldn't say out loud to anyone else.

"If Marcus is alive... if that's really him... then why would he come back like this?"

I swallowed, letting the words settle.

"I don't understand what I did. Or what I didn't do. I don't understand why he'd want to hurt the church. Or me. Or why he wouldn't just... come to me."

Memories flashed, one after the other—our shared room, our matching school uniforms, the times we whispered in the dark when we were too scared to sleep. Then the fights. The secrets. The distance that widened every year.

"We were boys once," I whispered. "We were brothers. And I know things got complicated. I know life wasn't fair to him. I know I didn't always defend him when I should have."

The words hit harder than I expected.

"I'm not pretending I was perfect. I wasn't. But does that really mean he wants to destroy everything? Is that the only path he sees now?"

My voice cracked, and I pressed a hand against my forehead, the oil from Mother Lavvy still faint on my skin.

"God, I don't know why he's doing this. I don't know what he wants. I don't know how to stop him without hurting him. And I don't want to hurt him. I just... I just want to understand."

Silence filled the sanctuary again, deep and unmoving.

I waited for something—comfort, direction, even conviction. Anything that let me know I wasn't alone in this. Instead, the only sound was my own breathing and the hum of the AC cycling on.

Eventually, I exhaled a long, shaky breath.

"If he's angry... show me how to reach him. If he's lost... show me how to bring him back. And if he really is the one behind all of this... give me the strength to face whatever comes next."

The sanctuary didn't answer, but for the first time all day, my thoughts felt a little less tangled.

I stayed there a while longer, eyes closed, hands open, trying to feel something—anything—that resembled clarity.

But the only thing I knew for certain when I finally stood was this: Marcus wasn't done.

And whatever he came back for... it wasn't reconciliation.

By the time I pulled into my driveway, the sky was the color of slate—one of those evenings where everything felt suspended, waiting for the next thing to break. I sat in the car for a few minutes, engine off, staring at my front door through the windshield.

I was exhausted, but it wasn't the kind of exhaustion sleep could solve. It was the kind that lived in the chest, pressing down, tightening everything a little more with each hour that passed.

I finally forced myself out of the car.

Halfway up the walkway, I saw it.

A small object sitting dead-center on my front porch mat.

I stopped cold.

The neighborhood was quiet. No cars passing. No kids outside. No porch lights on except mine. The object didn't look threatening—not at first glance. But something about the placement... the intention in it... made my heart slow and thicken.

I stepped closer.

It was a toy—an old plastic wrestler figurine.

A red mask. Blue boots. One arm taped at the shoulder where the plastic had cracked.

My breath caught.

There was only one other person in the world who knew about that toy.

When we were eight, Marcus and I fought over the last one in the store. Jeremiah bought it for me. Marcus got nothing. I tried to share it, but he didn't want it "secondhand"—so we broke it fighting over it in the living room, knocking the arm loose. I cried harder than he did because I thought our dad would blame him again.

He did.

I kept the toy hidden in a shoebox for years afterward, long after it stopped mattering. Marcus always said I held onto things too tightly.

Later, after he ran away, I tried to find that toy and couldn't. I thought I lost it in the move. Or maybe Mom threw it out.

But here it was.

Cleaned. Repaired with new tape.

Sitting on my porch.

Placed gently. Deliberately.

Cold slid down my spine.

I knelt slowly and picked it up. It felt heavier than I remembered— maybe because of what it meant now. Maybe because of who it came from.

There was a note under it.

A torn page from a spiral notebook.

My name written across the top.

MALIK

in handwriting I hadn't seen in years but recognized instantly.

My throat tightened as I unfolded it.

You always got what I wanted.

But don't worry... soon I will too.

No signature.

He didn't need one.

I stood there on the porch, the toy in one hand, the note in the other, the weight of both sinking into me. The air felt colder. The house felt smaller. The world felt wrong.

Marcus wasn't hiding anymore.

He was speaking.

He was remembering.

He was reaching back into our childhood and using our shared history as breadcrumbs to show me he'd been closer than I realized.

And he was making it clear this wasn't random.

This was personal.

I locked the door behind me once I stepped inside, though I knew it wouldn't matter. If Marcus wanted to get to me, a lock wouldn't stop him. It never would.

I leaned against the door, holding the toy to my chest, silently praying for clarity, strength—anything.

But the only thing I felt was the truth settling in:

He wasn't just alive.

He was coming for me.

Eight

MOTHER LAVVY

I woke up before sunrise, heart beating like somebody had run a revival service through my chest. Sweat soaked my edges clean out of their press. I sat straight up in bed and grabbed the nearest thing I could—my church fan with the picture of Old Pastor DeWitt on the front—because if any spirit was in that room that wasn't holy, I wanted at least one witness on my side.

The dream still clung to me, sharp as daylight.

Two men.

Same face.

Same height.

Same walk.

But one was headed toward the church… and the other away from it.

"I rebuke it," I whispered. Then I blinked twice. "But Lord, if it's from You… rebuke me back so I know."

I sat there fanning myself, thinking deeply.

"LeVerne Bolton," I told myself out loud, "the Lord been showing you some *STRANGE STUFF* lately."

I wasn't being dramatic—well, maybe a little, but that didn't mean I was wrong. Ever since Pastor Jeremiah got hauled out the sanctuary like he owed the feds child support, the spiritual atmosphere had been off. And yesterday at that board meeting? Whew. I felt confusion floating around that room like dust you can't quite sweep up.

Two sightings of Malik at once?

Reports of him at a club?

Rumors he was buying liquor?

Me seeing a shadow pass behind him but nobody else noticing?

No ma'am.

No sir.

Not on *my* watch.

That dream was the final confirmation:

The Holy Ghost FBI needed to launch a full investigation.

I grabbed my notebook labeled **"Prophetic Hunches – Do Not Throw Away"** and wrote at the top:

CASE #47: PASTOR MALIK OR MALIK #2??

I underlined it twice.

My dream replayed again in my mind—the two figures walking in opposite directions. One walking toward light, one stepping into shadow. Same face. Different spirit.

"Jesus…" I whispered, pressing my hand to my chest. "If I'm seeing double in the spirit, something ain't right in the natural."

I swung my legs off the bed and stood, popping my knees like bubble wrap.

"This calls for fasting," I said firmly. Then I paused. "A half-day fast. Until about… 12:15. After my stories go off."

I went to my mirror, slicked my hair back with some edge control, and tied my prayer scarf nice and tight.

If the enemy thought he could walk into Kingdom Rising with two faces and one agenda, he underestimated me.

"Oh, I'm gon' get to the bottom of this," I muttered as I grabbed my Bible, oil, and reading glasses. "The devil might be busy, but I'm retired—I got free time."

I stepped outside onto my porch, staring into the morning air like the answer might walk up the street in broad daylight.

Two men with the same face.

Two spirits.

Two paths.

And one church already hanging on by a thread.

Whatever was going on with Malik—and whoever that second man was—the Lord didn't show me things to ignore. So I straightened my shoulders and whispered:

"Alright now. Holy Ghost FBI, Operation Double Trouble is officially open."

And with that, I marched back inside to pray. Hard.

I had just finished tying on my prayer scarf when my phone buzzed on the nightstand. I snatched it up expecting another group message from the Mother's Board about who was bringing potato salad Sunday. Instead, it was a text from Simone.

URGENT BOARD MEETING. ONE HOUR.

I stared at the screen.

"Oh, Lord... something else done happened."

I got dressed quicker than I had in years. Pressed blouse, long skirt, comfortable shoes I could run, shout, or fight in if needed. I grabbed my purse, my Bible, my reading glasses, and my small can of pepper spray—because you never knew.

By the time I reached Kingdom Rising, my spirit was already stirred. I marched down that hallway like someone who had *business*. The board room door was half open. I didn't knock. I shoved it wide, stepped inside, and slammed my Bible on the table so hard Pastor

Rusty jumped.

"Alright now," I said, planting my hands on my hips. "Y'all ain't fooling ME. Pastor Jeremiah was laundering something and it wasn't salvation!"

Pearl gasped like she'd been personally indicted.

Simone froze mid-scroll on her tablet.

Rusty rubbed his face and muttered, "Lord, we need to get rid of her before she talks to the feds."

"I HEARD THAT!" I snapped. "Try it! I got prayer warriors AND pepper spray. I'll bind you AND blind you—don't play with me."

Rusty held up his hands defensively. "Woman, hush before you send the whole board into cardiac arrest."

Before I could pop off again, Pastor Malik entered the room, looking exhausted enough to pass out. The moment he stepped in, the noise simmered.

He cleared his throat. "Let's... bring the room to order."

Everyone sat up straighter.

Me included—though I kept my purse close. Just in case Rusty tried something slick.

The accountant, who usually kept quiet unless asked, cleared his throat and pushed his glasses up his nose.

"I, uh... I have an update from the federal liaison assigned to the case."

The room froze.

He continued, nervous but steady. "They released the main operating account this morning. They determined there wasn't enough evidence to hold it."

A wave of relief rolled around the table like a Pentecostal shout.

Pearl clutched her heart. "Oh, thank you Jesus."

Simone let out the breath she'd been holding.

Rusty nodded but stayed serious. "It buys us time. Thank the Lord for that."

I exhaled, lifting one hand toward the ceiling. "Well amen. Because I was about to go march down to that federal building myself."

Pearl rolled her eyes. "What were you gon' do, Lavvy? Storm the place?"

"With scripture and pepper spray," I replied. "The combination is lethal."

Malik finally sat down, shoulders sagging with relief. "This gives us enough to get payroll out and keep the lights on. We can stabilize while the rest of the investigation unfolds."

The atmosphere shifted from sheer panic to manageable anxiety.

Still heavy, but not hopeless.

Rusty leaned back in his chair. "This is good news. But it doesn't fix everything."

I waved a hand. "Let us have five minutes to celebrate, Rusty! The Lord done made a way; the least you could do is unclench your jaw."

A few board members snickered. Even Malik's lips twitched like he wanted to smile.

For the first time in days, the room didn't feel like we were one bad headline away from shutting the church down.

But underneath the relief, I felt something else. Something unsettled. The dream. The two faces. The strange sightings of Pastor Malik.

And the tug in my spirit that didn't let me rest.

Business as usual might return for the church—but something told me the real trouble was just getting started.

After the board meeting wrapped and everybody finished pretending like they weren't still worried, I made my way straight toward the choir room. If anything suspicious was happening in this church, the choir knew first. They were worse than group chats and prayer chains combined.

I paused outside the double doors, listening.

Arguing.

Laughing.

Something thudding.

Sounded like a normal Wednesday.

I stepped inside, quiet as a cat, and took a seat in the back row—no announcement, no greeting. The room went silent for three seconds before Wynter whispered loudly to Harmony:

"I told you! When Mother Lavvy sits in the back like that, she up to something."

Harmony smacked her arm. "Shh! She can hear you."

"I CAN," I said, folding my hands over my purse. "And I'm gon' hear more than that today."

Wynter gulped.

Harmony straightened her posture like she suddenly remembered God was watching.

Nova glanced at me with a nervous smile. "Mother Lavvy... everything okay?"

"Oh yes," I answered sweetly. "The Lord just put me on assignment."

That was all it took.

The entire choir froze.

I waited exactly four seconds—the perfect amount of pressure—before leaning forward.

"Now," I began, "I'm just asking questions. Collecting information. Ain't gon' accuse nobody. Ain't gon' spread nothing. I'm on a fact-finding mission."

Wynter whispered, "That's exactly what people say before they spread something."

"I HEARD THAT," I snapped. "And you right. But this time I'm serious."

Harmony cleared her throat. "Mother Lavvy, what kind of... facts are you looking for?"

I lowered my voice dramatically. "Anything unusual you've seen this week involving Pastor Malik."

The room went still.

Nova blinked. "Unusual how?"

"I ain't gon' lead the witness," I said. "Y'all tell me."

Wynter raised her hand like we were in Sunday school. "Well... I *did* think I saw Pastor Malik walking down the hallway earlier today, but then he came in from outside like it wasn't him."

Harmony gasped. "I SAW THAT TOO! And when I called his name, he didn't answer. He just kept going like he didn't hear me."

I scribbled in my notebook.

Wynter + Harmony: TWO SIGHTINGS OF FAKE MALIK.

Nova frowned. "Mother Lavvy, maybe it was just the lighting—"

"Sshh," I said, waving her off. "My spirit is collecting the details."

Harmony leaned closer. "And yesterday at rehearsal, I swear somebody who looked just like Pastor Malik walked past the choir stand, but he didn't say hi or nothing. And he ALWAYS says hi."

"That ain't like him," Wynter added. "Pastor Malik greets folks like he running for office."

I nodded, writing faster.

FAKE MALIK = RUDE.

I looked at Nova last.

"And what about you, baby? You seen anything strange?"

She hesitated. "Well... I did think I saw him standing near the hall by the nursery earlier. But when I walked toward him, he was gone."

My pen froze mid-sentence.

NOVA: THIRD SIGHTING. DISAPPEARS QUICKLY.

The choir stared at me, waiting for a reaction.

I closed the notebook slowly and stood.

"Well," I said, adjusting my scarf, "the Holy Ghost FBI is officially elevating this investigation."

Wynter's eyes widened. "What's that mean?"

"It means," I said, slipping my notebook back into my purse, "that something is walking around Kingdom Rising wearing Pastor Malik's face."

Harmony squealed and grabbed Wynter's arm.

Wynter shouted, "LIKE A SHAPESHIFTER?"

"Hush, girl!" I snapped. "This ain't sci-fi. This spiritual."

Nova bit the inside of her cheek, nervous.

I pointed at her gently. "And don't you worry, baby. Whatever it is, the Lord gon' reveal it."

Harmony asked, "To who?"

"ME," I said, picking up my Bible. "The Lord know who to talk to."

Then I walked out of the choir room with purpose, shoes clicking like a seasoned detective walking away from a crime scene.

After I left the choir room, I made my way to the parking lot with my Bible tucked under my arm and my notebook pressed tight against my purse. My mind was running fast—faster than it had in years—and the more I replayed those choir testimonies, the more convinced I became that something *serious* was happening.

Three separate sightings.

Three different hallways.

Three different behaviors.

And every single time, Pastor Malik was somewhere else entirely.

I knew what that meant.

"LeVerne Bolton," I muttered as I walked to my car, "you can't ignore this no more. The spirit been tapping you on the shoulder all week."

I stopped, hand on the car door.

"No…" I corrected myself. "The spirit been PUSHING."

I opened my notebook and wrote:

OPERATION SHADOW TRACKING: INITIATED.

Underneath it:

Step 1: Follow Pastor Malik discreetly for 24 hours.
Step 2: Document all sightings.
Step 3: Catch the devil slipping.

I snapped the notebook shut.

This wasn't gossip.

This wasn't speculation.

This was reconnaissance.

The Lord wasn't showing me dreams of double-walking men for entertainment. Something was loose in Kingdom Rising—something bold enough to wear our pastor's face—and somebody had to get to the bottom of it.

That somebody, clearly, was me.

I climbed into my car, adjusted the rearview mirror, and whispered: "Discreetly, LeVerne. Discreetly. Can't spook the boy."

* * *

The next morning, I arrived at Kingdom Rising thirty minutes before staff devotion. I parked far enough away to stay hidden, but close enough to keep an eye on every door. I pulled out my binoculars—the same ones I used at the church picnic last summer to confirm Sister Inez was cheating during the potato sack race—and I waited.

After ten minutes, I saw Malik's car pull up.

I straightened in my seat.

"There go the real him," I whispered. "I can tell. Spirit ain't uneasy."

He stepped out, adjusting his tie, shoulders weighed down. He looked tired. Not suspicious—just worn. That eased me a little. But worn men made easy targets, and I refused to let the devil take advantage.

When he walked toward the building, I scribbled:

REAL MALIK arrives 7:52 AM. Heavy spirit. Possible spiritual attack.

I waited another few minutes just to be sure.

Then I got out of my car and followed him at a distance.

Not close enough to get caught.

Not far enough to lose track.

I slipped behind bushes, pillars, and the big memorial stone engraved with "To God Be the Glory." I peeked around corners like a seasoned operative—even though my knees were voicing strong objections.

Every time Malik stopped to talk to someone, I blended in with whatever plant life was nearby. At one point I pretended to tie my shoe even though I was wearing slip-ons.

Did it look suspicious? Yes.

Did I care? Absolutely not.

This was holy work.

At one point I whispered to myself, "Lord, help me if this child catches me. He already think I'm extra."

By lunch, I had documented ten interactions, two phone calls, three hallway walks, and one moment he sat alone in the sanctuary staring into his hands like he was carrying the world on his back.

Everything he did felt normal.

But normal didn't calm my spirit—not when people swore they saw him in two places at once.

If there were two men with the same face, then one of them was walking around unchecked.

So as I ate my salad in the parking lot, binoculars balanced on the dashboard, I vowed:

"I'm gon' watch him all day. All night if I got to. Because the devil may be prowling..."

I took a bite and pointed my fork toward the building.

"...but I'm prowling too."

By mid-afternoon, I was feeling good about my progress. I had pages of notes, times, locations, behaviors, and one scribble that said "**Spirit uneasy from 11:42–11:45 — investigate later.**"

I told myself I was doing Holy Ghost recon with professionalism.

Then came the incident.

Pastor Malik left his office around three, heading toward the youth wing. I wasn't about to lose visual, so I followed. Quietly. Smoothly. With the precision of a woman who'd watched every episode of *NCIS* twice.

Or so I thought.

I ducked behind one of the big ficus plants in the hallway. Now, the plant wasn't tiny—but neither was I—and as soon as I crouched, I realized two things:

1. There was not nearly as much foliage as I imagined,
2. My bright purple church hat was sticking up behind the leaves like a lighthouse.

I tried to ease it down, but the hat was pinned too tight to my wig to move freely. Instead, the whole wig shifted half an inch to the left.

"Lord Jesus," I whispered. "I didn't train for this."

Malik turned slightly, like he sensed movement.

I froze.

The plant froze with me, but less convincingly.

He paused in the hallway, looking around.

Here I was, crouched behind a dying ficus with a lopsided wig and a hat that might as well have been blinking neon.

If he spotted me, I was finished.

The Holy Ghost FBI had rules:

Rule #7 — If caught, deny everything and blame spiritual warfare.

But I preferred not to use that card so early in the investigation.

So I did the only thing that made sense:

I became one with the ficus.

I held out my arms stiff like branches.

Tilted my head to mimic a leaf.

Tried to look leafy.

It didn't help that my purse slid off my shoulder and thumped loudly on the floor.

Malik turned fully then.

"Mother Lavvy?" he called.

I stayed frozen.

Maybe he'd think the ficus was talking to him.

Or the Spirit.

Or his imagination.

He took a few steps closer.

"Mother Lavvy... are you hiding behind that plant?"

I realized I had two options:

1. Admit it
2. Commit harder

I chose the second.

I closed my eyes and hummed lightly like I was deep in prayer. Maybe he'd think I was having a holy moment.

"Mother Lavvy," he said again, right beside me now, "why are you crouched behind a plant?"

I slowly lifted my head, wig still crooked, hat still pointing north, and answered with full confidence:

"I'm interceding."

He blinked. "Behind the ficus?"

"Yes," I said without hesitation. "This is... strategic intercession. You wouldn't understand."

He opened his mouth to respond, but I held up a hand.

"Don't interrupt the Spirit."

Then I stood—knees popping like frying chicken—and walked away with all the dignity I had left, clutching my purse and adjusting my wig as I went.

Behind me, I heard him sigh under his breath.

But I also heard confusion in it.

Concern.

And just a little bit of fear.

Good.

That meant the devil wasn't the only one unsettled.

Outside in the hallway, I fixed my wig properly, straightened my hat, and wrote in my notebook:

Surveillance Note #14:

"Plant was too small. Consider camouflage options."

Then I underlined it twice and added:

Malik suspicious. Increase stealth.

Even though "stealth" was clearly not my spiritual gift.

By the time I made it back toward the choir room, my knees were still complaining from the ficus incident, but the Holy Ghost FBI didn't clock out early. I needed intel, and the Lord usually revealed things through the most talkative members of the church.

Which was exactly why I stopped when I heard two familiar voices whispering... loudly.

Harmony and Winter.

They were standing just outside the choir room doors, leaning close together like they were hiding state secrets. Harmony's hands were flying dramatically as she spoke, while Winter nodded like she was taking mental notes.

I slowed my steps and listened.

"I'm telling you," Harmony said, "I saw Pastor Malik in the hallway, then two seconds later he was across the church. Beam me up, Scotty!"

Winter gasped. "But his twin dead. Maybe a clone? You think Jeremiah was running experiments?!"

Harmony smacked her arm. "Girl, don't be stupid. Jeremiah ain't smart enough for that."

"Oh. True."

Harmony lowered her voice. "I think there's TWO Maliks. Two! Like a—like a spiritual doppelganger."

Winter crossed herself. "I rebuke it."

Harmony continued anyway. "I heard somebody saw him buying liquor. And somebody else saw him at that club downtown."

Winter widened her eyes. "THE SAME NIGHT?"

Harmony nodded dramatically. "Baby, Malik is multiplying."

That was enough.

I stepped forward like a shadow of judgment.

Winter spotted me first. "Oh—Lord, Harmony—look!"

Harmony turned, saw me, and immediately started smoothing her hair like the Holy Ghost cared about her edges.

"Mother Lavvy!" she squeaked. "We were just—talking about— praise reports."

"The devil is a liar," I said, stepping into full motherly authority. "And so are both of you."

Harmony's shoulders slumped.

Winter hid her phone behind her back.

I folded my arms. "If y'all gon' spread gossip, at least make it intelligent gossip. Ain't no clone. Ain't no hologram. And if the Lord made two Pastor Maliks, He would've told ME first."

Winter whispered, "She right..."

I pointed at them both. "This church is in the middle of a storm. Pastor Jeremiah locked up. Pastor Malik barely sleeping. And y'all out here turning the sanctuary into an episode of Blue's Clues."

Harmony blinked. "We just said what we heard—"

"And I'm saying hush," I cut in. "Before y'all open a spiritual door you can't close. Words carry weight."

Winter nodded meekly. "Yes, ma'am."

Harmony sighed, deflated. "Yes, Mother Lavvy."

I lifted my purse. "Now go inside and rehearse. And don't let me hear nothing else about 'Two Maliks.' The next time y'all wanna talk, talk to God."

They both scurried into the choir room like chastened toddlers.

I stood there a moment, letting my spirit settle.

Because the truth was… even though they were messy, they weren't completely wrong.

Something *was* off.

And that unsettled me more than their rumors.

* * *

By the time I got home, the sun was setting, and my house felt too quiet. I put down my purse and Bible on the kitchen counter, kicked off my shoes, and sank into my recliner.

My body was tired, but my spirit was pacing.

I closed my eyes.

"Lord," I whispered, "You gon' have to show me what all this means. I'm seeing double. Hearing double. Feeling double. Is it deception? Confusion? Something worse?"

I waited.

Silence stretched across the room.

So I prayed again—this time more quietly, from the center of my chest.

"Jesus... cover Malik. Whatever is coming for him, don't let it take him. And give me eyes to see what I need to see. Even if it scares me."

A soft wind moved through the house.

Not a window open.

Not an air vent running.

But I felt it—something brushing past me, settling like a whisper on my shoulders.

Then I saw it.

Not a dream.

Not a vision.

Just a flicker—like a shadow crossing the wall where no one stood.

Two silhouettes.

Same height.

Same head.

Same shoulders.

Walking in opposite directions.

My breath caught.

The silhouettes faded, leaving the wall blank again... but the message stayed.

Two Maliks.

But only one carried light.

I pressed a trembling hand to my chest.

"Lord... what are You trying to show me?"

Only one sentence rose in my spirit:

All that looks familiar ain't family.

I didn't understand it fully—but I knew this:

My investigation had just shifted.

Whatever was wearing Malik's face wasn't just a threat to him...

It was a threat to Kingdom Rising.

And the Holy Ghost FBI needed to stay on the case.

Nine

NOVA

❧

I stayed late after choir rehearsal because I needed the sanctuary still. We've doubled up on practices with everything going on. That payroll hit, so people aren't complaining as much this week.

Quiet.

Empty.

No Harmony dramatics.

No Winter foolishness.

No board members pacing holes into the carpet.

Just me, the mic, and the song that refused to come out of my throat.

I stood at the pulpit, eyes on the stained-glass cross above the sound booth, and tried again.

"Yet will I praise You..."

My voice cracked.

Not just cracked—collapsed.

I clutched the microphone tighter and tried again, but the note dissolved into a sob I couldn't swallow fast enough. My knees buckled. I dropped onto the front pew, letting the mic roll onto the cushion beside me.

My ex had DM'd me twice already that day, taunting me with memories I'd begged God to bury. And now, the church I loved—the church that saved my life—was unraveling. Pastor Jeremiah in handcuffs. Board members panicking. Rumors everywhere.

And Malik...

Trying to stand in the middle of a storm meant for giants.

I buried my face in my hands.

"I can't do this," I whispered. "God, I can't even *sing* without falling apart."

Footsteps echoed behind me.

I wiped my face fast, hoping whoever it was would turn around and pretend they didn't see me.

But of course... fate had a sense of humor.

"Nova?"

Malik's voice was soft. Too soft. The kind of soft that meant he hadn't slept in days.

I straightened and adjusted my hair, hoping my eyes didn't look as red as they felt. "Hey, Pastor. I was just practicing. Long day, that's all."

He didn't respond.

Instead, he walked down the aisle and sat beside me—close enough that I could feel the weight he carried, but not close enough to make it awkward.

He didn't ask me to explain.

He didn't push.

He just sat there, breathing in the quiet with me.

After a moment he said, "You don't have to hide your tears from me."

I swallowed hard. "I didn't want to make things heavier than they already are. I don't know how you're standing, Malik. I can't even sing without falling apart."

He rubbed his palms together slowly, staring at the floor.

"I'm not standing," he admitted. "Not really. I feel like I'm losing pieces of myself every day. This church... my dad... the board... and now Taz—"

He cut himself off. Too fast.

Like he hadn't meant to say that part.

My heart dropped a little. "Taz... Moreno?"

He didn't confirm it.

Didn't deny it.

He just kept talking, voice low and frayed around the edges.

"I feel like I'm holding everybody else together with tape and a prayer, but when I'm alone? I can barely breathe. I keep wondering if I'm even supposed to be doing this... standing in my father's place. Preaching sermons I'm not ready for. Leading people who expect me to have answers."

His hands trembled slightly.

"And then," he said, exhaling slowly, "I come in here and find you crying, and all I can think is... I'm failing you too."

My chest tightened. "Malik, you aren't failing anyone."

He gave a bitter little laugh. "Feels like I am."

"You're human," I told him. "And you're hurting. That doesn't mean you're failing—it means you're still standing in spite of it. That's strength."

I didn't touch him, but I wanted to.

Not in a romantic way—just... human to human.

He leaned back in the pew and stared up at the ceiling.

"Do you ever feel like God put something on your life that you're too fragile to carry?"

I let out a shaky breath. "Every day."

We sat there in silence, both of us watching the sanctuary lights shift against the stained glass. The emptiness of the room didn't feel empty at all.

It felt honest.

Unmasked.

"I wish I could just be enough," he whispered.

"You already are," I replied before I could stop myself.

He closed his eyes like the words hit a place he didn't want to admit existed.

For a moment, we were two people drowning quietly in the same ocean.

No titles.

No expectations.

Just pain and breath and truth.

"Nova?" he asked softly.

"Yeah?"

"Don't give up on your voice. Even when everything else is shaking."

I nodded, wiping another stray tear.

"Only if you don't give up on yourself."

His eyes opened—tired, haunted, hopeful.

"I'll try," he said.

And for the first time all day... I believed him.

For a few minutes after Malik opened up, the silence between us felt almost peaceful. Not light—not easy—but shared. Like we were holding the same cracked thing between us and trying not to let it shatter.

I picked up the mic again, more out of habit than hope.

"Maybe I should try one more time," I murmured.

Malik nodded gently. "Only if you're ready."

I wasn't.

But I didn't want him worrying about me when his world was already collapsing.

I inhaled, tightened my grip—

And my phone buzzed.

Once.

Then again.

Then a third time like a knock that wouldn't stop.

I tried to ignore it.

Buzz.

Buzz.

I set the mic down and pulled the phone from my pocket, already bracing myself.

It was him.

My ex.

I didn't even open it yet, but the preview alone made my stomach drop.

"I know you still think about us. Don't pretend church erased everything we did."

My fingers trembled.

Another message lit up instantly:

"You never moaned like that with anybody else."

My heart slammed against my ribs.

And then a third:

A picture.

Not explicit enough to break laws—

But suggestive enough to rip open every soul tie God had tried to cauterize.

My throat closed.

For a second I forgot how to breathe.

I locked the screen so fast my hand shook, but not fast enough to hide the way the blood drained from my face.

Malik saw.

Of course he did.

He leaned forward, voice low, worried. "Nova? What was that? Are you okay?"

I swallowed hard, forcing the phone deeper into my pocket like I could bury the shame with it.

"I—I'm fine," I lied, too quickly.

He didn't buy it.

"Nova."

Just my name.

Firm, gentle, grounding.

I felt exposed.

Like every wall I kept up around my testimony—my past—my struggles—had cracked open.

I shook my head. "It's nothing. Just… someone I used to know. Being disrespectful."

"Disrespectful how?" he pressed softly.

I closed my eyes.

A memory hit me—my ex's hands, my own voice I barely recognized, a version of me I worked hard to bury.

Tears burned the back of my eyes.

"I can't talk about it," I whispered. "Not right now."

Malik didn't touch me—not even accidentally. But he shifted closer, elbows resting on his knees, posture protective without crossing a line.

"You don't have to tell me," he said. "But whatever that message was… it shook you."

My breath hitched.

He had no idea.

"It's just…" My voice broke. "I thought I was free from that life. From him. From the things I did before God pulled me out."

Malik watched me with an intensity that wasn't judgment—just heartbreak.

"You *are* free," he said quietly. "Triggers don't mean bondage. Fear doesn't mean failure."

I covered my mouth to keep the sob from slipping out.

He noticed anyway.

"Nova..."

I kept shaking my head because I could feel myself unraveling, and I hated it. I hated that this man—this good man—was seeing a side of me I promised myself nobody in leadership would ever see again.

Another buzz.

I flinched hard.

Malik heard it.

His jaw tightened. "That's him again, isn't it?"

I didn't answer.

I didn't have to.

Something shifted in his eyes—not jealousy, not anger—but a kind of protective fury that surprised me. A quiet one. Dangerous in its silence.

"Nova," he said, voice low. "Whoever he is, he doesn't get to have space in your spirit like this."

My chest rose and fell too fast.

Malik exhaled shakily, like he was pushing down his own storm.

"You're fighting battles alone that you shouldn't have to fight alone," he whispered. "You help everybody else, but who's helping you?"

My lip trembled.

Another buzz.

I nearly dropped the phone.

Malik's hand moved—just an inch, like he wanted to reach for it, or maybe reach for me—but he stopped himself, fingers curling into a fist instead.

"Do you want me to stay?" he asked softly. "You don't have to be by yourself right now."

Something in my spirit tore open.

But before I could answer—

A shadow passed across the sanctuary doorway.

Malik didn't notice.

But my skin prickled.

I froze.

Because for just a second...

I could've sworn that same face—the same height, same silhouette—passed by again.

Not Malik.

But *him.*

The other him.

My breath stuttered.

"NOVA?" Malik asked again, alarmed now.

I looked back at him, heart pounding.

"I—"

I swallowed.

"I think something's... wrong."

Malik was still watching me, concern written everywhere on his face. His shoulders were tense, his jaw clenched like he was fighting thoughts he couldn't manage. He leaned forward slightly, waiting for me to explain why I suddenly froze.

I opened my mouth, but nothing came out.

My pulse was thudding so loudly I could hear it in my ears.

Malik frowned. "Nova? What did you see?"

I swallowed hard, my gaze drifting toward the sanctuary doorway even though the shadow was gone now—like it had never been there at all.

"I..."

My voice trailed off.

"Nova." His tone sharpened—gentle, but firm. "You're scaring me.

What happened?"

I finally forced myself to say it.

"I saw you," I whispered.

He blinked. "I'm right here."

I shook my head quickly, tears burning behind my eyes.

"No. I saw *you*. In the doorway. Just now."

Malik's face went still.

Completely still.

Color drained from his expression in a way I'd never seen. His breath hitched almost imperceptibly as he turned his head toward the doorway, scanning the empty hall beyond it.

"Nova," he said carefully, "are you sure?"

My hands trembled. "I know what I saw, Malik. Same height. Same build. Same... everything. It was you—but it wasn't."

He closed his eyes briefly, like something inside him cracked open. When he looked at me again, his voice was a rasp.

"Nova... you can't tell anyone else you saw that. Not yet."

The fear in his eyes wasn't for himself.

It was for me.

My heart sank. "What does that mean?"

He looked down at his hands—shaking now—and exhaled through clenched teeth.

"It means I think I know who you saw."

My breath caught. "Who?"

He didn't answer right away.

He looked haunted.

Conflicted.

Terrified.

Finally, barely above a whisper, he said:

"Marcus."

My entire body went cold.

"Malik… your brother is… dead."

His voice broke in a way that made the room feel smaller.

"No," he whispered. "He isn't."

I stared at him, disbelief and fear tangling in my chest.

"You think Marcus is alive and—what? Stalking the church? Following you? Playing… games?"

Malik rubbed his forehead like the weight of the truth was physically hurting him.

"He's been spotted twice already," he admitted softly. "I didn't want to believe it at first. But now… Nova, if you saw him—then he's not just watching me."

He met my gaze.

"He's watching everything."

My fingers wrapped around the edge of the pew to keep myself steady. "Why? What does he want?"

Malik shook his head. "I don't know. But Marcus never did anything without purpose. If he's here… it's because he planned it."

I shivered.

A chill ran through the sanctuary, and I wasn't convinced it was imagination.

"Malik," I whispered, "does anyone else know?"

"No," he said immediately. "And they can't. Not yet. The board would panic. The congregation is already fragile. And if Marcus is dangerous enough to fake his death…"

He trailed off before finishing the sentence.

He didn't have to.

The implication was heavy enough.

My voice came out soft. "What do we do?"

He looked at me—really looked at me—as if anchoring himself to my presence.

"You pray," he said quietly. "You stay alert. And you don't walk anywhere alone in this building."

"And you?" I asked.

He exhaled and leaned back, eyes distant.

"I figure out why he came back."

But beneath that calm determination... I heard the truth in his spirit.

He wasn't just scared Marcus was alive.

He was scared Marcus wanted to replace him.

And I was scared Malik might be right.

* * *

By the time I got home that night, my whole body felt like it was holding someone else's heartbeat. My nerves were rattled. My spirit was unsettled. And the look in Malik's eyes when he said Marcus's name... it followed me all the way up the walkway to my apartment.

My keys rattled loudly in the lock, louder than they should've.

I stepped inside and locked everything—deadbolt, chain, even the patio door. Not because I thought Marcus would be waiting for me on the sofa, but because...

Because I didn't know what he was capable of now.

I placed my purse down slowly.

Turned on the lamp.

Took a breath.

I needed prayer.

Not the polite kind I said before meals—real prayer.

Raw.

Honest.

Desperate.

I sank to my knees beside the couch, clasped my hands tightly, and whispered, "God... I need You."

The words were simple, but they cracked something open inside me.

"I'm scared."

My voice wavered.

"I'm scared of my past coming back. I'm scared of my desires waking up again. I'm scared of what I saw tonight—of what's stalking Malik… stalking this church."

I closed my eyes.

"Please cover him. Please cover us. Please—"

The air shifted.

Subtle at first.

Like a draft from under the door.

Then heavier.

Thicker.

My breath froze in my throat.

I opened my eyes slowly.

Nothing looked different—but everything *felt* different.

The room had weight.

Like someone else had stepped into it.

I pressed a hand to my chest.

"Jesus…?"

The lamp flickered.

Just once.

But enough to make my heart thud painfully.

I shook my head, trying to clear it. "No. No, Nova, you're tired. You're overwhelmed. You're jumping at shadows."

But when I closed my eyes again to pray—

A pressure settled behind me.

Not touching.

Not close enough to call physical.

Just… present.

Watching.

Listening.

My throat tightened.

Something in my spirit whispered, *Get up.*

I rose slowly to my feet, legs trembling. The air behind me felt colder—like walking past a freezer door someone left open.

I turned.

Nothing there.

But that didn't comfort me.

Because the heaviness remained.

I grabbed my Bible off the coffee table, holding it like a shield against something I couldn't see.

"God is not the author of confusion," I said under my breath. "Nor fear. Nor torment."

But fear was climbing my spine anyway, steady and slow.

I opened the Bible randomly.

My eyes landed on Isaiah.

"When the enemy shall come in like a flood, the Spirit of the Lord shall lift up a standard against him."

A shaky breath escaped me.

"Okay… okay. Lord, I hear You."

I tried to pray again.

"Cover my mind. Cover my home. Cover my—"

A soft vibration startled me.

My phone.

Across the room.

I didn't want to look.

Didn't want to see his name again.

Didn't want to know what new temptation or poison my ex had sent.

But something in my chest said *check it.*

I took a few steps toward the table, hesitant.

The notification preview lit up.

Not my ex.

A new number.

No contact saved.

Just one sentence:

"You left something at the church."

My blood ran cold.

Another message came immediately after.

"Tell Malik I said hello."

I staggered back a step.

The atmosphere behind me—the pressure I couldn't explain—tightened.

Not violent.

Not angry.

Just there.

Just watching.

I clutched my Bible harder and whispered through trembling lips:

"God... what is happening?"

Because deep down, past fear, past confusion, past all of it—

I already knew who sent the message.

Marcus had found me too.

Ten

MALIK

I didn't sleep.

I closed my eyes, but my mind wouldn't stop replaying Nova's fear, the shadow she swore she saw, and the truth I finally said out loud:

Marcus was alive.

By dawn, my chest felt bruised from the weight of everything pressing on me. But Thursday morning prayer couldn't run itself, and I wasn't about to give anyone another reason to question my stability.

When I walked into the sanctuary, only a few church mothers were scattered across the pews. Some were praying quietly. Some were whispering. Some were staring at me like I was the morning headline.

I tried to steady my breathing.

"Good morning, saints," I said gently.

Two mothers marched toward me immediately—Mother Jenkins and Sister Arlissa. Both of them looked furious. Not disappointed. Not confused.

Furious.

"Pastor Malik," Sister Arlissa said, voice trembling with anger, "I need to speak with you RIGHT NOW."

Mother Jenkins crossed her arms. "Same here. You owe us some explanations."

I blinked, caught off guard. "Of course... what's wrong?"

Arlissa stepped closer. "You told my husband to leave me."

My stomach dropped. "What?"

"You DM'd him on Facebook!" she snapped. "Saying the Lord showed you our marriage wasn't ordained!"

Mother Jenkins chimed in, voice rising. "And YOU told me God said my son should move out my house because I'm 'stunting his spiritual growth!' He's FIFTEEN, Malik. FIFTEEN!"

I stared at both of them, stunned. "I... I never said that. I never messaged either of you."

Arlissa shoved her phone toward me.

A screenshot.

My name.

My profile picture.

A message reading:

"Sister Arlissa, the Lord says separation is necessary for the next season. Obey quickly."

My throat tightened.

This wasn't gossip or misinterpretation.

This was deliberate.

Calculated.

Marcus.

He wasn't just impersonating me around the church—he was infiltrating the congregation one by one, planting poison in my name.

Mother Jenkins shook her head. "You got the whole internet talking about fake prophets and abusive leadership. You better fix this before

Sunday, Pastor."

I exhaled slowly, fighting the nausea crawling up my chest. "Listen to me... I did not send these messages. Any of them."

Arlissa scoffed. "So somebody just pretending to be you?"

"Yes," I said, firmer this time than I expected. "That's exactly what's happening. The board discussed it already. Someone is impersonating me to make Kingdom Rising look worse than it already does."

They paused.

The anger wavered—but the confusion thickened.

Mother Jenkins lowered her phone slightly. "But who would do something like that?"

Someone who wanted to destroy me.

Someone who wanted to dismantle this church.

Someone who shared my face and my blood.

I swallowed hard. "We believe it's someone targeting the church during a vulnerable time."

I forced myself to keep my voice steady. "But it won't work. God is still here. And the truth always rises. Always."

Arlissa's expression softened.

Mother Jenkins sighed, long and heavy. "I hope you're right, Pastor... because if somebody's tryna tear this church apart, they're doing a good job."

She walked away slowly.

Arlissa followed, shaking her head.

I stood there alone, pulse hammering, dread squeezing every breath out of me.

Marcus wasn't hiding anymore.

He was escalating.

He wasn't just stalking me—

He was speaking for me.

Acting as me.

And if he could manipulate people with a screen...

It was only a matter of time before he stepped into a room and spoke with my voice.

I pressed a hand to my chest and whispered, barely audible:

"God... please don't let him destroy what's left."

But even as I prayed it, something deep inside me knew:

The destruction had already started.

And Marcus hadn't even begun.

Thursday morning prayer felt like walking through fog: thick, heavy, and disorienting. I went through the motions—scripture, intercession, petitions—but my mind kept circling the same thought.

Marcus was no longer testing boundaries.

He was crossing them.

And he was using my face to do it.

When prayer ended, I stepped out of the sanctuary before anyone else could corner me again. I needed air. I needed silence. I needed something to feel normal for five minutes.

My phone buzzed.

A reminder to visit Sister Danielle at the hospital.

Her husband, Mr. Harold, had suffered a stroke late Wednesday night. Solid man. Quiet. A regular usher on fourth Sundays. The kind of church member who kept everything steady even when folks around him wavered.

I left immediately.

The drive to the hospital was a blur—red lights, street signs, all of it passing too quickly and not quickly enough. My thoughts felt swollen, too large for my skull. Every passing window reflected my face, but it didn't feel like my own. The idea that Marcus could've been anywhere I'd been... speaking to people I cared about... making decisions in my name...

A cold, crawling dread settled in my chest.

By the time I reached the hospital room, I had rehearsed what I'd say. Something comforting. Something pastoral. Something that would soothe without promising miracles I didn't have the strength to believe in.

But the moment I stepped inside, the air snapped tight.

Mr. Harold lay hooked up to machines, pale beneath the fluorescent lights. His chest rose and fell in slow, assisted rhythms. Tubes. Wires. The steady rhythm of a heart monitor. It was heartbreaking, but familiar.

What wasn't familiar was the way his wife turned when she heard me step in.

Her face blanched, then twisted.

Before I could say a word, she screamed.

"GET OUT!"

The sound cracked through the room with so much grief and fury it stunned me in place. She rose from the chair so fast it collided with the wall behind her.

"I mean it, Malik. Get out of here! You've done enough."

I stood frozen, both hands raised slightly, palms out. "Sister Danielle... I just got here. I came as soon as I could."

She shook her head—wild, unmoored. "Don't lie. You were here last night. Looking over his bed like he was already gone. Telling me it wouldn't be long now. What kind of pastor says something like that?"

My mouth went dry.

"Sister Danielle, I wasn't here," I said carefully. "I haven't been to the hospital this week. I'm seeing him for the first time today."

Her eyes flooded with tears. "You're lying. You stood right there"—she pointed to the foot of the bed—"and spoke to him like he was already slipping away. You told me to 'prepare myself.' Do you know what that did to me?"

My stomach twisted. "I promise you... that wasn't me."

A nurse stepped toward us, a middle-aged woman with kind eyes that now held suspicion. She lowered her voice but didn't bother hiding her expression.

"Pastor... you were definitely here," she whispered. "We nearly had to sedate her because she was so distraught."

My skin prickled. A chill spread down my spine, slow and nauseating.

Marcus had been here.

In *this* room.

Standing where I stood.

Looking down at a dying man and using my voice to speak death over him.

The realization hit me so hard I felt my knees weaken.

I turned to the nurse. "Did... did he say anything else? Anything unusual? Did he sign in?"

She frowned. "You came straight up. Security let you through because, well... you're known here. And you left quickly after upsetting Mrs. Daniels. Wouldn't stay to explain anything."

My pulse thudded in my ears.

Of course he wouldn't stay.

Chaos was the point.

Mrs. Daniels stepped closer, grief twisting her features into something raw and jagged. "Just leave, Malik. Please. I don't want to see you right now."

My throat tightened, but I nodded. Her pain wasn't anger—it was confusion, betrayal, heartbreak. She couldn't tell the difference, and I didn't blame her.

"I'm so sorry," I said softly. "I truly didn't come until now. But I'll give you space."

She turned back to her husband, pressing a trembling hand to his arm.

I stepped into the hallway, and the moment the door closed behind me, the air left my lungs.

Marcus wasn't impersonating me anymore.

He was weaponizing me.

Every step he took, every place he visited, every lie he planted—it was sinking the knife deeper into everything I'd built. Everything the church believed about me. Everything I held sacred.

I pressed my hands to my face and tried to breathe through the sickness twisting inside me.

He was dismantling my life one encounter at a time.

And if he had the courage to walk into a hospital room, face a grieving wife, and talk like her husband was already gone...

He wouldn't stop.

He wouldn't slow down.

He was escalating.

I lowered my hands and whispered the truth I could no longer ignore.

"I have to find him. Now."

Because if I didn't— he would burn this entire church to the ground, one stolen conversation at a time.

By the time I left the hospital, my nerves were shot. My hands wouldn't stop shaking. My breath felt shallow and tight. And every hallway mirror, every window reflection, every surface that caught my image made my stomach twist.

Because I didn't know if it was me.

Or him.

By noon, I stopped pretending I could think clearly. There was only one person alive who understood Marcus well enough to predict what he might do next.

My father.

I drove to the federal facility in silence, replaying the hospital room again and again. The devastation on Sister Danielle's face. The certainty in the nurse's voice. The way Marcus had mimicked not just my appearance but my tone—the calm cadence of pastoral authority.

He knew exactly where to hit.

Exactly where to fracture the ministry.

And the more I thought about it, the more I realized how blind I'd been to just how deep his resentment must run. Resentment born long before he ever ran away.

Resentment that Jeremiah helped cultivate.

I checked in, passed through security, and was finally led to the visitation booth. My father stepped into the opposite side a minute later, dressed in an orange jumpsuit that looked wrong on a man who'd always paraded across a pulpit in designer suits.

He sat with a slow, heavy exhale, the weight of humiliation etched into every line of his face.

"You shouldn't have come," he said without greeting.

"I didn't come for you," I answered quietly. "I came for answers."

He looked up sharply, and for a moment I saw the father from my childhood—the one who expected obedience, not conversation.

"About the case?" he asked.

"No. About Marcus."

His jaw tightened.

"Don't start with that," he snapped. "He's dead."

"No, he's not," I said, keeping my voice steady. "He's alive. And he's impersonating me. In the church. In the city. Everywhere."

Jeremiah's expression flickered—shock, denial, fear—but he smothered it quickly.

"That's impossible. The medical examiner—"

"Was paid off," I cut in. "You knew the remains weren't identifiable. You knew the report wasn't clean. You wanted closure so badly you accepted a lie."

My father's eyes narrowed. "You don't know what you're talking about."

"Then help me understand," I said. "Because Marcus is out there—hurting people. Destroying what's left of our name. And I need to know why he's doing this."

Jeremiah leaned back in his seat, folding his hands. "Marcus always wanted to hurt someone. He came out angry. Nothing I did changed that."

I shook my head. "You didn't change him. You crushed him."

His jaw flexed.

"He needed discipline," he said. "You needed structure. Marcus... needed deliverance."

I stared at him, stunned at how effortlessly he rewrote the past.

"Do you hear yourself?" I asked. "Marcus wasn't possessed. He was a kid starving for attention. Every time he acted out, you punished him. Every time I acted out, you excused me."

Jeremiah didn't respond.

He didn't deny it either.

"And now," I continued, "he's come back to make both of us pay. And he started with you."

My father bristled. "What has he done?"

"He visited a hospitalized member and told his wife to prepare for death. He's sending messages to the congregation under my name. He's slipping in and out of the church pretending to be me."

Jeremiah's face drained of color.

"He's escalating," I said. "He's precise. Calculated. And he's been planning this for years. What did he want from you after he ran away? What did he say? Did he ever reach out?"

Jeremiah didn't answer immediately.

When he finally spoke, his voice came out quieter than I expected.

"He came to me once," he said. "Years ago. I told him if he wanted redemption, he needed to come home sober, stable, and repentant."

My hands curled into fists. "So you sent him away."

"He wasn't ready," Jeremiah insisted. "He was wild. Violent. Full of rage."

"You were supposed to be his father," I said, voice breaking despite myself. "Not his judge. He needed you."

Jeremiah looked away.

"He hated you," I said softly. "But he hated you because he wanted you to love him. And now… now he's using your neglect as fuel."

Silence stretched between us.

Thick. Bitter. Uncomfortable.

"Did he ever say he blamed me?" my father asked quietly.

"Yes," I said honestly. "But he blames me too."

Jeremiah's eyebrows furrowed. "Why you?"

"Because I got everything he wanted," I whispered. "Your approval. Your praise. The future you told him he'd never deserve."

My father pressed a hand to the glass. Not tender—almost pleading.

"Malik… if Marcus is alive, you need to protect yourself. He wasn't right. Something was always… off."

"No," I said. "Something was broken. And we left him to fix it alone."

Jeremiah swallowed hard, guilt flickering over him like a shadow.

"Find him," I said. "Or he'll burn Kingdom Rising to the ground."

Jeremiah nodded slowly. "If he's come for you… he's not finished."

I stood to leave.

As the guard opened the door, my father called after me.

"Malik?"

I turned.

"Be careful," he said. "Your brother was always dangerous. But now… he has nothing left to lose."

I stepped into the hallway, my pulse tight, my chest aching, and a single truth echoing in my mind:

Marcus wasn't just after my life.

He was after my identity.

By the time I got back to Kingdom Rising, my hands were still trembling from the conversation with my father. I closed the door to Jeremiah's office behind me and leaned against it, breathing hard, trying to gather the pieces of myself that felt scattered.

The office was too quiet.

Too familiar.

Too heavy with everything my father had been—and everything he'd forced me to become.

I moved toward the desk, the same desk I'd sat across from as a child when I was praised and scolded in unequal measure. I pressed both hands against the surface, bowing my head.

Marcus.

Alive.

Watching me.

Speaking like me.

Walking where I walked.

Taking every fracture in this church and driving a wedge deeper.

I felt nauseous.

My reflection caught my eye in the small decorative mirror hanging near the bookcase—the one Jeremiah used to straighten his tie before stepping onto the pulpit. I turned toward it.

My reflection stared back, but something felt wrong—like I was looking at a version of myself slightly out of place, slightly distorted, slightly... distant.

For one terrifying second, I wondered if someone else might mistake Marcus for me... because I was starting to mistake *myself* for him.

I stepped closer to the mirror.

The circles under my eyes were darker than ever. My shoulders were slumped. My jaw tight. I didn't look like a pastor. I didn't look like a leader. I didn't even look like someone in control of his own life.

I looked like a man losing his identity one stolen moment at a time.

A surge of frustration rose inside me so quickly I didn't recognize it until it was too late.

My fist slammed into the edge of the desk.

Pain shot up my arm, sharp and sudden, but it felt grounding—real—something I could control when everything else was slipping out of my hands.

"Where are you, Marcus?" I whispered. "What do you want from me?"

He wasn't answering.

He was moving.

Manipulating.

Infiltrating.

And I was reacting like a man being hunted.

I raked a hand through my hair, pacing the length of the office, heart pounding. Every beat echoed the same truth:

I had no idea where to start looking for him.

He could be anywhere.

With anyone.

In any space I used to occupy.

I sat down, then stood back up. The walls felt like they were closing in. The office smelled like old cologne and polished wood—Jeremiah's scent, Jeremiah's world—but the pressure around me felt like Marcus.

I needed answers.

I needed direction.

I needed someone who knew the version of Marcus I never did—the version he became after he left home.

And there was only one person alive who fit that description.

Every warning, every gut feeling, every logical instinct told me not to do it.

But I didn't have the luxury of wisdom anymore. I was running out of time. Out of allies. Out of clarity.

My chest tightened.

Against my better judgment—

against everything I'd ever sworn I'd avoid—

I pulled out my keys and headed toward the door.

If I wanted to find Marcus, if I wanted any hope of stopping him, I had to start where he ended.

With Taz.

The man who built him.

The man who used him.

The man who might be the only one who knew where Marcus would strike next.

As I locked Jeremiah's office behind me, the bitter truth settled in: To save my life, my reputation, and my entire church...

I was going to have to walk straight into hell and ask a devil for help.

Taz's club sat wedged between two abandoned warehouses, the kind of place that always looked like it was waiting for a raid or a funeral. The neon sign flickered weakly in the late afternoon light, casting a red pulse over the cracked pavement like a warning.

I pulled into the back lot, parking where Taz's men had eyes on every corner. My heartbeat was a slow, heavy thud against my ribs. Going to him felt reckless. Stupid, even. But the hospital room, the false DMs, and Nova's fear replayed in my mind again and again until I couldn't talk myself out of it anymore.

If Marcus learned to disappear under Taz, then finding Taz was the only place to start.

I cut the engine, sat for a moment, and tried to steady my breath.

My phone rang.

The sound startled me enough that I flinched. Nova's name flashed across the screen.

Part of me considered ignoring it—because the last thing I wanted was to lie to her. But I answered.

"Nova?"

Her voice came through soft at first, but edged with tension. "Malik... where are you?"

I closed my eyes briefly. "At Taz's."

There was a long, thick pause, so heavy it felt like the air inside the car tightened around me.

"You're at *Taz Moreno's* club?" she asked, her tone barely controlled.

"Yes."

"Why would you go there alone?" Fear cracked through her voice, not dramatic, not exaggerated—real fear, stitched with something she wasn't saying. "Malik, listen to me. Men like Taz destroy everything they touch. Once you step into his world, it's hard to come back out untouched."

"I'm not stepping into his world. I just need answers."

"No," she said sharply. "You need protection. And wisdom. And distance from men who treat violence like language."

I rubbed my forehead, looking toward the back entrance of the club where two guards lingered, watching my car with slow suspicion.

"Nova, I don't have a choice. Marcus is impersonating me. He's already hurt people. He's unraveling this church one thread at a time. I can't sit back and do nothing."

"You think Taz cares about that?" she asked softly. "You think he'll hand you anything without taking something from you first? Malik, I've known men like him. Men who swallow good people whole. They're charming when they want to be, helpful when it benefits them, and merciless when you're no longer useful."

Her breath shook.

"I don't want that happening to you."

Her words struck me harder than they should have. It had been a long time since someone worried about me without expectation. Without obligation. Without ulterior motives.

"Nova," I said quietly, "thank you for caring. Truly. But Marcus isn't going to stop. And if I don't find him soon, he'll burn this church to the ground and stand in the ashes with my face."

Silence again.

Then, barely above a whisper, she said, "Just… come out alive, okay?"

"I'll do my best."

"Malik—"

"I have to go."

I ended the call before I could lose my nerve.

I stepped out of the car. The air smelled like cigarette smoke and oil. Taz's men followed me with their eyes as I approached the back door.

The door swung open before I reached it.

Taz Moreno stood there in a charcoal blazer, cigar in one hand, annoyance in his eyes. He looked me over like I was an interruption, not a visitor.

"Well, well," he said. "If it isn't the church boy. You must be real desperate to show up here after the other night."

His gaze sharpened with curiosity, irritation, and something colder— a recognition shaped by history he shared with Marcus, not me.

"What do you want, Malik?"

"I need information."

He stepped back, letting me in with a dismissive wave. "Of course you do. Everybody wants something when they come to me."

Inside, the music was low, the lights dim, and the scent of liquor soaked into the walls. He gestured toward a private room.

"Before we get into your problems," he said, "let's talk about mine."

I stiffened. "What problems?"

Taz's smile was humorless.

"My two point seven million dollars," he said. "Your father froze it when the feds came knocking. And you—you owe me answers. Because if Marcus is back in play, then somebody needs to tell me where my money is."

I swallowed hard.

This was why Nova had been afraid.

This world didn't do compassion.

It didn't do grace.

It barely did negotiation.

"Taz," I said carefully, "I'm not Marcus. I never ran your numbers. I never touched your money."

He exhaled smoke and leaned forward. "That's the funny thing about twins. Same face." He tapped ash off his cigar. "Same consequences."

My pulse hammered in my throat.

Taz smiled without warmth.

"Now... let's talk about your brother. And why he play dead."

And just like that—

I realized the truth:

Whatever answers I thought I'd get here...

They were going to come with a price.

Inside Taz's office, the air felt stale and heavy, thick with cigar smoke and the same danger Marcus had once lived in. Every instinct in me screamed I didn't belong here, but turning back wasn't an option. I needed answers, and Taz was the last person alive who had them.

He watched me the moment I stepped in — not casually, not curiously, but like a hunter studying prey he couldn't decide whether to manipulate or devour. I felt that assessment travel across my skin.

"You shouldn't have come here alone," he said as he eased back into his chair, cigar balanced between his fingers. "People like me don't hand out mercy because someone walks in scared."

The words landed, not because they were intimidating, but because they were true. I was scared. And he saw it before I admitted it to myself.

"I'm not here for mercy," I said. "I just need the truth."

Taz let out a sound that wasn't quite a laugh. "Truth? You came looking for truth in a place built on lies." His gaze sharpened. "You're too fragile for this world, Malik. Your brother... Marcus... he grew teeth in here. You didn't. If he's coming after your church, you don't stand a chance against him."

Heat crawled up my neck — frustration, fear, anger tangled together. "Don't talk about me like I'm weak."

"I'm not talking," he replied calmly. "I'm observing. And telling you what Marcus already knew."

It struck something in me that I didn't want to acknowledge — the idea that Marcus had always viewed me through Taz's eyes. Soft. Sheltered. Untested. It twisted in my stomach.

"You took him in," I said. "You shaped him. You fed whatever darkness he had. So don't stand here and pretend you're just an observer."

Taz raised an eyebrow. "Shaped him? No. I recognized what was already there. Marcus didn't need training — he needed purpose. Rage is a resource when someone knows how to use it."

Hearing that — hearing a stranger claim ownership of pieces of my brother I'd never even known — made something inside me snap.

"You used him," I said. My voice shook, but the anger was steady. "You took a teenager running from pain and turned him into something worse."

"Everybody gets used," Taz answered. "Marcus wasn't a victim. He was hungry for someone to see him — even if what they saw was broken."

I wanted to hit him.

I wanted to walk out.

I wanted to pretend none of this was real.

But instead, I pushed past the sick feeling rising in me and asked the question I came for.

"What was Marcus running from when he faked his death?"

That made Taz go still.

For the first time since I walked in, he looked wary.

Then he said a name I'd never heard before.

"Lysander."

The room felt colder instantly.

"Who is that?" I asked.

"A man you should hope never to meet," Taz replied. "Your brother owed him. More than he ever owed me. And Lysander doesn't settle debts through negotiation."

My chest tightened.

"How did Marcus end up tied to someone like that?"

"Long story," Taz answered. "But here's the short one: Lysander found value in your brother's invisibility. That chip on his shoulder made him reckless, but it also made him fearless. Lysander gave him a choice — disappear or die."

The words landed like a blow.

"So faking his death was survival," I said quietly.

"It was obedience," Taz corrected. "Lysander turned Marcus into a ghost. A cleaner. A courier. Someone who could move without being seen, without raising suspicion. He made Marcus disappear from every life he ever touched."

I felt sick. Truly sick.

"Did Marcus reach out? At any point?" I asked. "Even once?"

Taz studied me for a long moment before answering.

"No," he said. "Ghosts don't look backward. They don't revisit graves."

I swallowed, forcing down the ache. "But he's looking back now. He's impersonating me. He's hurting members of the church. He's trying to destroy everything connected to my name and my father's."

"That's not destruction," Taz replied. "That's reclamation."

I blinked. "What does that mean?"

"It means your brother spent years watching life move on without him. He watched you become everything he was told he could never be. And now that Lysander is gone…" Taz leaned forward. "There's nothing controlling him. Nothing holding him together. Nothing keeping his darkness aimed in the right direction."

I felt my breath stall.

"And you're telling me," I asked quietly, "that I'm supposed to… what? Fight him? Outrun him? Catch him?"

Taz shrugged. "You're supposed to be smart enough to realize this won't end with a sermon."

His words lodged deep in my chest.

"He wants something bigger than revenge," Taz added.

"What?"

Taz lifted his chin, eyes hard.

"Your life. Your ministry. Your identity. Marcus didn't just come back to punish you, Malik." A long pause. "He came back to replace you."

My stomach clenched.

Every sighting.

Every impersonation.

Every lie he planted in my name.

Taz saw the realization hit me and didn't soften the blow.

"If you want to stop him," he said, "you need to stop hoping he's still your brother. He's not."

I stood there, heart pounding, understanding settling in with terrifying clarity.

Marcus wasn't hiding anymore.

He was becoming me.

And if I didn't find him soon—he would finish the job he started.

When I stepped out of Taz's club, the late afternoon sun hit me like a shock. It felt wrong—too bright for the darkness I had just walked through, too warm for the cold settling under my skin.

My legs were unsteady. My hands wouldn't stop shaking. I reached the car and leaned against the door, trying to steady my breathing, but nothing seemed to land. My heart kept climbing into my throat, my thoughts running too fast to catch.

Marcus wasn't just angry. He wasn't just reckless.

He was trained.

He was sharpened.

He was unbound.

And he was coming straight for everything connected to me.

The parking lot felt too open. Every shadow looked like movement. Every sound felt like a clue I couldn't decipher. I pressed a hand against my chest, trying to push the panic back where it belonged, but it kept rising.

Before I even realized what I was doing, I pulled out my phone.

My thumb hovered over Nova's name.

There were other people I could've called—elders, deacons, ministry friends—but none of them would have understood the kind of fear that sat in my bones right now. And none of them would have answered with anything other than expectation.

Nova didn't expect anything from me.

She just… showed up.

And right now, I needed someone who wasn't pulling on me, demanding from me, or collapsing in front of me. I needed one steady voice in the middle of a day that had turned into chaos.

I hit the call button before I could think myself out of it.

She picked up on the second ring.

"Malik?"

The sound of my name in her voice was like air finding its way back into my lungs.

I swallowed hard. "Hey."

There was a pause—not long, but enough for her to hear the strain I couldn't hide.

"Are you okay?" she asked quietly. "Just tell me you're safe."

I closed my eyes. The concern in her voice softened something in me I didn't realize had turned rigid.

"I'm alright," I lied first, out of habit. Then the truth slipped through. "I'm... not great."

Another pause, this one heavier.

"Did something happen?" she asked. "You sound... shaken."

I rubbed a hand over my face, staring at the cracked pavement. "I went through with the meeting with Taz."

The breath she took on the other end wasn't loud, but I heard the fear in it. "Malik... I told you—"

"I know," I said, cutting her off gently. "But I had to go. He knew Marcus better than anyone. And there were things I needed to hear. Even if I didn't want to."

"Did he hurt you?" she asked, voice rising, tight with worry.

"No," I said quickly. "Nothing like that. But I... I'm trying to wrap my head around what Marcus became. And what he's capable of now. I thought I understood the danger. I didn't."

I sat in the driver's seat but didn't start the car. The silence between us wasn't uncomfortable—it felt like a space she allowed me to breathe in.

"Nova," I said quietly, "do you ever feel like something is pulling your life out from under you? One thread at a time?"

Her voice softened. "Yes. More times than I want to admit. And that feeling doesn't make you weak... it makes you human."

I felt my throat tighten. I hadn't realized how close I was to breaking until she said that.

She continued, "You don't owe me details, but you sound like you're carrying more than one person should."

"I can't let the church collapse," I said. "I can't let Marcus destroy what little stability we have left. And I'm running out of options."

"You don't have to figure it all out tonight," she said gently. "And you don't have to figure it out alone."

Something in me cracked at that, something I'd been holding together through force and habit.

"I didn't call for advice," I admitted. "I just... needed to hear a voice that wasn't angry or afraid of me."

She was quiet for a moment. Then she said, "You called the right person."

The words landed deeper than she probably meant them to.

I let out a slow exhale. "Thank you, Nova."

"You're welcome," she replied with a warmth that steadied me. "Call me when you get home so I know you made it safely."

I allowed myself a small nod even though she couldn't see it. "I will."

And for the first time all day, the ground beneath me felt a little less unstable.

I hung up the phone, started the engine, and pulled away from the club—still shaken, still uncertain, but no longer alone in the dark.

Eleven

KYRIE CHAMBERS

By the time I made it home, my head was still buzzing from everything happening at Kingdom Rising. Pastor Jeremiah in cuffs, Malik suddenly carrying the whole church on his shoulders, Mother Lavvy threatening to tase people for the Holy Ghost — it was too much mess over the past couple of weeks.

But something had been nagging me since Sunday.

Something I couldn't shake.

Some of the choir members said they'd seen Malik in the hallway before service… but Malik had been in the pastor's office with me, mic'ing up, and then walked straight to the pulpit.

Impossible.

Or… it should've been.

I kicked off my shoes, grabbed a Sprite from the fridge, and opened my laptop. If somebody was impersonating Pastor Malik, then the cameras would catch them. People lie. Footage doesn't.

I pulled up the sanctuary feed from Sunday.

Clicked through timestamps.

Fast-forwarded past altar call rehearsal, musicians clowning around, and Winter arguing with Harmony about who stole whose wig glue.

Then I hit the timeline between noon and one — the most chaotic hour of the entire service.

I scrubbed through the footage.

12:15 PM.

And my entire body went cold.

On the left balcony camera, clear as day, a man slipped into the sanctuary through the side door. Hoodie up. Head low.

But the second he walked under the light—

I froze.

I knew that face.

I *knew* that face.

Pastor Malik.

Except... Malik was preaching at 12:15.

I remembered the exact timestamp because I edited the livestream. He was mid-sermon, voice cracking about "standing firm in the day of trouble."

So how in the world—

My Sprite nearly slipped out of my hand.

"Nah... nope..." I muttered as I zoomed in so far the pixels screamed for help.

Same jawline. Same walk. Same build. Same everything.

"What—what the—did we clone this man? Did Jeremiah have a secret son? Was Malik part of a lab experiment?!"

I scrubbed back.

Played it again.

Played it a third time.

Every angle showed the same thing:

A man who looked EXACTLY like Pastor Malik had entered the sanctuary at 12:15 PM... while the real Malik stood on the pulpit preaching live.

I leaned back hard in my chair.

"Oh no. Ohhhhh no no no—"

My chest tightened.

My skin prickled.

My mind raced.

Marcus was dead.

DEAD.

Closed casket, funeral program, people crying off-key at the repast — dead.

So unless the Cross brothers were actually triplets and somebody hid one in the wilderness for twenty years...

This wasn't possible.

"This is some Holy Ghost X-Files mess," I whispered.

My hands shook as I grabbed my phone. I didn't want to call Malik... but how could I not?

Something wrong was happening at Kingdom Rising.

Something big.

Something dangerous.

And I had just found proof.

I clicked the footage one more time — just to be sure — and the man turned slightly toward the camera.

Same face.

Same expression.

But the eyes...

They weren't Malik's.

Not even close.

My drink finally slipped from his hand and splashed across the floor.

"Oh, Pastor... you are NOT gonna believe this."

I didn't even give myself time to think.

The second the Sprite hit the floor, I snatched my phone and hit

Pastor Malik's contact so fast I almost FaceTimed him by accident.

He picked up on the second ring.

"Hey, Kyrie. Everything alright?"

"No. No, sir. Absolutely *not*. Pastor, listen—are you alone? You need to be alone for what I'm about to say. Matter fact, sit down. Actually, NO—stand up. You ever faint before? Because this—this right here—"

"Kyrie," Malik said slowly, "breathe."

"BREATHING ISN'T THE ISSUE, PASTOR. I GOT FOOTAGE OF YOU—BUT IT AIN'T YOU—BUT IT *IS* YOU—BUT IT CAN'T BE YOU—"

"Kyrie."

"YES, SIR?"

"Tell me what you saw."

I ran both hands down my face. "Pastor… there's somebody walking into the sanctuary Sunday. Twelve-fifteen. And I zoomed in. And I checked the timestamp on the livestream. And unless you got cloned at the county fair, we have a PROBLEM."

Silence on his end.

The calm kind.

The kind that made my left eye twitch.

Then Malik exhaled and said quietly, "Kyrie… that was my brother."

"Your—" I froze. "Your WHAT?!"

"My brother," he repeated. "Marcus."

I shot up out of my chair so fast it rolled backward and hit the wall.

"PASTOR, THAT MAN IS DEAD! DEAD-DEAD! We prayed! We cried! We ate potato salad at the repast—THE ONE WITH MOTHER LAVVY MADE! Are you telling me we threw an entire funeral for a man who's out here walking around like a—like a—WHAT IS THIS?! A resurrection?! A divine prank?! A *glitch in the Holy Ghost matrix*?!"

"Kyrie." Malik's voice was firmer. "Calm down."

"CALM DOWN? Pastor, the man you buried is wandering around

the church like he's Lazarus straight out the tomb!"

"Kyrie."

I forced myself onto the couch. "Okay. Alright. I'm listening. But my spirit is rattled."

"I know this is a lot," Malik said gently. "But you can't tell anyone. Not one board member. Not Lavvy. Not Harmony. Not anyone in media. Understand?"

I nodded even though he couldn't see me. "Yes, sir. Lips sealed. Zipped. Stitched shut in the spirit."

"Good," he said. "I'm working on handling it. But I need you to do something for me."

I straightened up. "Say the word."

"I need you to check the footage for patterns," he said. "See if there are certain exits or entry points Marcus is favoring. Any blind spots. Any angles he returns to."

My stomach flipped. "Oh Lord... Pastor, your brother got favorite *entrances* now? Like he got a PREFERRED DOOR? This is—this is demonic."

"Kyrie."

"Right, sorry. Patterns. Got it."

"And I've already contacted security," Malik continued. "We're changing all the locks. Marcus's old fobs are being deactivated. Jeremiah's access is also revoked. If you need camera adjustments— different angles, new equipment—coordinate with security immediately."

I blinked.

"You already did all that?"

"Yes."

"Pastor... when did you have time to—never mind. That's none of my business. That's between you and the Lord."

I took a long breath and ran a shaky hand over my forehead. "Alright.

I'll start pulling footage tonight. If Marcus sneezes too hard near a doorway, I'll catch it."

"Thank you, Kyrie."

"No problem. But Pastor?"

"Yes?"

"If your dead brother starts talking through the speakers at choir rehearsal, I'm quitting. I don't do ghosts. I don't do spirits. I don't do supernatural twins. I'm not built for that."

Malik actually laughed under his breath — small, tired, but real.

"I'll do my best to prevent that," he said.

"You better," I muttered. "Because I ain't trying to get dragged into a Lifetime movie."

We hung up, and I stared back at the paused footage on my laptop.

Same face.

Different man.

And he walked like he belonged in the shadows.

"Lord," I whispered, "if this ends with two Maliks fighting on the pulpit, I will NOT be able to handle it."

And then I got to work.

Twelve

NOVA

I should've prayed longer before I left the house.

Maybe fasted.

Maybe done anything other than drive straight across town with my heart pounding and my old instincts clawing their way up my spine.

But I was tired.

Tired of the late-night DMs.

Tired of the spiritual attacks.

Tired of fighting the same temptation with the same man who had once wrecked my soul and taken pieces of my identity with him.

So I pulled into the lot of Asonta's barbershop on a Saturday morning — the worst possible day to confront a man like him.

The place was packed.

Men standing outside waiting for cuts. Music thumping through the glass. Laughter spilling out with the smell of aftershave and hair spray. And the moment I stepped through the door, every head snapped in my direction.

Because they remembered me.

Not the Nova who led worship.

Not the Nova who prayed with people until her throat was raw.

Not the Nova who begged God to deliver her from soul ties that felt like chains.

They remembered *her.*

The girl who used to sit on Asonta's lap in that same shop.

The girl who flirted in the mirrors.

The girl who let attention fill the holes in her heart.

Heat rose in my cheeks as I walked in.

A few of the older barbers nodded politely.

Some of the younger ones whispered.

Someone in the back muttered, "Dang... ain't seen her in a minute."

I wanted to disappear.

Asonta turned around in his chair like he already knew I was coming.

That same slow smile slid across his face — the kind of smile that once made my knees go weak before I knew how dangerous it was.

"Well look who the Holy Ghost brought back," he said, voice low and smooth. "My favorite little church girl."

I clenched my jaw. "I need to talk to you."

"Oh, do you?" He stood, wiping his hands on a towel. "You finally ready to stop pretending you ain't miss me?"

Some of the men snickered.

My stomach twisted in humiliation.

"Asonta," I said sharply, "I'm not here for that."

He chuckled, unbothered. "Mhm. Sure you're not."

He was taller than I remembered. Or maybe he'd always been this tall and I just used to look up at him too much. Tattoos peeked from under his sleeves. Confidence dripped from him like cologne.

And when he stepped a little closer, his eyes dragged over me the way they used to — slow, possessive, like he still had claim on something

God had already freed me from.

"Can we talk in your office?" I asked through my teeth.

His smile widened like he'd just won.

"Oh, now you wanna go behind closed doors. That's interesting."

A few guys in the shop made quiet comments, and embarrassment burned hot in my chest.

I leaned in enough so only he could hear me. "Either we talk alone, or I say what I need to say right here. In front of everybody."

That got his attention.

He raised a brow, amused but curious. "Alright then, church girl. Let's go."

He led me through the back hallway — the same hall I had walked down too many times before. Every step made my skin crawl. Memories leaked through the walls. My spirit screamed that I shouldn't be here.

But I kept walking.

Because running from my past wasn't working anymore.

We stepped into his small office, and he closed the door behind us.

"So," he said, leaning against the edge of his desk, arms folded. "What's got you popping up like old times?"

I met his eyes, steadying my breath.

"This ends today."

His smile vanished.

Good.

Because I wasn't the same girl he used to manipulate.

And God wasn't about to let me go backwards.

Not now.

Not with everything happening around Malik.

Not with Marcus lurking in shadows.

Not with dangers rising on every side.

I squared my shoulders.

"I need you to stop contacting me. Now. And for good."

As soon as the door shut behind us, the air in Asonta's office thickened with the same suffocating energy I used to confuse for excitement. The same walls. The same dim light. The same smell of cologne and clippers.

He leaned against his desk like he'd been waiting for me.

"So," he said, smirking, "you came all the way across town just to tell me you miss me? That's cute."

I folded my arms. "I said this ends today."

He chuckled, low and smooth. "Nova... you always did talk crazy when you were trying to convince yourself you didn't want me."

"I'm not that girl anymore."

"Sure you aren't." He pushed off the desk and took a step toward me. "But that girl sure knew how to pull up in the middle of the day lookin' like this."

I stepped back. "Asonta. Stop."

He paused, gave a slow mocking blink, then tilted his head.

"You serious?"

"Yes," I said. "Completely."

Something flickered in his eyes — irritation first, then disbelief, then something sharper.

"So let me get this straight," he said, his tone shifting. "You pop up at *my* place of business, in front of all my barbers, walk back to my office like you used to, just to tell me you're done?" He laughed once, humorless. "Nah. You want attention. You always did."

"I came to tell you to leave me alone."

"Or what?" he said quietly.

My hands curled at my sides. "Or I'll take steps. And I won't warn you again."

That caught him off guard — but only for a second. Then he laughed, slow and mocking.

"You know…" he said, crossing his arms, "I could tell people a whole lot about the *old* you. The things you begged for. The things you did right in this office. In my car. In that little apartment you swore was temporary."

My stomach twisted.

Shame tried to crawl up my throat… but I didn't let it.

"I'm not afraid of my past," I said. "I've been delivered from it."

He smirked. "Delivered? Nova, please. You left me, not the other way around. And if anybody wants to know the truth, I got screenshots, texts, videos—"

"Stop." My voice cracked, but I held steady. "You don't get to threaten me anymore."

He stepped closer. Way too close.

"You think some church songs make you holy now? You think Pastor Malik gonna save you?" He leaned in, lowering his voice. "Because he won't touch you like I—"

My hand moved before my mind did.

I slapped him.

Hard.

The sound cracked through the room like a whip.

His head jerked to the side, and for a brief moment, the entire world went silent.

Even I was shocked — not because I didn't mean it, but because I finally did what Past Me never had the courage to do.

Slowly, he turned back toward me.

"Wow," he whispered. His jaw tightened. "You really gone."

"Yes," I said, voice steady, breath shaking. "I am."

He approached again, but this time I didn't back up. I stood my ground.

"You don't own me. You don't control me. And whatever power you used to have — it died the moment I gave my life back to God."

His nostrils flared, anger rising.

"You got one more time to DM me," I continued. "One more time, and I promise you I won't be the one regretting it."

I stepped past him and grabbed the doorknob.

"Nova," he called behind me, his voice lower, darker. "You walking out doesn't mean this is over."

I looked back only long enough to make sure my words landed.

"It does for me."

Then I opened the door and walked out into the crowded barbershop, head high, shame lifting with every step I took toward the sunlight.

I didn't look back.

Not once.

The sunlight outside the barbershop felt too bright, almost violent.

I kept walking, fast, refusing to look back, refusing to let Asonta's words stick anywhere they could take root again.

I made it to my car before the trembling started.

Not fear.

Not regret.

Just… release.

Whatever spell he used to have on me, whatever soul tie I had begged God to break — I felt the last thread snap.

My phone vibrated just as I shut the door.

Malik.

I hesitated, wiping the tears I didn't even realize were slipping down my face.

"Hello?" My voice was barely steady.

"Nova?" His voice was low, rough around the edges. "What happened?"

I closed my eyes, breath shaking. "Nothing. I'm fine."

"You're not," he said. "I felt… something. I don't know how to explain it, but something hit my spirit hard."

Of course he felt it.

Of course he did.

The timing with him was always strange — inconvenient, uncanny, intimate in a way I didn't know how to define.

"Where are you?" he asked.

"I'm leaving somewhere I shouldn't have gone," I whispered.

He didn't judge. He didn't ask questions.

"I'll meet you at your place," he said. "Drive safe."

"I don't want to—"

"Nova," he interrupted, gentler, "let me be there. Please."

I didn't argue again.

He was waiting on my porch when I pulled in — hands in his pockets, shoulders tense, eyes scanning the driveway like he expected danger to crawl out of the bushes.

When I stepped out, he didn't smile.

He just studied my face, and whatever he saw there made him step toward me without thinking.

"Come on," he murmured. "Let's go inside."

I unlocked the door with unsteady fingers.

The moment we stepped in, I tried to hold myself together. I really did. But everything — the barbershop, the humiliation, the slap, my past clawing at me, Marcus lurking in the shadows of this church mess — it all crashed into me at once.

My knees gave out before I could stop myself.

Malik caught me before I hit the ground.

"Nova—hey—hey, look at me," he said, his arms firm and warm around me. "It's okay. You're safe. I'm right here."

The words broke something open inside me.

I buried my face against his chest and let the sobs come — raw, ugly, shaking. I hadn't cried like that in years, not even when I got saved.

He held me through all of it.

Not tight.

Not possessive.

Just present.

His hand moved slowly across my back, not to comfort me like a man trying to fix something, but like someone making space for me to finally breathe.

"You didn't do anything wrong," he whispered. "You don't have to carry all this alone."

I grabbed fistfuls of his shirt, desperate for steady ground. "I'm trying, Malik. I'm trying so hard to stay free of the things that used to pull me under. But today—today was too much."

"I know," he said quietly. "I know."

Eventually the sobs slowed.

My breathing evened.

But neither of us moved.

When I finally lifted my head, his face was right there — close enough to feel his breath, close enough to see the exhaustion buried in his eyes, close enough to remember that in the middle of everything falling apart around him... he still showed up for me.

His hand came up, hesitated, then brushed a tear from my cheek.

The air between us shifted.

It wasn't lust.

It wasn't temptation.

It was the ache of two people carrying too much and finding a moment where the weight didn't feel quite as heavy.

Our faces leaned in — not fully, not intentionally, just drawn together by something warm and fragile.

Close enough that if either of us inhaled too deeply, our lips would touch.

That was what snapped me back.

I stepped back first.

He closed his eyes briefly and exhaled, like he was pulling himself out of something dangerous.

"Nova…" he whispered.

"I know," I said quickly. "I know. We can't."

He nodded, running a hand through his hair. "I shouldn't have—"

"You didn't do anything wrong," I said. "We're just… tired. Overwhelmed. And too close to the fire."

He gave a faint, sad smile.

"I should go," he murmured.

I nodded even though a small part of me didn't want him to.

"I'll check on you tomorrow," he said as he walked toward the door.

"Okay."

He paused before leaving, like he wanted to say more but knew he shouldn't.

Then he stepped out, closing the door behind him.

And for the first time all day, the silence felt safe.

Thirteen

MARCUS

I didn't expect her to walk into that barbershop.

I had been following Malik all afternoon, studying his movements, his voice, the little ticks he hadn't outgrown. I knew he was breaking — I could feel it. All that pressure Daddy placed on him was finally cracking through his skin.

I planned to push a little harder. Maybe show up at the church again, maybe leave something on his desk, maybe slip into rehearsal just to watch him squirm.

But then *she* walked in.

Nova.

Light in her eyes even when she was fighting tears.

Shoulders squared even though every step wobbled from the weight she carried.

I'd only seen her at a distance before — a supporting character in Malik's world, useful but forgettable.

But up close?

There was something else there.

Fire under restraint.

Wounds pretending to be healed.

A softness that didn't match the hardness of her past.

And the way she talked to that man — Asonta — the way she commanded the room?

It stirred something in me I didn't expect.

At first, she was just a pressure point.

A way to squeeze Malik.

People like him fall apart when someone they care about is touched.

But watching her walk out of that barbershop, shoulders trembling but lifted high?

Yeah.

There was more to her.

More that I wanted.

More that I would have.

So I followed her home.

Parked where she wouldn't see me.

Waited while she cried in her car, wiping her face like she was begging God not to let her fall apart again.

Pathetic.

Beautiful.

Then Malik's car was parked at her house, and I had to sink back into my seat.

I watched him guide her inside, watched her crumble in his arms like I should've always been the one to hold her.

I hated him for that.

Hated her for trusting him that way.

Hated how he stood in the doorway when he left, staring at her like she was some blessing meant just for him.

But when he drove off, I finally moved.

I slipped into the driver's seat of the car that matched his — the same model, same color, same shine. Bought it the moment I came back, because presentation matters when you're stealing someone's life.

I checked my mirror.

Hair trimmed the same way.

Clothes identical to what he wore earlier.

I practiced the expression — soft, tired, burdened.

His burden.

Not mine.

Then I walked up the steps and knocked.

Nova opened the door, eyes red, hair slightly messed from crying. And the moment she saw my face, relief washed over her.

"Malik?" she whispered. "Why'd you come back?"

God, the power in that.

I stepped inside like I belonged there.

I softened my voice to match his tone from earlier.

"For this," I murmured.

I lifted my hand to her cheek.

Her breath caught.

She didn't pull away.

Not yet.

I leaned in slowly — not because I doubted the disguise, but because savoring the moment mattered. Her eyes fluttered closed, her lips parted just slightly, and her hand lifted, like she was about to touch my chest the way she touched his when she needed grounding.

I was close enough to smell the faint sweetness of her perfume, close enough to feel her warmth against me.

Close enough to take what should've never belonged to him.

My lips crashed against hers and the flood gates opened. Clothes dropped to the floor in puddles and I took full advantage of Nova thinking I was Malik.

Shortly into the interaction I quickly understood why that dude from the barbershop was stalking her. Nova may be saved but her body remembered sin.

Honestly, I didn't have time to hold her because it was time I met with my brother face to face. I had to ask myself what would Malik do?

So, I stayed and held Nova. Personally I thought she would've had a rush of conviction that made her fold and cry, but she didn't. Nova had waited on this exact moment with Malik, but she got it with me.

When I take over as Malik fully this would be a sweet memory for her. The moment she secured her spot at First Lady of Kingdom Rising.

"Do you have any regrets?"

Our eyes tangled momentarily. "Not one."

"What does this mean?" She asked.

"It means that we have decided to be there for one another in the way we needed the most. I don't take it lightly and I cherish this moment Nova. I have some errands to run, but I'll check on you when I'm done."

"Okay. Please watch out for your crazy brother."

I flinched and prayed she didn't notice.

"I'm not worried about him. This will all be over soon."

"I hope so."

"I'll lock the door on my way out."

"Okay."

I headed to Malik's house. The only place he'd be before service tomorrow.

I shouldn't have left Nova's doorstep needing more.

I should have been satisfied with how close I got, how her breath caught under my hand, how she leaned toward me before her spirit recognized the wrongness in my skin.

But instead, driving away from her house, something in me ignited

— something sharp, jealous, starving.

She didn't choose me.

She *felt* me.

And Malik?

He was the one she cried on.

He was the one she trusted.

He was the one she looked at like he had the right to comfort her.

She would never look at me like that. Not unless I was him.

So I went to his house.

Not by impulse.

By instinct.

The same house Daddy used to boast about — the one "for family," the one he kept Malik in while I slept on floors and hustled to survive.

I parked my matching car across the street, stepped out in the same clothes, same haircut, same posture.

I wanted him to see himself when he looked at me.

I wanted it to cut.

Malik's headlights appeared at the end of the street.

His car slowed the moment he saw mine.

Good.

He knew.

He parked crooked in his own driveway.

Didn't even close the door before he stepped out — chest heaving, hands clenched, eyes wide as he saw me standing in the dark on his porch.

"Marcus," he breathed.

I tilted my head. "Hello, brother."

He didn't move at first.

Just stared like he was seeing a ghost he prayed would stay buried.

"You went to her house," he said. Not a question. A charge.

I smiled. "She let me in."

He flinched — not because he believed it, but because the *suggestion* was enough to break him.

"You stay away from Nova," he said, stepping closer. "You hear me? Stay away from her."

"Oh Malik," I murmured, "you don't get to make demands. You don't get to protect anything. Not anymore."

He walked right up to me, practically nose to nose.

The porch light flickered above us, and for a split second, our shadows merged on the siding like God wanted to remind us we were made from the same clay.

"What do you want?" he asked.

"Everything you have," I said simply.

"The love. The calling. The church. The life that should've been mine. I want it all."

"You abandoned us."

"No," I snapped. "YOU abandoned me. And He did too."

I jabbed a finger toward the sky as my voice cracked.

"You were Daddy's Isaac. His answer to prayer. And I was the goat he tied to the altar."

"Marcus—"

"No. No more preaching. No more excuses."

I stepped closer until we shared the same breath.

"I'm going to bring you to your knees, Malik. You. And Kingdom Rising. And anyone who tries to stand between us."

His fist hit me before the scripture rolled off his tongue.

It snapped my head back, split my lip.

I tasted blood and laughed — a deep, wild sound that had been caged too long.

"There he is," I said. "The golden boy finally fights back."

He swung again, faster this time, and we crashed into the porch rail, wood splintering under our weight.

I grabbed his hoodie and slammed him into the front door so hard the glass rattled.

"You think being chosen makes you strong?" I growled.

"It makes you soft."

"You think suffering makes you righteous?" he shot back.

"It makes you cruel."

I dragged him down with me as we tumbled off the porch into the grass.

He tried to pin me — failed.

I tried to choke the fight out of him — failed.

We rolled like children who were never allowed to fight the first time, finally unleashing years of unspoken resentment.

He threw an elbow.

I threw a knee.

He grabbed my wrist.

I punched his ribs.

We rose at the same time, panting, faces inches apart, identical and furious.

"You will never be me," he whispered.

I smiled slow, bloody, unbothered.

"I don't need to be you," I said.

"I only need to replace you."

His breath caught.

Then he lunged — and I dodged, stepping back into the shadows near my car.

"See you soon, brother," I said.

Then I got into the mirror-image car — *his* car, copied down to the scratches — and drove off into the night.

Leaving him staring after me.

Shaking.

Scared.

Exactly where I wanted him.

I should've gone home after I left Malik bleeding on his own porch.

Should've taken the win, cleaned my split lip, replayed the satisfaction of watching the golden child crack.

But rage is a fuel I learned to live on.

And obsession is momentum.

So instead of driving toward silence, I drove to the one place that raised me after Daddy threw me out.

Taz's club glowed in the dark like a warning light on the dashboard of Hell.

The bouncer clocked me the second I stepped out of the car, but he hesitated.

Recognition flickered in his face — not of me, but of Malik's reflection.

Good.

Let it confuse him.

Inside, the bass shook the floor.

Lights strobed over faces that didn't matter.

I cut through the crowd, straight to the back hall, and knocked once on Taz's office door.

He opened it himself.

His eyes scanned me, taking in the matching car, the fresh bruises, the split lip.

His smirk crawled across his face like a scar.

"You really are your brother's shadow," he said.

"No," I corrected, brushing past him into the room. "I'm what happens when the shadow learns how to walk in daylight."

He closed the door and leaned against it, amused but cautious.

He was always cautious around me — even when I was fourteen.

Especially now.

"What do you want, Marcus?"

I turned, hands in my pockets, calm as a man asking for a glass of water.

"I want you to kidnap Malik."

Taz let out a short, sharp laugh.

"Boy… you really came back wrong."

"I came back intentional."

I stepped closer, lowering my voice so he didn't mistake any of this for emotion.

"Keep him alive. Keep him contained. Keep him out of my way until I decide he's not useful anymore."

"And what makes you think," Taz said slowly, "that I'd risk crossing a pastor, a congregation, and the Feds just to snatch your brother?"

"Because I'm going to give you something Malik never will."

His eyebrow lifted.

"Your two point seven million," I said. "With interest."

Taz went still.

He wasn't afraid of much — but he respected money more than bullets.

"And how exactly," he asked carefully, "do you plan on getting that, when the Feds froze it and Malik ain't got a violent bone in his body?"

I smiled.

A calm, cold, effortless smile.

"Malik doesn't know how to open doors that shouldn't exist."

"And you do?"

"I've been opening them for years."

He studied me for a long moment, trying to measure whether I was bluffing.

But I wasn't the boy he used to intimidate.

I was the man Lysander trained.

Finally, Taz pushed off the door.

"You really are one cruel soul."

I laughed.

Not loudly.

Not theatrically.

Just enough for him to hear that there was no remorse left in me.

"Cruelty is a language," I said. "And I speak it fluently."

He crossed his arms. "So what's the plan?"

"I'll handle the church. I'll handle the narrative. You handle Malik."

"And when do you want this done?"

I tilted my head, thinking of the last moment I saw Malik — breathless, bruised, desperate enough to cling to Nova as if she could save him from the storm standing in front of him.

"Soon," I said. "Before he gets too bold."

Taz nodded slowly. "Alright, ghost boy. You got yourself a deal."

I walked toward the door, paused, then turned just enough for him to see my grin.

"And Taz?"

"Yeah?"

"Make sure you catch my livestreams every Sunday."

He frowned. "Why?"

"Because you're about to watch a kingdom crumble. And I want you to enjoy the show."

I left him standing there, half-amused, half-unsettled, fully committed.

Just like I wanted.

* * *

I woke before dawn, restless, wired, adrenaline still humming under my skin from last night's fight on Malik's porch.

He fought better than I expected.

Bled better too.

But even bruised, even shaking, even flinching at the sight of my face — he still dragged himself to preach this morning.

Predictable.

Pathetic.

Righteous to a fault.

I poured coffee, sat on the edge of my hotel bed, and pulled up the Kingdom Rising livestream on my tablet.

The sanctuary came into view — thinner crowd, worried faces, too much gossip bouncing off the walls. The scandal had bruised the church just like I'd planned.

And there he was.

Malik.

Standing behind the pulpit with a carefully pressed suit, a Bible open, and eyes still swollen from crying or praying or both. He tried to hide the bruising along his jaw, but the camera caught the shadow of it anyway.

Good.

Let them wonder.

I leaned back, studying him like a scientist examining a flawed experiment.

He wasn't as strong as people thought.

He wasn't as wise.

He wasn't as anointed.

He just had the benefit of love—

love I never received,

love I never forgot,

love I was willing to burn down the world to correct.

I watched the live chat roll in:

✧ *We love you Pastor Malik!*

✧ *You're carrying the mantle well!*

242

✧ *We're praying for you!*

Disgusting.

Then I saw *her.*

The camera panned across the choir, and Nova stood behind her mic, head bowed, hands clasped. Even from the livestream angle, I could tell she was praying for him. Not the public kind — the private kind. The kind she gave to people who mattered.

My jaw clenched.

She lifted her head when Malik started speaking, and her eyes locked on him with something I recognized instantly:

Admiration.

Devotion.

Tenderness.

A kind of spiritual intimacy that belonged to me now — whether she understood that yet or not.

How dare she look at him like that.

My irritation spiked, hot and sharp.

I zoomed in on the screen without thinking.

Nova's mouth softened into a small, proud smile as Malik read scripture, the kind of expression that said she believed in him even when she shouldn't.

No.

That was mine.

She didn't get to look at him like that.

She didn't get to give him her loyalty, her prayers, her trust.

Not after last night.

Not after the way her breath hitched when I touched her face.

Not after the way she leaned toward me as if her soul knew me before her mind could register something was wrong.

She was supposed to be confused today.

Torn.

Unsteady.

Not admiring Malik from across the sanctuary like he hung the moon.

I leaned closer to the screen until my reflection glared back at me beside Malik's image.

"Stop looking at him," I muttered under my breath. "You don't even know who he is."

But she kept looking.

And Malik kept preaching like he earned that gaze.

I felt my irritation slide into something colder — possessive, hungry, ancient as Cain himself.

A man watching Abel receive favor he was denied.

Then Malik did something unforgivable:

He smiled at her.

Not a big smile — just a small, exhausted one, brief enough that most people wouldn't notice.

But Nova noticed.

Her eyes softened even more.

And I felt something snap in my chest.

"No," I whispered. "No, no, no."

That look—

that connection—

that unspoken thread between them—

It did not belong to Malik.

He didn't deserve her hope.

He didn't deserve her prayers.

He didn't deserve her voice supporting him when she should have been trembling at the thought of me standing in his skin.

The livestream continued, but I no longer heard the sermon.

I only saw Nova.

And the way she looked at him.

I set the tablet down so hard it rattled the bedside table.

"Oh, brother," I murmured, a slow smile forming. "You have no idea what war you just declared."

Because now this wasn't about Kingdom Rising.

Or Daddy.

Or the mantle I was denied.

This was about Nova.

And I always take what I decide is mine.

Fourteen

MALIK

Service ended in a blur. I barely remembered the benediction. My ribs ached every time I breathed, and the bruise on my jaw throbbed under the heat of the sanctuary lights. People swarmed me as I tried to make my way to my office—hands on my shoulder, voices asking if I was okay, whispers floating through the air like gnats I couldn't swat away. Everyone meant well, but the attention made my skin crawl.

Halfway down the hall, Mother Lavvy intercepted me like a linebacker sent from Heaven's special forces. She planted herself squarely in front of me, eyes wide, hand on her hip, fanning herself like she was revving up revelation.

"Pastor Malik," she said, narrowing her eyes, "what happened to your face?"

I swallowed and shifted my jaw like the movement might make the bruise disappear. "Nothing, Mother Lavvy. I'm fine."

She leaned in closer until her glasses nearly tapped mine. "That bruise is not 'fine.' That bruise is a ruckus. A disturbance in the spirit. A manifestation of warfare!" She poked my chest with alarming accuracy. "Who you been tusslin' with?"

I stepped back before she could prod me again. "No one. Really. I bumped into something this morning."

She sucked her teeth. "Uh-huh. And I'm the Queen of Sheba." She crossed her arms. "If you don't want to tell me, just say that. But don't lie to the Holy Ghost."

I sighed, murmured something polite, and hurried past her before she started oiling her hands. The last thing I needed was a public exorcism performed on a fight I didn't win.

Inside my office, I shut the door and pressed my back against it. The silence hit me like a weight sliding off my shoulders. I was exhausted. Irritated. Embarrassed. And for the first time since the confrontation with Marcus, I felt something ugly stirring in me—self-blame. If I were stronger, he wouldn't be able to do this. If I were smarter, I could find him. If I were truly called, I wouldn't feel so lost.

I sank into my chair, rubbing the side of my face, when a soft knock broke the moment.

"Come in," I said, trying to straighten up.

Nova stepped inside cautiously, closing the door behind her. Her eyes moved over my bruised jaw, worry tightening her features. I opened my mouth to reassure her, but she spoke first.

"Malik... we need to talk about yesterday."

I frowned. "Yesterday?"

She nodded slowly, clasping her hands together like she was steadying herself. "When you came back to my house."

My heartbeat stuttered. I rose halfway from my seat.

"Nova... I never came back."

The words landed between us like something heavy and irreversible. Her posture stiffened immediately. Color drained from her face so quickly it looked like someone pulled the spirit right out of her body.

"What...?" she whispered. "No. No—Malik, you—"

But she didn't finish.

Her eyes went wide with a kind of terror that made the back of my neck prickle. Whatever she remembered, whatever she felt when she opened that door—it wasn't me. It was Marcus.

She stumbled back, shaking her head, breath quickening. "I—I have to go."

"Nova, wait—what happened? Talk to me."

But she was already at the door, hand trembling on the handle.

"Please don't follow me," she murmured.

Then she slipped out before I could stop her.

I stood there frozen, dread creeping into my bones.

Marcus had gotten closer than I ever imagined.

And Nova had seen him.

I didn't know what terrified me more—

that he'd gone to her house...

or that she couldn't bear to tell me what happened when she opened the door.

I didn't bother waiting for the rest of the ministers' meeting.

Didn't bother changing clothes.

Didn't bother pretending I was okay.

The second Nova ran out of my office, I went looking for the only person in the building who might be able to help me track a ghost.

Kyrie was in the media room, surrounded by monitors and half-finished sermon graphic thumbnails. He had his headphones on, bobbing his head like he wasn't supposed to be editing worship sets.

I knocked on the doorframe. "Kyrie."

He jumped so hard one of his AirPods flew out.

"PASTOR JESUS!" he yelped. "Warn a man before you sneak up on him with spiritual warfare in your eyes."

"Sorry," I muttered. "I need your help."

Kyrie paused, eyes narrowing. He took one good look at my face—bruised, tired, pacing by reflex—and suddenly lost the jokey smirk.

"What happened?"

"No time," I said. "I need to know if you caught Marcus leaving the church on any of Sunday's footage. Or Monday. Or today."

Kyrie blinked. "Leaving? Pastor... you think he's still coming in and out the building like we ain't upgraded security since Noah built the ark?"

"Yes," I said flatly. "It would've looked like *me*. He drives the same car. Different plates. May be on some old footage."

"Same car?" Kyrie's eyes bulged. "Ohhhh that boy bold."

"He's... mimicking me," I forced out. "Every detail. Down to the car."

Kyrie didn't laugh this time. He swallowed like the reality finally hit him.

"Aight. Say less." He spun in his chair, waking up all the screens. "Let's pull the Marcus folder."

"Marcus folder?"

He shrugged. "I label everything. Footage, timestamps, screenshots—listen, when you got a dead twin showing up on film like a BET special, you make folders."

He clicked through several files until the screen filled with clips of the mystery figure slipping into hallways, lingering in doorways, walking through back entrances.

Except it wasn't a mystery anymore.

It was Marcus.

"Pause there," I said quietly.

Kyrie froze the frame at the exact second Marcus stepped into a shadow near the east exit—my height, my stance, my face.

He zoomed in. "I knew that wasn't you. I prayed real hard before I exported this, too."

"Do you have a shot of his plates?"

"Oh, I got EVERYTHING." Kyrie pulled up a clear freeze-frame of the car parked across the street—the same make, model, color, down to the dirt on the bumper. "I started tracking the plates just in case."

"How?" I asked, even though I already knew I wouldn't want the answer.

Kyrie smirked nervously. "Well... remember how I told y'all I used to run in some tech circles before Jesus saved me?"

"Yes."

"Yeah, so... I might still have a few accounts on some networks that Jesus didn't fully shut down." He cracked his knuckles. "But ain't nothing wrong with a little hacking for the Kingdom."

I stared at him. "Kyrie."

"What?!" He lifted his hands. "David fought Goliath with a slingshot. *This* is my slingshot."

Before I could argue, he was already typing—fast, efficient, like his fingers had been waiting years to sin in a holy direction.

"License plate search... bouncing the IP... scrubbing the trace..." He muttered under his breath like he was praying and committing a felony at the same time. "Okay, okay. The car pinged at two locations this morning. One was the church lot. The other..."

He froze.

"What?" I stepped closer.

"Pastor..." He swallowed. "The other ping is tied to hotel guest Wi-Fi. Real expensive spot, too. Only criminals and rich folks stay there."

"Give me the address."

He typed again, hesitation growing by the second. "This is... too easy."

"What do you mean?"

Kyrie slowly turned toward me. "Easy means deliberate. He wanted to be found."

A chill crawled down my spine.

"Room number?" I asked.

Kyrie exhaled and clicked one final panel. "Marcus Cross is in Room 214."

My stomach dropped.

Kyrie sat back, wiping sweat from his forehead. "Pastor... are you sure you want to go? 'Cause this don't feel like a rescue mission. This feel like a setup. Like—Old Testament levels of setup."

"I need answers," I said.

"Answers? Or vengeance?" Kyrie asked softly.

I didn't respond.

He nodded slowly, understanding the silence.

"I'll text you everything. But Pastor..." His voice lowered. "Don't go alone."

I didn't want to.

But the truth was I wasn't sure anyone could help me with what waited on the other side of that door.

The drive to the hotel felt longer than it should have been.

Maybe it was the silence — that thick, haunting kind that sank its teeth into the back of your neck.

Maybe it was the weight of everything I didn't know.

Or maybe it was because every mile I drove felt like I was walking deeper into a story I was never prepared to be part of.

Room 214.

Marcus.

Alive.

Watching me.

Stalking the church.

Standing on my porch.

Standing where I should've been protecting the people I cared about.

Standing in my skin.

I gripped the steering wheel harder, my knuckles pale against the leather. My ribs ached from the fight last night, and the bruise on my jaw throbbed in rhythm with my heartbeat, a reminder of how unready I really was.

"God..." I whispered, swallowing the dryness in my throat. "I need You. I really need You right now."

Nothing answered except my own breath.

I started praying anyway.

Not one of those polished, pastoral prayers people expect from a preacher.

No scripture woven neatly through the syllables.

Just desperate, broken honesty.

"Lord, I don't know what he's become. I don't know what's in him. I don't know how to stop him. But please—keep me from doing something I can't come back from."

The light ahead turned red and I slowed to a stop.

That's when it hit.

A pressure.

Heavy.

Low in my chest, like something cold slid into the seat beside me even though I was alone.

I reached instinctively for the locks even though I didn't know what I was protecting myself from.

The feeling wasn't physical.

It wasn't emotional.

It was spiritual.

A presence.

Dark.

Familiar in the worst way.

Marcus.

I didn't even know how I knew — I just did.

The same way Nova sensed something was wrong in her home.

The same way my spirit jolted the night of his death.

The same way our fight felt less like fists and more like prophecy.

Even now, miles from the hotel, miles from wherever he was, his presence brushed against my nerves like fingers dragged along a piano wire. A broken chord. A warning.

"God…" I whispered again, gripping the steering wheel. "Help me. Please."

The light turned green but I didn't move.

My breath came shallow, panic scratching at the edges of my mind.

What if I wasn't ready?

What if I walked into that hotel and never walked out?

What if facing Marcus meant I wouldn't survive him?

I forced myself to shift gears, easing into the intersection.

Nova's face flashed in my mind — drained, terrified, unable to speak about what happened the night before. The fear in her eyes wasn't the kind that faded overnight.

He'd violated her peace.

He'd invaded her home.

He'd scarred something in her spirit.

And suddenly, fear wasn't the strongest thing in me anymore.

Anger took its place.

Real anger — sharp, heavy, born of something deeper than rivalry.

Nothing righteous.

Nothing holy.

Just raw, unfiltered fury.

He touched her.

He followed her.

He tricked her into letting him inside.

"Not again," I muttered. "Not one more person."

I pressed the gas harder.

The hotel sign appeared ahead — expensive cars lined up front, men in suits, the kind of place people stayed in when they needed secrecy and safety.

A perfect place for Marcus to hide.

I parked at the far edge of the lot, hands trembling as I cut the engine. My chest tightened again — that same pressure, closer now. He was here. He was expecting me.

I bowed my head one last time.

"God... I don't know if this is a battle I can win. But please don't let me face it alone."

Still nothing.

No warmth.

No clarity.

No reassurance.

Just silence.

And the knowledge that my brother was waiting.

I stepped out of the car and the night air wrapped around me like a warning.

Every instinct screamed to run.

Every responsibility told me to walk forward.

And every ounce of fear in my body whispered the truth I didn't want to admit:

Marcus didn't just want to destroy my life.

He wanted to trade places.

I squared my shoulders, breathed in deep, and walked toward Room 214.

Whatever happened inside that room, I already knew—

Only one of us would walk out the same.

I didn't go straight to the front desk.

Didn't bother asking questions.

I didn't want Marcus hearing my name whispered through the lobby or feeling my presence before I got close.

Instead, I waited.

Patience wasn't my strength, but adrenaline sharpened my instincts in a way nothing else could. I lingered near the vending machines until a housekeeper came pushing a cart down the hallway. She was small, older, humming softly as she worked.

"Excuse me," I said gently, stepping close enough to seem harmless. She startled, clutching her chest. "You scared me, baby."

"I'm so sorry," I whispered. "I'm in 214, but my keycard stopped working. Can you let me in? I don't want to go all the way back to the desk."

She didn't even question it — just gave me a tired smile and handed over a spare key. "Just bring it back when you're done, sweetheart."

"Thank you," I murmured.

My heart pounded as I walked down the hallway with the card in my palm. Every step felt like walking deeper into a storm. I stopped at the door and stared at the brass numbers like they were mocking me.

Room 214.

I swallowed hard, slid the keycard through the lock, and waited for the click.

The door eased open with a soft groan.

I stepped inside.

The room was dim, curtains drawn tight. A faint smell hung in the air — soap, expensive cologne, something metallic beneath it that made my skin prickle. The bed was unmade. The sheets twisted like someone had tossed and turned all night.

But Marcus wasn't there.

For a moment I just stood in the doorway, anger draining through me, leaving only exhaustion. I'd come all this way. I'd prepared myself for confrontation, for violence, for answers.

Instead, I was staring into a hollow room.

I stepped inside and shut the door behind me.

My eyes scanned everything — the dresser, the nightstand, the open closet. There were clothes missing. The closet hangers swayed slightly, as if he'd just been here.

A sick twist churned in my stomach.

He knew I was coming.

I crossed to the nightstand and yanked open the drawer. Empty. No wallet, no papers, no receipts. The trash can had nothing but a crumpled wrapper. The bathroom counter was dry. No toothbrush. No shaving kit. No lingering condensation from a recent shower.

He'd wiped the place clean.

I knelt beside the bed, checking underneath. Nothing but dust and a forgotten sock from whoever stayed before him. I searched behind the curtains. Under the sink. Inside the dresser drawers.

Nothing.

I sat on the edge of the bed, burying my face in my hands.

The defeat hit hard.

He was always one step ahead.

Always sharper.

Always faster.

Always slipping through my fingers.

"God," I whispered, "why can't I find him? What am I supposed to do?"

Silence pressed against my ears.

I raked my fingers through my hair and forced myself to breathe. I couldn't give up. Not when he was hurting people. Not when he had already gotten close to Nova. Not when he was unraveling everything my father built — even if my father built some of it on lies.

I stood again, refusing to leave empty-handed. I looked around one last time.

And that's when I noticed it.

A small indentation on the pillow.

A faint shadow of a headprint.

Still warm.

He had been here minutes before I arrived.

My heart slammed against my ribs.

He wasn't running.

He was playing.

And I was already moving exactly how he wanted me to.

I backed away from the bed, palms damp, sweat chilling the back of my neck. Every instinct inside me screamed that I was prey in a game I didn't understand.

I turned toward the door, ready to get out of that room—

And something crunched under my shoe.

I froze.

Looking down slowly, I lifted my foot.

A single slip of paper.

Blank on one side.

But when I turned it over, my stomach dropped.

It was a photograph.

Of Nova.

Taken from outside her living room window.

My hands shook as I stared at it.

Marcus wasn't hiding.

He was escalating.

And he wasn't finished.

Fifteen

TAZ

M y patience was hanging by a thread.
I paced the length of my office, cigar clenched between my teeth, staring at the frozen bank account number glowing on the screen like God Himself was mocking me.

$2.7 million. Frozen.

Jeremiah was in jail.

The church was in chaos.

And somehow *my* money was still locked up in a holy chokehold. If Marcus could get my money I ain't care who we had to snatch up to make it happen.

I slammed my fist on the desk hard enough to rattle the bottles behind me. Two of my lieutenants jumped like they were brand-new to my temper.

"I'm tired of this church-boy clown show," I muttered, smoke curling out of my mouth. "Jeremiah was supposed to keep that place clean. One job. ONE. And now I can't get a dollar out."

Deuce cleared his throat carefully. "We've been watchin' Malik, boss.

He walks a tight lil' triangle—church, hospital, home. Doesn't even stop for gas long enough to blink."

"Too damn clean," I said. "A man that clean either a saint or a liar."

I dropped into my chair, leaned back, and let the cigar burn slow.

"Bring Malik to me," I said. "Tonight."

Nobody spoke.

"No noise," I continued. "No mess, no bodies, no scene. Bring him quiet. I'll handle the rest."

They nodded and moved.

That's what I liked about my men—quick feet, quiet mouths.

It didn't take long before my phone started vibrating across the desk.

– We got eyes on him in an alley near the church.

– Target isolated.

– Moving in.

I smirked and took another drag of my cigar. Finally—something going right.

Then the phone rang again.

Deuce's voice came through tight. Too tight.

"Boss... we got him, but—uh—we got a problem."

I sat forward. "What problem?"

"He looks like Malik, boss. Same car. Same face. Same everything... but when we threw the bag off his head—man started *laughing*."

My grip on the cigar froze.

"Put him on."

There was shuffling, a grunt, and then—

"Tazzy."

My whole spine went cold.

Marcus.

The dead twin.

The ghost.

The boy I once molded until he turned snake on me.

"These idiots grabbed the wrong twin," he said, voice smooth as sin. "I see you ain't had good help since I left."

"You weren't the target," I growled.

"You sure?" he laughed. "Because your boys grabbed me like they missed me."

I gritted my teeth. "Where's Malik?"

"Around," he said. "Praying. Panicking. Pretending. Tripping over a kingdom he was never meant to inherit."

My jaw flexed hard enough to crack.

"You're playing a dangerous game, boy."

"It's only dangerous," he murmured, "if you can't do your part."

Deuce returned to the line. "Boss… what you want us to do with him?"

I stared straight ahead, a slow burn rising in my chest.

Marcus wasn't afraid.

Marcus wasn't hiding.

Marcus LET himself get taken.

"Let him go and find the right one," I said. "And make sure he's still breathing when you get here."

Deuce hesitated. "Even after what he said?"

"Deuce," I growled, "if I wanted him dead, we wouldn't be having this conversation."

The call ended.

I sat there in the silence, cigar smoke swirling around me like a warning.

I'd planned to break Malik tonight.

But Marcus…

Marcus was a different kind of animal.

And now he was in *my* hands.

The question was—

Was I holding a threat?

Or a bomb waiting to go off?

I was halfway through pouring myself a drink when my phone buzzed again.

At first, I ignored it — I'd already dealt with enough stupidity for one night.

But it kept buzzing.

And my men knew better than to double-call unless something important finally happened.

I snatched it up.

"Boss—" Deuce's voice came through ragged, breathless, like he'd been sprinting.

I straightened. "If this is another problem, I swear—"

"We got him," Deuce said. "The real one. Malik."

A slow, satisfied heat spread across my chest.

"About time."

"He fought," Deuce added. "Hard. Nearly cracked one of the boys' ribs. The pastor finally snapped."

I grinned despite myself.

Good.

I *wanted* him angry.

I wanted him unhinged.

Angry men make mistakes — and mistakes make leverage.

"Where is he now?" I asked.

"Warehouse. Room three. Hood off. Out cold."

I chuckled low. "Now we have a party."

"He clowned all the way in the van," Deuce muttered. "Kept yelling he wasn't paying you a dime, that you ruined his family, that—"

"Good," I said. "Let him scream. Makes it easier when they burn out."

As soon as I hung up, I dialed Marcus.

He picked up on the second ring.

"Well?" he said, voice smooth and too calm.

"We got your brother," I told him. "The right one this time."

There was a pause — not long, but long enough for me to picture the smile forming on his face.

"Is that so?" he asked.

"He's in my warehouse," I said. "Angry. Loud. Breakin' things. Looks like he hit the edge and jumped clean off."

"So Malik's finally cracked." Marcus exhaled like he'd been waiting years to hear it. "Good. He should."

I leaned back in my chair. "I thought you might want to know."

"Oh, I do," Marcus murmured. "Very much."

"You comin'?" I pressed.

Another beat of silence, but not hesitation — it felt like anticipation. Calculation.

A man already picturing the moment.

"I'm on my way," Marcus said. "Don't start without me."

"Anything particular you plan to say to him?" I asked.

Marcus's tone dropped to something darker.

"Just a few words," he said. "A little brother-to-brother clarity. Then I'll let you handle whatever business you need to."

My eyebrow lifted. "Just words?"

"That's all it ever takes," Marcus replied. "Two brothers. Two destinies. One of us always had to fall."

The line clicked dead.

I stared at the phone, a cold ripple sliding down my spine.

I'd seen dangerous men.

I'd raised dangerous men.

But Marcus Cross?

He was something else entirely.

And now he was walking straight toward the brother he wanted to destroy.

I didn't trust the silence after Marcus hung up.

Didn't trust the calm in his voice.

Didn't trust the way he said he was "on his way" like this was a family reunion instead of a setup waiting to happen.

I'd dealt with snakes before.

Trained some of them myself.

But Marcus Cross?

Marcus wasn't a snake.

He was the shadow behind the snake.

The thing you didn't see until it bit you.

I gathered my men, jerking my chin toward the door. "Saddle up. We're heading to the warehouse."

Everyone moved fast — guns checked, radios clipped on, engines revving outside.

Before I stepped out, I turned and gave them a look I didn't have to explain.

The kind of look that said: *If tonight goes wrong, don't expect mercy.*

When we rolled out, gravel popping under the tires, I finally said what needed to be said.

"Y'all keep your eyes open," I warned. "I don't trust these Cross twins. Either one of 'em."

Tank glanced over from the passenger seat. "Marcus the worst of the two?"

I let out a humorless laugh. "Worse? Malik might fight when he's pushed, but he got limits. Marcus ain't got no limits. Marcus is the kind of man who figures out where your bedroom window creaks just for fun."

The car fell silent for a moment.

"Boss," Tank said slowly, "if Marcus needs Malik out the way... then what he need *you* for?"

Exactly the thought I'd been chewing on since the phone call.

"Power first," I said. "Money second. Revenge third. Marcus is stackin' all three."

"And when he's done?" Tank asked.

I stared out into the dark road ahead, headlights slicing through the shadows.

"When Marcus finishes with Malik," I said, "I'll be next on his damn list. No question."

Deuce shifted uneasily. "So why we helpin' him at all?"

"Because I need Malik out the way too," I said. "And because Marcus ain't gettin' the chance to pull the trigger. Soon as I get my two-point-seven million back?" I tapped the gun resting against my hip. "I'm puttin' him in the ground myself."

The men in the back tensed, exchanging looks.

Good.

They needed to understand the kind of war we were walking into.

Marcus was playing nice now because he needed space.

He needed distance cleared.

He needed pieces moved off the board.

But once Malik was gone?

Taz Moreno would be next.

I wasn't about to sit around and wait for that.

As the warehouse came into view — big, black, silent except for the dim security lights — a cold certainty washed over me.

Marcus wasn't walking into my trap tonight.

I was walking into *his*.

And I'd be damned if I didn't walk out again.

Sixteen

MALIK

I woke up to pain.

Not sharp, not sudden — the deep, throbbing kind that settles into your bones like it plans to stay awhile. My head hung forward, chin against my chest, and when I tried to lift it, fire shot down the side of my neck.

Cold metal bit into my wrists.

A chair.

Zip ties.

Concrete floor.

A single spotlight overhead that burned my eyes the moment I opened them.

For a few seconds, I didn't even remember how I got here.

Then it all rushed back — the struggle outside, hands grabbing me, a hood over my head, fists, darkness.

My lip was bleeding again. I tasted iron thick on my tongue.

I forced myself to breathe. Slow. Quiet. Prayer forming in my mind even though my voice couldn't find it.

"God, please… please be with me."

A low voice cut through the darkness.

"Well, well. Pastor Malik finally woke up."

I jerked my head up, flinching at the pain.

Taz Moreno stood a few feet away, arms crossed, looking at me the way a man looks at something venomous — interesting enough to study, dangerous enough to kill.

Every hair on my arms lifted.

"Taz—" My voice cracked. "This… this isn't necessary—"

"Oh, it's real necessary," he said, stepping closer. "You cost me money. You cost me time. And you out here actin' like you don't owe nobody nothin'."

"I don't have your money," I whispered.

"I know." Taz leaned down so his shadow swallowed my face. "That's why this is happening."

I closed my eyes. My heart pounded so loud I could hear it echo in the rafters.

"Look at me," Taz ordered.

I forced myself to.

His eyes were cold.

Calculated.

Done playing games.

"You wanna pray?" he asked. "Go ahead. But prayer ain't what's gon' save you tonight."

Before I could respond, a laugh drifted out of the far corner of the warehouse — a slow, deliberate laugh that made my stomach drop.

It wasn't Taz.

It wasn't any of his men.

I knew that laugh.

Even before he stepped into the light, my body seized with instinctive recognition.

Marcus.

Taunting.

Amused.

Smiling like this moment was his coronation.

He walked out of the shadows with the confidence of a man who had already won. His eyes slid over me like I was a piece of furniture he'd finally gotten around to dismantling.

"All this time," Marcus said, shaking his head. "All these years. You still look at me like you don't recognize what you did."

My throat tightened. "Marcus... why—"

"Oh save it," he snapped. "I'm not here for a confession. I'm here for closure."

He crouched down in front of me, face inches from mine.

The same face.

My face.

Twisted into something I didn't recognize.

"It's time, brother," he whispered. "Tomorrow morning, I become Malik Cross."

My breath stalled.

"I'm walking into your life," Marcus continued, voice dripping satisfaction. "Into your pulpit. Into your congregation. Into everything you failed to become."

"That's not— you can't—"

"Oh, but I can," he murmured. "And I will."

He stood up and paced in front of me like a professor teaching a class I never asked to attend.

"You couldn't rebuild Kingdom Rising," he said. "Not really. But I can. And once I get them all worshiping the ground I stand on?" He smiled, slow and cruel. "Then I'll tear the whole thing down again. With joy."

My chest tightened, panic clawing at the inside of my ribs.

"That's not what God wants," I whispered.

Marcus paused.

"God?" he echoed, turning back to me with a dark grin. "I stopped believing in God when I realized my twin brother got all the prayers and I got all the punishment."

I shook my head, tears stinging. "Marcus... I never—"

"No," he said sharply. "You never did anything to stop Jeremiah from treating me like a demon in the house. You never stood up for me. You never once said 'Marcus isn't the problem.' And now?" His smile widened. "Now you pay for it."

Taz cleared his throat loudly.

"Don't forget about my damn money," Taz barked. "Two point seven million."

Marcus didn't even look at him.

"You'll get your money," he said casually. "With interest."

Taz nodded, satisfied... for now.

But I saw the suspicion flicker in his eyes.

He didn't trust Marcus.

And he shouldn't.

Marcus turned back to me.

"You know what the best part is?" he asked softly. "When this is over... nobody will even miss you."

Something inside me shattered.

He leaned in one last time.

"Sleep well, Pastor," he whispered. "Tomorrow... Malik Cross is reborn."

He stepped away, fading back into the shadows he crawled out of.

And for the first time in my life, I prayed not for victory.

I prayed for survival.

When the warehouse door slammed shut, the darkness settled over me like a weight — thick, suffocating, alive.

The single light overhead flickered once, then died, leaving me swallowed in shadows.

I couldn't see my hands.

I couldn't see the walls.

I couldn't even see the chair I was tied to.

All I could hear was my own breathing — shallow, uneven — and the echo of Marcus's voice repeating in my head:

Tomorrow I become Malik Cross.

I let out a strangled breath and bowed my head as much as the restraints allowed. My lip throbbed, my ribs ached, and the cold concrete floor beneath my feet stole whatever warmth I had left.

"God..." I whispered, voice cracking, "please... please don't leave me here."

The words sounded small — smaller than they ever had in my life.

I'd prayed for people.

Prayed with people.

Prayed in hospital rooms, at altars, in emergencies, in joy, in grief.

But I had never prayed like this.

Never prayed from the edge of fear so deep it tasted like metal on my tongue.

"I don't know what to do," I whispered. "I don't know how to fight him. I don't know how to survive this. God... I'm scared."

The confession tore something open inside me.

Humility.

Desperation.

A kind of brokenness I didn't know I was capable of.

I wasn't praying to preach.

I wasn't praying to be strong for others.

I was praying because I was a man in a chair in the dark and I might not live to see the morning.

My breath hitched.

Tears slipped down the sides of my face.

I tried to wipe them, forgetting my hands were tied.

"Please…" I choked out. "Please help me."

Silence pressed against my ears.

No warmth.

No whisper.

No comfort.

Just silence.

I inhaled shakily, trying to keep my courage from shattering completely. That's when I heard it—

Footsteps.

Slow.

Measured.

Coming from the hallway outside.

My entire body went rigid.

I held my breath as the steps drew closer — not rushed, not angry, but deliberate… like someone wanted me to hear them coming.

Click.

A boot sole against concrete.

Click.

Another.

My heart hammered so violently the chair vibrated beneath me.

"God…" I whispered, "please…"

The footsteps stopped right outside the door.

A shadow moved beneath the crack — long, still, waiting.

For me.

For the right moment.

For whatever came next.

Then—

The doorknob twitched.

My breath froze in my chest.

Sweat rolled down my spine.

Every prayer I knew tangled together in my mind.

The doorknob turned again.

Slow.

Controlled.

Almost curious.

My pulse thundered in my ears.

I didn't know if it was Taz.

I didn't know if it was Marcus.

I didn't know if it was someone worse.

All I knew was that whoever stood behind that door?

Was coming for me.

And God help me...

I wasn't sure He was coming with them.

The doorknob turned slowly, and I braced myself for Marcus's silhouette, or Taz's shadow filling the frame.

But when the door opened...

My breath left my body.

"Deacon Rusty...?"

He stepped inside like he'd been invited, like this warehouse was a Sunday board meeting instead of a kidnapping scene. His suit jacket was still on, still buttoned. His Bible tucked under his arm like he came here directly from the pulpit.

Behind him stood Marcus, leaning against the doorframe with an amused smile — like this was the punchline he'd been waiting to deliver.

My stomach twisted so hard I felt dizzy.

"Rusty... what are you doing here?" My voice cracked under the strain of disbelief. "How—how do you even know about this?"

Rusty didn't answer.

He simply closed the door behind him, walked a few steps into the room, and studied me with an expression I'd only ever seen from him when he thought the choir was flat.

Disappointment.

Judgment.

Authority he never should've had.

"Malik," he said, shaking his head slowly. "I told myself I wouldn't let my heart get soft over this."

Rusty's voice sounded almost paternal.

Almost.

But the words were knives.

"I prayed long and hard once Marcus came to me," Rusty continued. "And the Holy Ghost made it plain. Clear as daylight. Kingdom Rising has been operating out of order for years."

My mouth went dry. "Marcus... came to you?"

Marcus smirked from the corner like a proud son.

Rusty set his Bible on a table and folded his hands behind his back.

"I'm an old man, Malik. I don't get many surprises anymore. But when that boy walked into my home—alive, strong, clear-minded—and told me the truth about Jeremiah?" He exhaled deeply. "I knew God was leading me to help."

My head spun. "Truth about what?"

Rusty's eyes hardened.

"About the betrayal. About how your father chose you for that pulpit before you could even crawl. About how Marcus was treated like a curse instead of a child. About how he was cast aside instead of guided."

"That's not true," I whispered. "Marcus had choices—"

"He had no father," Rusty snapped. "Not a real one. And he certainly didn't have a brother who fought for him."

The words hit harder than any punch I'd taken.

My chest tightened.

My vision blurred.

"I—I tried..." My throat closed up. "You don't know what it was like growing up with Jeremiah—"

"Oh, I know exactly what it was like," Rusty said. "That man ran this church with an iron fist and a blind eye. And he raised you to be the same kind of leader — timid, apologetic, indecisive. Always second-guessing. Always folding under pressure."

His voice rose with each word, sharp and cutting.

"You were never fit to lead Kingdom Rising. Not then. Not now. Not ever."

I felt something inside me crack — not pride, not ego... something deeper. Something I didn't even have a name for.

"Rusty..." My voice barely carried. "I thought you supported me."

"I supported the position," Rusty corrected. "Not the man."

Marcus stepped closer now, folding his arms, enjoying every moment.

Rusty continued, calmer this time — which somehow made it worse.

"For years, Kingdom Rising has been fooled. We poured our prayers, our money, our anointing into the wrong twin. The wrong vessel." His gaze flicked to Marcus with something dangerously close to reverence. "The anointed one has always been Marcus."

A cold wave rolled through my entire body.

Rusty nodded solemnly.

Like this was holy.

Like this was righteous.

Like this was God.

"Tomorrow," Rusty said quietly, "Marcus will step into his rightful place. The place God intended. And Kingdom Rising will finally have the shepherd it deserves."

My jaw trembled.

"And you?" Rusty added, looking down his nose at me. "You will finally be out of the way."

Marcus smiled.

My heart broke.

I wasn't terrified of dying.

I was terrified that they truly believed this was God's will.

* * *

I must've blacked out again, because when I opened my eyes, the warehouse was different.

Quieter.

Brighter — but only slightly, a sliver of dawn leaking through a boarded-up window.

I didn't know how long I'd been out.

Hours?

A night?

A lifetime?

My wrists throbbed where the zip ties had cut into my skin. My shoulders screamed from being pinned behind me for so long. Every muscle in my body felt like it had been dragged through concrete.

But I was awake.

Alive.

Barely—but alive.

The door creaked open and one of Taz's men stepped inside, rubbing sleep from his eyes.

He looked irritated, bored, like this was just another shift in a job he hated.

"You gotta piss or what?" he grunted.

I didn't answer.

I just stared at him, waiting for the right moment.

He sighed heavily, walked behind me, and sliced the zip ties off with a knife. The blood rushed back into my hands so fast I nearly passed out again.

"Come on," he muttered. "Boss said keep you alive. Didn't say keep you comfortable."

He yanked me up by my arm.

That was his mistake.

The second my feet hit the ground and my balance returned, I swung.

I didn't think.

Didn't breathe.

Didn't pray.

I just moved.

My elbow connected with his jaw — a sickening crack. His head snapped back, and he staggered. Before he could recover, I grabbed the closest thing I could reach — a piece of wood leaning against the wall — and brought it down across the back of his skull.

He dropped instantly.

I stood there panting, shaking, adrenaline burning so hot it blurred my vision.

"God... forgive me," I whispered. "But I can't die here."

I stumbled to the door, every step pounding through my ribs. I pushed through the hallway — empty. Either everyone was gone or asleep. I didn't stop to question. I followed the draft, the faint noise of traffic, until I found the exit.

When I burst outside, the sunrise stabbed my eyes.

But I didn't stop.

I ran.

My legs felt like they were made of fire and gravel, but I ran anyway.

Down the street.

Past the warehouses.

Past anything that looked like danger.

Toward the only place that mattered.

Kingdom Rising.

If I could just get there...

If I could just get inside...

If I could warn them...

If I could expose Marcus—

My lungs burned.

My throat tasted like blood.

Every breath felt like it scraped the inside of my chest.

But the church rose into view at the top of the hill, gold cross catching the morning light like hope itself.

I pushed harder.

"Please..." I begged God, gasping. "Please let me get there..."

The parking lot was already filling. Sunday service. I had no idea what time it was until I saw people walking inside, chatting, greeting each other like it was just another morning.

A wave of relief almost knocked me to my knees.

I was going to make it.

I could save them.

I could expose him.

I could—

A hand clamped around my mouth from behind.

Another arm wrapped around my chest, lifting me clean off my feet.

I kicked wildly, muffled screams tearing from my throat.

I was three steps from the side door.

Three steps.

"Thought you could outrun us, Pastor," a voice growled into my ear. "Boss said keep you alive... not let you loose."

I fought harder, but my body betrayed me — too weak, too slow, too depleted.

I saw the church door.

I saw the worship team warming up on stage through the stained glass.

I saw people taking their seats.

I was right there.

And still unreachable.

Tears spilled hot down my face as they dragged me backward.

"No—no, please—" I choked behind the hand smothering my screams. "Let me go—please—"

The world tilted as they shoved me into a van, slammed the door shut, and darkness swallowed me whole again.

I had escaped hell only to be dragged right back into it.

And now Marcus had a head start.

They shoved me into the van so hard the air left my lungs. The door slammed, metal echoing like a coffin lid sealing shut.

My chest heaved. My wrists burned. My vision blurred in and out as the engine roared to life.

But none of that compared to what I felt when I looked through the back window—

The church doors opening.

Members filing inside.

The choir preparing.

The morning sun hitting the stained glass like nothing was wrong.

And then—

A figure stepped into the light.

My face.

My walk.

My suit.

Marcus.

Already there.

Already stepping into my pulpit.

Already taking my place.

My stomach twisted so violently I thought I might pass out.

He wasn't preparing.

He wasn't planning his entrance.

He was already living my morning.

Already breathing my air.

Already wearing the name *Malik Cross* like he had earned it.

And nobody inside that church would know the difference.

As the van pulled away, the sanctuary shrank in the distance — the life I'd built disappearing behind me like a bad dream I couldn't wake up from.

I pressed my forehead to the cold metal wall, shaking uncontrollably.

"God... please... don't let him destroy them."

But even as I prayed it, one truth sank deeper than the pain in my ribs:

Marcus had already begun.

Seventeen

MARCUS

I stood in the pastor's office — *my* office now — adjusting the collar of Malik's suit jacket in the small mirror above the bookshelf.

It fit perfectly.

Of course it did.

We were born in the same skin.

I straightened the tie. Smoothed the jacket sleeves. Practiced the quiet, humble smile Malik used when he wanted to look sincere. The congregation loved that expression — the soft, earnest one, like he carried their souls in his hands and felt honored by the weight.

I tried it on.

It was laughable how easy it came.

Behind me, Kyrie's graphics for the morning sermon flickered across the monitor:

RESTORATION SUNDAY — Pastor Malik Cross

I let the title sit on my tongue.

Pastor Malik Cross.

Perfect.

I heard footsteps in the hall and turned to see Rusty peeking in, face serious, eyes shining like he'd just watched the Second Coming stroll through the parking lot.

"They're ready for you," Rusty whispered. "The Spirit is already stirring."

Of course it was.

Nothing stirs a church more than a lie they're hungry to believe.

I walked past him, and he followed close, almost reverent. He looked at me with a kind of pride he'd never shown my brother. A kind of pride he claimed came from God but really came from resentment, bitterness, and years of wanting control.

"Remember," Rusty murmured, "speak from the heart. The congregation needs steady leadership. Confident leadership. Something your brother never possessed."

I smiled.

"I won't disappoint you," I told him — in Malik's exact tone, soft and steady.

Rusty shivered.

We reached the sanctuary doors. Worship was ending, the choir repeating the last chord of their praise break. The energy was high, electric. People were on their feet, clapping, shouting, hands lifted.

The perfect moment to walk into the spotlight.

The perfect moment to become him.

Rusty reached for the door handles, but before he pushed them open, he asked quietly:

"You're certain you're ready?"

Ready?

I'd been preparing for this since the day Jeremiah looked at me like I was the devil's child.

I forced Malik's gentle smile again.

"God has prepared me for such a time as this."

Rusty exhaled like those were the holiest words he'd ever heard.

He pushed the doors open.

Light hit me.

The choir faded out.

The congregation turned in unison.

A hush fell over the sanctuary.

And every face — every single one — softened with relief when they saw me.

They didn't see me.

They saw the Malik they trusted.

The Malik they adored.

The Malik they expected to lead them through the storm.

And I stepped forward, letting the weight of their belief wash over me.

For the first time in my life...

The world looked at me with reverence.

I was Pastor Malik Cross now.

And I intended to savor every moment before I destroyed everything he ever touched.

The applause hit me like a wave the moment I stepped toward the pulpit.

All those faces — desperate, hopeful, hungry — lifted toward me as if God Himself had walked through the sanctuary doors.

They had no idea.

Rusty slipped into the front row, nodding like a proud father.

The choir settled.

The musicians quieted.

Silence rolled through the church, thick with anticipation.

I rested Jeremiah's Bible on the podium and looked out over the sea of believers who truly thought their pastor had survived the storm.

I gave them Malik's smile — small, trembling with sincerity, the smile that said, *I'm humbled to stand before you.*

The church melted.

People cried just seeing my face.

It was almost too easy.

I opened the Bible, though I didn't need it. I already knew the scripture Malik had planned for today.

"Joel, chapter two," I said softly, letting my voice break just the right amount. "Verse twenty-five."

A few mothers shouted instantly — they loved that verse.

I laid my hand on the page like the Word was pulsing beneath it.

"'And I will restore to you the years...'"

A swell of emotion surged through the room.

I paused deliberately, lowering my head as if the weight of God's presence had just landed on me.

Truthfully, I was savoring the manipulation.

"'The years the locusts have eaten.'"

People stood.

Hands lifted.

Tears flowed.

I gripped the edges of the podium and leaned forward the way Malik always did when he wanted to drive a point home.

"Kingdom Rising..."

I let the words tremble.

"...we have lost some things."

A murmur of agreement washed through the sanctuary.

"We have faced embarrassment. We have faced destruction. We have faced attacks on our house, our name, our faith."

The roar grew louder — shouts of *come on, pastor, teach!*, *yes, Lord.*

"And yet... we are STILL HERE."

The room erupted.

I raised my hands slightly, palms outward. "But hear me —

restoration is not about returning to what once was. It is about stepping into what God intended ALL ALONG."

Rusty jumped to his feet.

Harmony screamed.

Kyrie nearly dropped his camera.

I could've told them God was quitting the ministry and they'd have praised anyway.

Emotion.

Not spirit.

It was beautiful.

"You think the enemy attacked this house because we were weak?" I asked, voice rising. "NO. He attacked us because we are dangerous."

They were shouting now.

Stomping.

Crying.

I gave them Malik's raw vulnerability — the illusion of a breaking man finding strength.

"He thought he could destroy us. He thought he could tear us apart. But what the enemy MEANT for EVIL—"

The building shook from the collective shout.

"—God is about to turn for GOOD!"

They lost it.

I mean *lost it.*

People ran laps around the sanctuary.

Mothers fell out.

Musicians jumped back in on cue.

Rusty sobbed into a handkerchief like revival had hit Houston.

And all I did was feed them a performance.

A beautiful one, yes — but a performance nonetheless.

I lowered my voice until the room strained to listen.

"And the greatest restoration," I whispered, "is not in your finances.

Not in your reputation. Not in your circumstances."

I placed a hand over my heart.

"It is in your leader."

Gasps rippled through the room.

"God did not bring me this far... to leave me now."

Someone screamed.

A woman fainted.

The choir started speaking in tongues.

I looked out over the sea of faces — adoring, trusting, desperate — and felt a rush of triumph surge through me.

They believed.

Every word.

Every gesture.

Every lie.

This church — Malik's precious Kingdom Rising — was mine now.

Not because I stole it.

Because they handed it to me with open arms.

And the moment they finished praising?

I would begin tearing down everything they worshipped.

One brick at a time.

If worship was loud, the praise after service was louder.

Hands shook mine until my fingers went numb.

Women cried into my suit jacket.

Men hugged me like I'd just snatched the whole church out of the devil's jaws.

They called me *anointed.*

They called me *chosen.*

They called me *their pastor.*

And I accepted every word with Malik's humble smile.

The high was intoxicating.

Adoration always is.

By the time I slipped back into the pastor's office — *my* office — my heart was still thundering with victory. I loosened the tie and admired my reflection again.

Perfect.

Flawless.

Undeniable.

The door creaked open.

I didn't turn at first — I assumed it was Rusty, ready to gush.

It wasn't.

A soft clack of heels entered behind me, followed by the familiar scent of peppermint oil and White Diamond perfume.

Mother Lavvy.

I forced a smile before I faced her.

"Mother Lavvy," I said in Malik's gentle tone. "You blessed me today. Your prayers—"

She held up a hand.

Not shaking.

Not trembling.

Steady.

Strong.

And unwavering.

"Save it," she said.

My smile faltered.

She stepped closer, her eyes narrowing the way only an old mother of the church can — like she was looking straight through the flesh and into the soul you wished you didn't have.

"I came in here to tell you something, Pastor Malik."

She tilted her head.

"Or whoever you is today."

The words cut sharper than a blade.

My throat tightened.

"What do you—"

"Don't play with me, baby," she snapped. "I been in church longer than you been alive. I done seen wolves shout louder than sheep. I done seen demons run laps around sanctuaries while folks called it the Holy Ghost." She pointed a finger right between my eyes. "And I know — without a shadow, without a doubt — something in the milk ain't clean."

Heat crawled up the back of my neck.

Lavvy stepped even closer, lowering her voice until it felt like prophecy dripping through her teeth.

"The whole church might be fooled by your hollerin' and hoopin'... but not me. I felt the spirit shift. I felt heaven pull back from that pulpit." She tapped her chest. "And God told me... *watch him.*"

I swallowed, forcing Malik's softness back into my expression. "Mother Lavvy, I assure you—"

"ASSURE?" she barked, eyes wide. "Baby, you can't assure me of nothin'! The Holy Ghost showed me TWO shadows walkin' and only one had a face Heaven recognized. And you—" she pointed at me again, "—WASN'T the one."

My entire body stiffened.

Lavvy leaned in until her breath warmed my cheek.

"You might've fooled the saints... but you didn't fool the Spirit."

She straightened her hat.

"And I'm gon' pray until the truth walks itself back through that door."

She turned to leave, but paused in the doorway.

"Oh, and another thing," she said without facing me. "Whatever mess you think you about to pull? Baby, just know — God always unmasks a wolf."

She walked out, heels clicking, leaving the office colder than before she entered.

I stood frozen.

For the first time since stepping into Malik's life...

I felt something crack at the edges of my triumph.

Not fear.

Not guilt.

Something worse:

A direct challenge.

Because if Mother Lavvy could sense the truth it was only a matter of time before someone else did.

And I couldn't allow that.

Not now.

Not ever.

I didn't move for a long time after Mother Lavvy left.

Her perfume still hung in the air — peppermint oil, White Diamond, and holy irritation.

A spiritual cocktail I should've dismissed.

But I couldn't.

Her words replayed themselves with irritating clarity:

"Two shadows walkin'... and only one had a face Heaven recognized."

"You wasn't the one."

"I'm gon' pray 'til the truth walks itself back through that door."

I clenched my jaw.

Of all the people in Kingdom Rising, it had to be *her.*

Not Kyrie.

Not Harmony.

Not Winter with her Instagram Bible verses.

Not Nova — though she looked at me strange once or twice during service.

It was Mother Lavvy, the one woman everybody wrote off as a spiritual nuisance until her prayers actually shook something loose.

Her intuition wasn't just inconvenient.

It was dangerous.

A soft knock tapped the doorframe.

Rusty stepped inside, closing the door behind him like we were discussing church renovations instead of spiritual treason.

"You did beautifully," he said with quiet awe. "Absolutely beautifully. The congregation... I haven't seen them that unified in years."

I didn't smile.

Not fully.

"Sit," I told him.

He obeyed immediately, straightening his tie like he expected praise.

Instead, I let silence settle between us — heavy, deliberate.

Rusty finally shifted, sensing I wasn't basking in the afterglow of my own performance.

"Something wrong?" he asked carefully.

I leaned forward.

"I had a visitor," I said. "Someone less... persuaded by my sermon."

His brows furrowed. "Who?"

"Mother Lavvy."

Rusty let out a slow, exasperated sigh. "Oh, Lord. Of course. That woman sees demons in dust bunnies. Ignore her."

"No," I murmured. "I won't."

His eyes sharpened. "Marcus... Malik..." He corrected himself quickly. "Pastor. What exactly did she say to you?"

"She said she wasn't fooled."

I watched that land.

"She said the Spirit didn't recognize me."

Rusty swallowed hard.

"She said she'll pray until the truth walks through the door."

Rusty's face drained.

I lowered my voice.

"She's a problem, Rusty."

He nodded once, understanding the tone beneath my words.

"And we can't have problems," I continued.

Rusty hesitated. His hand twitched on his knee. "She's... beloved. Long history with the church. But she can be... redirected."

"Redirected?" I asked, raising an eyebrow.

He wet his lips. "I can talk to her. Pull her off your trail. Make her think she misunderstood God."

That wasn't enough.

Not by a long shot.

I leaned in closer.

"No," I said softly. "I need you to handle her."

He blinked. "Handle—"

"Yes."

I didn't repeat myself.

Rusty's voice dropped, almost a whisper. "What exactly do you mean by 'handle,' Pastor?"

I held his gaze, letting the silence fill in the answer I didn't need to speak aloud.

Finally, Rusty exhaled — long and trembling — the realization dawning like a burden he wasn't sure he wanted but felt obligated to accept.

"For the sake of Kingdom Rising," he said quietly, "I'll take care of it."

I nodded.

"Good."

He rose slowly from the chair, adjusting his jacket with shaking hands.

Before leaving, he looked back at me — the faintest crack of fear slipping through his loyalty.

"Pastor... what do I tell her?"

I smiled — not Malik's gentle one this time.

My smile.

The real one.

"Tell her God wants her quiet."

Rusty flinched, nodded once, and slipped out of the office quickly.

The door clicked shut behind him.

And just like that…

The first person who saw the wolf

was marked for silence.

To be continued…